D1450207

OPTICS

A NOVEL ABOUT WOMEN AND WORK AND
MIDLIFE MUDDLES

GAIL REITENBACH

Published by Moonsong Press, an imprint of Right Hand Communications LLC. For information: info@righthandcom.com.

First Print Edition 2020

ISBN 978-0-9786842-2-8

K

The letter filling the lighted screen in front of her was still recognizable. The letters on her phone screen, not so much. She'd have to catch up with email later.

"Good to see you again, Kris," Dr. Ortiz said, as he extended his hand for a shake.

"You, too, Dr. Ortiz—though you're a little blurry."

"Sorry we had to dilate you, but I understand you're concerned about some floaters that suddenly appeared. Tell me about that." He listened as he tapped at his computer keyboard. Ortiz, just thirty-one, had been Kris's optometrist for the past five years, since he took over the practice from his father.

"We spent most of the weekend outside, and as we were hiking yesterday, I noticed something swimming around in my field of vision. I'm not sure exactly when it started, but I notice it most when there's strong sunlight coming in from the left side of my sunglasses."

"Any pain?"

"No."

"Any flashes of light?"

"No."

"Has your left eye had its vision obstructed by what looks like a dark curtain moving down or across it?"

"No."

"OK, let me take a look." He rolled his stool so he was facing Kris on the other side of the swing-armed optical equipment and instructed her to look in every direction as he shone a red light in her left eye. Their bodies were close, and he was looking intently in her eye, but he wasn't looking at *her*. His interest was solely in her eye tissue—as, of course, it should be. Still, she couldn't shake the sense that he hadn't seen her as a person first and a patient second. That was the way with all medical professionals these days. Everyone hustled to book as many appointments as possible and spent more time entering data than they spent interacting with you. All to satisfy the insurance companies. At least she had a good vision care policy through her job.

"I have an important work trip next week, so I wanted to get this situation addressed as soon as possible." The comment was classic Kris. Zero procrastination. Deal with problems head-on. Don't let unforeseen developments get in the way of personal or professional commitments. In this case, though, her no-nonsense demeanor masked a flutter of anxiety. She'd always been healthy. This eye thing unnerved her.

"It's as I suspected. You have a PVD—a posterior vitreous detachment. Luckily, you don't have any retinal damage, but you will have that semi-translucent vitreous material floating in your eye from now on. Over time, you'll get used to it and won't be as aware that it's there."

"What causes it?"

"Nothing in particular, usually. It's a common problem with middle-aged, near-sighted adults. You should know that you'll probably experience the same thing in your other eye eventually."

Middle-aged. He threw the word out so matter-of-factly. Lately, she'd come to hate it. She didn't feel middle-aged, or middle anything. She just felt like herself. The label seemed to imply that it was all downhill from here. "Is there anything I need to do? Will it be visible to others?"

"No on both counts. But I do want you to come back right away if the number of floaters suddenly increases, if you see flashes of light, or if the same thing happens in the other eye."

After checking out and paying her small deductible, Kris decided she had time to browse the frame cases. She'd worn prescription glasses since fourth grade. By middle school she was replacing both lenses and frames yearly. Annual new prescriptions were common for children, but frames were another matter. Blame it on being a tomboy. Blame that on Kevin.

Having a brother just a year older had sparked Kris's interest in sports and all things outdoors. All that physical activity—especially on the basketball court—was rough on frames. By middle school she was participating in every seasonal team sport at their suburban Boston public school. But it was individual sports she excelled at; tennis and running let her focus completely on the elements she alone controlled. She'd picked up those loves from Kevin too. He was her first practice partner on the tennis court, and—until he hit junior year of high school—he'd even let her run with him.

But Kevin eventually went off to college and law school, following in their father's wingtips. His first Christmas home from Yale Law, he brought Elizabeth, a Boston Brahmin who was getting her masters in art history at Yale. She was perfectly kind to the rest of the family, but never warm—though she must have been to Kevin. They married a week after he graduated with his law degree, and they moved to New York. Ever since, he and Kris had been in a weddings-and-funerals sort of sibling relationship. He never called or emailed. He'd changed. People change, she told herself. Nothing to fuss over. Same with eyes, apparently.

As she browsed the optical shop, she began to grow anxious. She wasn't in the market for new frames right now, but it troubled her that she wasn't seeing what she was looking for. There was a decent variety of brands for the size of the shop. Coach, Kate Spade, Burberry, and more of the clothing designer brand extensions as well as the dedicated frame makers—Flexon, Oliver Peoples, LaFont, and the like. But no Klassik frames.

As soon as the optician was free, she made eye contact. "Hi, Janey. How have you been?"

"Great. And you? Are you in for your annual?"

"No, I just learned I have PVD."

"Oh, too bad. But really, it's not such a bad condition. Many of our older patients have experienced PVD, and they usually find they get used to it quite quickly."

Kris tried not to wince at *older*. From Janey's millennial perspective, did she really qualify as older? Well, yes, older than Janey, but the implication was that PVD was a medical condition associated with being *old*. She wasn't *old*. She had as much energy as she'd had twenty years ago. And as for medical conditions, she'd avoided doctors' offices for all but the most routine care her entire life. Did she *look* old? Snapping back to business, she asked, "I was just browsing your current selection, and I'm not seeing any Klassik frames. Did I miss them?"

"No …" Janey's customer service smile relaxed and her eyes darted away from Kris's face momentarily. Now she was the one who looked uncomfortable. "The truth is, we recently stopped carrying them. They just weren't selling enough to warrant the display space."

"Oh." Kris was momentarily taken aback. "I hadn't heard anything from our sales staff. Ken's your rep, isn't he?"

"Yes, but it's not his fault. It's just that the frames don't seem to appeal to our patients."

"I see." Kris debated about pushing the issue further and decided there was nothing to lose. "It would help me back at the office if you could share more details about why you think Klassik frames weren't moving. We always want to improve."

"Honestly, we kept carrying the brand longer than we otherwise would have just because we wanted to support a local Albuquerque business," Janey offered. "The lower price range is pretty saturated these days, so even budget brands are looking for ways to distinguish themselves with design or materials. The Klassik styles just didn't seem to change much season to season, and we recently had been getting complaints about poor quality."

Just then Kris heard her phone buzz. She pulled it out of her front tote pocket. After checking the sender, she added, "Thanks, Janey, I appreciate your candor. I'll see you in a couple of months when I'm in for that annual appointment."

Before heading out into the blinding late-afternoon sun, she dug into her leather tote and traded her dark brown tortoise-shell frames for wire-framed prescription sunglasses. People had told her they liked her retro aviators. Though her glasses evoked the classic Ray-Ban aviators, they were Klassiks—at half the cost of the better-known brand.

＇

Kris waited to read the email from Ashley until she was seated behind her Subaru's tinted windows. Mentoring the new marketing assistant was one of her recently added job responsibilities. More than that, it was a precondition for a potential, long-overdue promotion. Six months ago, she'd met with Roger, her boss and CEO, along with Sandy, the HR director, and made the case for a promotion from marketing director to vice president of sales and marketing.

Aside from being one of the longest tenured employees at Klassik Eyewear, she was the most well-rounded, she reminded them in that meeting. She had risen quickly in her early years under the company's founder, advancing from marketing assistant to marketing manager and marketing director. Between the first two positions, she made a year-long lateral move into sales—just for the experience of interacting with customers—but marketing was her real love. It drew on her understanding of all the other business functions, from supply chain to customer service to finance.

Since Roger had taken over as CEO five years ago, she noted—being careful to avoid any hint of complaining or whining—she had taken on more work (the result of layoffs that pink-slipped Andrew, who had been her marketing manager for four years). She had found inventive ways to stretch a shrinking marketing budget. (Initially, she had voluntarily proposed a few changes to their marketing strategy after Roger opened up about how hard a hit the balance sheet had taken; after that first voluntary reallocation, Roger imposed increasingly draconian budget cuts each subsequent quarter.)

She had regularly offered brand-extension and revenue-building proposals: a line of reading glasses for wider distribution beyond their traditional optical shops, decorative glasses holders, and more. (This was after she floated the idea of launching a luxury line, which would have warranted higher price points and profit. Roger, adamant about "dominating the affordable frames segment," dismissed that idea as too far beyond their core business.) And she always made time to consult with others who asked for her help. She'd even gone on several sales calls over the past couple of years to demonstrate extra attention to troubled accounts. On such occasions, most of which required multiple nights out of town, she also kept up with her own responsibilities, no matter how late she had to remain tethered to her laptop.

Even among the newest staff—some of whom saw her as competition for budget dollars—no one would have disputed Kris's dedication, effectiveness, acumen, and loyalty.

Except for Roger and Sandy. Not that they said so in so many words. Instead, Roger leaned back in his high-backed leather chair and babbled on about how the economy had never really recovered sufficiently after the 2008 financial crisis. The company still had a lot of rebuilding to do. Budgets were tight for both operating expenses and salaries. (What he paid himself, she didn't know. It was a privately held firm, so when he shared bad financial news with his department heads, she knew the prognosis was bad.)

At the end of the meeting, Sandy suggested that she and Roger discuss Kris's request and get back to her in about a week. As Sandy dismissed her from Roger's office, she raised her left hand to gently grasp her frames, as if to reposition them higher on her nose. Though Sandy's oily T-zone probably did make her green plastic cat-eye frames slide a bit, the gesture had become an affectation, always accompanied by a slight tilt of the head, as if to convey superiority. Or something.

A week later Kris was summoned to Roger's office, where Sandy did most of the talking. The bottom line was that they had more hurdles for her to clear before they'd revisit the promotion decision. But there was a very good chance she'd get the promotion, Sandy said. It was just that they had to be extra-prudent with all things budget-related for a few more months. To that end, Sandy argued, they wanted to hire a recent college grad to serve as marketing assistant. Beefing up their marketing efforts was key to renewed profitability, Roger added. How well Kris managed to mentor this new (low-salaried) hire would figure into their promotion decision a year hence.

As if Kris wouldn't naturally mentor a new hire who reported to her. As if she hadn't mentored multiple staff in every department over the years. As if! It was nearly impossible not to take that condition as personally insulting. Bridling her Boston Irish, she had calmly responded in perfect professionalese, "Of course. I look forward to the opportunity."

As she sat in her car, air conditioner blasting, her light-sensitive eyes struggled to focus on the small, blurred type of the email. Even though Ashley, the new marketing assistant, sat just beyond Kris's open door, she rarely communicated in person even when Kris was in the office. Every question or comment required an email. Kris wondered if it was a CYA reflex but decided Ashley was too young to have adopted that politically motivated behavior. *Roger is asking if all the booth materials have been shipped to Vegas. He wants an answer right away.*

Good God, Kris thought, *both of them knew I had a doctor's appointment this afternoon. I don't know who's more clueless—*

Airhead Ashley or Roger. (She had resisted giving her boss a nickname. Despite his manifold shortcomings, she was determined to make the best of her professional situation, and she couldn't afford to let a sour note accidentally slip publicly.) *Ashley had helped prepare the shipping forms; how could she not know everything was en route? And I had this checked off on my pre-event checklist outside my door. I've never missed a marketing deliverable. Doesn't Roger have anything more important to worry about?*

She'd made her eye appointment late in the afternoon to minimize schedule disruptions. She'd planned to head home after the doctor's visit, but maybe she should circle back to the office in case there was something more serious behind the email that required her attention.

Squinting to shade her dilated eyes, she grimaced. Not a good look to hold for twenty minutes when you're trying to minimize crow's feet and frown lines.

2

September had always seemed to Kris the real start of a new year. Not January. Not spring. September was when lives got a reset—a new grade in school, a recommitment to work disciplines after flexible summer hours, updated family routines and social schedules. She loved the promise of fall colors, cooler nights after cloudless days, and the way donning a sweater—which wouldn't be necessary for another month—gave her extra energy to walk briskly. Not even a bad boss could spoil her seasonal joy—or so she thought.

Kris grabbed her iPhone from the night stand, silenced the alarm thirty seconds before it was set to go off at 6 a.m., sat up, and tapped the Outlook icon. It showed thirty-five new emails, the number highlighted in red. Next to her, Mike groaned and muttered, "Five more." She leaned over, kissed his head, and threw off the covers on her side of the bed.

Scrolling through the inbox as she headed toward the bathroom vanity, she glanced at one marked "Important" with its red exclamation point and rolled her eyes. It was from Roger.

He'd sent it at 11 p.m., knowing she'd have stopped checking messages an hour earlier last night. He'd misplaced her monthly report but claimed she hadn't sent it. "He can't even manage his mail, let alone a business," she muttered to herself as she navigated to the "missing" message she had Bcc-ed to herself. And he hadn't said anything about needing her report when she showed up at the office yesterday just before closing.

Then she went on auto-pilot. After pulling back her honey-blonde hair and splashing her face, she donned workout glasses—an old, silver wire-rimmed pair with soft nose pads that kept the frames from sliding down her face when she broke a sweat. In the kitchen, the coffee maker had gone into action on timer mode at the same time she had. Kris poured a half cup and headed to the workout room.

Though it had originally served as guest bedroom, when they turned fifty Mike suggested they convert it to a workout space. Kris hadn't been fond of the idea originally, but without a basement, they had no other option. That left Kate's bedroom as guest quarters when their daughter wasn't home from college; when she was home, Kate or the guests slept on an air mattress squeezed into the workout room.

Kris and Mike had both been lifelong runners, but when they hit fifty—midlife, as they reckoned it, given that all four parents were still going strong in their seventies and eighties—they'd decided to diversify their activities and protect their knees so they could stay active well into old age. Climbing Machu Picchu was high on their retirement wish list, though at fifty-five, retirement at seventy was too far in the distance to be seen even with corrective lenses. They bought an elliptical machine on the advice of an older friend who said it was gentler on his knees than running yet still gave him a serious aerobic workout. Then they added some free weights because they'd heard maintaining muscle mass past fifty is harder. Kris had taken some yoga classes over the years, but she hated breaking up her work day for a trip to the studio, so she developed her own circuit of poses that she practiced each weekday. Having grown up around water, she missed the feel of oars, so they squeezed in a rowing machine, and within a month, Mike was using it as much as Kris. In the far corner, visible from all the equipment, was a wall-mounted TV.

That morning in mid-September, Kris turned on the local news and got moving: five minutes warming up on the rowing machine; fifteen minutes of high-impact interval training on the elliptical; and ten minutes of yoga.

The top news story was about the strong economy, yet on its heels was a darker piece about the thousands who had stopped looking for work and, hence, weren't counted in labor statistics. Traffic was backing up around construction on her route to work. It was a short commute, but she hated to be late for anything. She couldn't dawdle.

On her way to the kitchen, she checked for messages. Kris and Kate had a weekday routine of texting while Mom was getting ready for work and Daughter was on her way to her first class of the day. Kate was loving her fall courses as a senior at Boston College, her mother's alma mater. She was taking the last required course for her economics major (she was her mother's daughter when it came to organization and deferred gratification) and was finally able to coast a bit by filling in remaining electives.

Some friends are already talking about skiing at TG break. Could I invite Carly home so we can ski Taos? She's never been West.

Of course. Would be fun to see her again.

THX!

Are the leaves staring to turn? I miss them.

Want me to press some for U?

Yes! Love U!

Mike was putting the finishing touch on breakfast. "Mmm," Kris cooed as she leaned over the plate of scrambled eggs he'd made for her, loaded with green chile, a bit of jack cheese, and avocado on the side. She scooped it all into a warm flour tortilla, rolled it shut, and took a bite. "I know I should cut the carbs," she said between bites, "but I just can't make it through the morning without some ballast!"

"I really think you should stop worrying about carbs," Mike chided. "Carbs are an issue for men more than women. Besides, you're not overweight—"

"For my *age*," she interrupted.

"I was going to say that you're not overweight, you look great, and you feel good, right? That's what matters."

Rolling her eyes in grudging agreement, she headed for the shower.

It had always been hard for her to accept compliments. Her mother had held such high expectations of her (hell, she still did) that—even though she never exactly said so—nothing Kris ever achieved seemed quite enough. As she became a mother and then a middle-aged woman (she knew she was midlife, middle-aged, but she still hated when others used the "MA" designation), Kris started to understand her mom a bit better. Her grandparents hadn't been exactly poor, but they couldn't scrape together enough money to send Margaret to college after they'd already sent her two brothers, so secretarial school it was. Once she had kids, Margaret took a break and only went back to work after Kris started college. In retrospect,

Kris suspected her mother had chafed at being relegated to support positions rather than the management roles she was wired for. Her pushiness with Kris? She probably just wanted to see her daughter take full advantage of the opportunities her generation of women had. Intellectually, Kris got it. Emotionally, like many of her generation, she resented the pressure and had learned that having it all took its toll. She wanted, and got, a terrific husband and child. The tradeoff had been limiting her career to a city where her husband's higher-paying career was firmly rooted. Not so unlike her mother after all.

One last text went to a group: *See U Fri for G7!*

Before stepping into the shower, she set out everything she'd need five minutes later: firming, hydrating, and eye creams, plus sun protection. Then a light foundation, eye liner, mascara, and her moisturizing "work" lipstick in an opaque neutral that the woman at the Sephora counter had recommended for her coloring and age. "Too bright or glossy and it draws attention to the creases framing your mouth; too dull or matte and it makes you look tired," she said with the confidence of a twenty-year-old who'd absorbed the makeup training but couldn't imagine being thirty, let alone fifty.

One eye on the time, Kris checked for stray eyebrow hairs as the hot rollers cooled. She didn't mind being post-menopausal for the most part, but the hair migration issues were annoying. Her eyebrows had always been dramatic, dark, and perfectly shaped. She'd rarely paid attention to them until recently. Now she had to monitor hair length as well as new growth above and below her normal arch.

After shaking out the soft curls in her medium-long hair, she reached for her work uniform: black skinny-leg dress pants, fresh-from-the-cleaner tailored white shirt, and a funky strand of pearls and silver beads, all anchored by power heels —not so high as to look sexy but lofty enough to prove she could dress like a woman and kick ass like a man. Digging into a basket of eyewear cases, she grabbed one containing a pair of *au courant* heavy black-rimmed glasses and put them on. A quick glance in the mirror and she was out the door.

3

Roger Kohl sauntered into the conference room. He liked to think he was an affable guy. A guy's guy, but also sensitive to women. He believed the laconic gait he'd adopted right out of college gave him a confident cool. Though beards were in fashion again—especially in the design field—he kept his face clean-shaven. Wouldn't want to reveal how gray he'd become. It was creeping up into his temples, and that was bad enough. At least he wasn't balding, like a lot of other men in their mid-forties.

He set his blank notepad and coffee cup on the table. "Aim High!" the cup ordered, in bold script.

"Ashley, would you pass me a pen?"

The twenty-three-year-old marketing assistant reached across the conference table, which made her blue Banana Republic shirt gape just enough for Roger to glimpse her black bra and a bit of cleavage. Though Kris hadn't been sold on Ashley's abilities during the interview process, Roger insisted the bubbly blonde brought just the right youthful ideas to the table.

Ashley selected a blue ballpoint from the cup of writing utensils, handed it to Roger, and sat back down on his immediate right. "Thanks! How's it going with the marketing plan for next quarter?"

"Great!" she replied. "I'm going to do more-frequent email blasts, because our customers aren't very active yet on social media," she said, raising her left eyebrow, as if to imply they weren't very young and hip. "And I've got an idea for a new distributor competition."

"That's great!" the CEO gushed. "Attitude is everything!" he said, gesturing at and reading the caption on a poster featuring a rock climber. It was one of those ubiquitous motivational posters developed, one imagined, for multilevel marketing companies. Roger had ordered it placed next to the door so staff would see it at the end of every meeting. Roger had never been particularly athletic, but he knew climbing was cool, especially in the West.

"OK, let's get started." Roger cleared his throat as the last three attendees took their seats. "Let's be sure we're all clear on what we're doing for the big show next week." He'd asked all the department heads plus a couple of extras to the meeting. Over the past couple of years, the staff had fallen into the habit of arranging themselves on Roger's left if they'd been hired before he arrived as CEO of Klassik Eyewear or on his right if they'd been hired after. If Roger noticed the staff picking sides, he didn't seem to care. That put Kris, Liz Martinez (controller), Diana Delgado (receptionist and customer service), and Terry Wilkins (IT) on the left. On the right, next to Ashley, were Eugene Pullman (vice president of supply chain), Mark Chavez (vice president of sales), and Sandy Blair (human resources director and office manager).

"Let's go around the table, starting on my right, and briefly review what you're doing next week. Ashley?"

"I'll be working the booth, greeting people as they walk by, modeling our frames, trading business cards, and—"

"Partying late in Vegas!" Roger interrupted, laughing at his own comment.

"Probably," Ashley continued. "The after-parties can be a good way to connect with people."

"And I see you've already got 112 connections on LinkedIn. Well done!" Roger smiled at her. "Eugene?"

"Well, I've been setting up meetings with our suppliers to see if we can get some additional price breaks. Problem is, we can't capture volume discounts because we're not selling the numbers we need."

Mark interrupted, "Sales are stuck because our brick-and-mortar customers are getting hammered by online retailers. That's why I think we need to extend our payment terms," he said, looking across the table at Liz. "I'm afraid we may lose more of our key accounts if we can't provide additional flexibility. I'd really like to have that sweetener to offer them in Vegas."

Liz countered, calmly, "I can see how that might be appealing to our delinquent customers, but we have to focus on our own cash flow. There may be one or two accounts where we could work a custom payment plan, but only for those we know are solid. I'm going to email you a list today of which accounts are overdue and by how much. Rather than continually extending credit to shaky retailers, we could use some *new* accounts or new revenue streams."

"We're all aware that it's a challenging time for sales," Roger jumped in, protective of Mark, whom he liked to call a rainmaker, though his throughput was more like a sprinkle.

"But we need to stick to our core business during downturns."

"Is there a way Marketing could provide more support for Sales to help increase our visibility?" Sandy asked, looking at Ashley. "Maybe something a bit more eye-catching, especially at next week's event?"

Kris responded before Ashley could open her mouth. "We are always looking at new ways to support Sales, but I'm afraid we don't have enough time to develop any additional materials for next week. The booth has already been shipped to Nevada, and the printer is sending our collateral tomorrow. Besides, our marketing budget was cut for the third year in a row, so we're already trying to do more with less."

"Hm. OK. Just trying to help." Sandy sulked and leaned back in her chair.

"One thing I'm going to focus on this year," Mark continued, "is identifying the international reps and planting some seeds for more foreign distributors."

"Let's hope they're fast-sprouting seeds!" Eugene couldn't help adding, even though he knew every comment from him annoyed Mark.

Terry jumped in to avoid being left out: "Before most of you leave for the convention, I'll be sending instructions on how to connect to our new VPN. Remember, you will not be able to access any of your work files or presentations on our server unless you install the new VPN." As Mark rolled his eyes, Terry continued, "Especially when you are around an international crowd on open wireless networks, you cannot be too careful. It's super easy for anyone with moderate tech skills to spy on what you're doing online if you don't use a VPN." He rested his case with a soft "N," like the son of New Orleans he was. He'd made his way to New Mexico after losing his home in Hurricane Katrina and had never gone back. Kris didn't roll her eyes—she liked and respected Terry—but she wanted to snark that Klassik Eyewear had nothing worth stealing.

"I'll be here, fielding calls, as usual," said Diana.

"Holding down the fort, as it were," Roger grinned, always the biggest fan of what he understood to be his clever quips. It was the sort of comment Diana had come to expect from the CEO. Not a direct dig about her weight, but easily interpreted as a double entendre. The only time she'd heard him talk about her size directly was not long after he had bought the company from the founder. Roger was talking with Sandy in his office when Diana passed the open door. They both had their backs to her, huddled over an org chart on the desk. "We need a new receptionist," Roger said. "An overweight, middle-aged woman who doesn't wear our glasses doesn't make a good first impression. The optics are bad." She couldn't catch Sandy's response, but some argument the HR director made must have changed his mind, and Diana kept her job.

"I'll be running some budget scenarios for next quarter that I'll finalize once I see the list of orders from Vegas," Liz said, looking at Mark.

"And I'll be working our booth as well as walking the exhibit hall to gather intel," said Kris. "I've already found that many of our competitors are rolling out virtual reality websites where customers can try on different eyewear to see what they look like. It's mostly online retailers, but some manufacturers are also exploring this strategy for building consumer interest."

"Cute idea, but I heard Neweyes paid $1.5 million for their 3D interface. Plus, that technology will just drive online sales and throttle store traffic. We're in the business of supplying our Main Street customers, so we don't want to siphon off their business." As Roger made his anti-tech pronouncement, Kris caught Terry slowly raising his eyes to the ceiling. It wasn't an eye roll, and it was slow enough for plausible deniability, but she recognized the movement for what it was.

"I hear you," Kris said. She didn't bother to correct the overstated expense. Either Roger's sources were inflating costs to discourage him from pursuing the latest technology, or he was throwing out the first huge number he could think of and assuming his minions would take him at his word. "But what if we were able to offer online try-ons *and* in-store sales? Once someone has virtually tried on two pairs of frames, our website could be programmed to display a pop-up that encourages that person to visit a local distributor to ensure they'll get a proper fitting. We could do that, right, Terry?"

"Absolutely. It's easy."

"Hm. That's a thought," Roger mused. "But I still don't see how we could develop something like that on our own."

Terry and Kris had talked about this idea repeatedly over the past couple of years, and they'd pitched it to Roger formally twice before. Each time, he rejected it as too expensive to outsource and too complicated for "internal resources"—a not-too-subtle diss of Terry, who actually had developed a feasible implementation plan. Always in the background was the foundational problem—one Kris had been forced to acknowledge about six months into Roger's tenure as CEO: Roger rarely gave the green light to any idea that wasn't his own. Employees hired under his reign had slightly higher odds than those who were "left over" from the founder's era, but even they seldom were praised for their contributions. Any new initiative only advanced when Roger announced it as his own brainchild. His behavior went beyond the familiar phenomenon of a man repeating and appropriating a woman's idea; Roger was non-sexist in his appropriation of other people's creativity.

"There are companies that specialize in coding for virtual fitting apps. I can find out who others are using, if you like. I can ask around when I'm at the show," Kris offered.

"OK ...," Roger said slowly, "though we mostly need you coordinating the booth traffic and capturing leads when Mark is in customer meetings.

"That about does it then," Roger began his wrap-up. "I'll be meeting with our board and investors next week, so text me with any good news! For all of you headed to Vegas, remember to tell everyone you meet that Klassik Eyewear is top dog in the frames game! We offer the best pricing around."

Kris held her tongue, though she couldn't stop the voice in her head from retorting, *You don't convince anyone of your product's excellence by* saying *it's excellent. You have to be able to* demonstrate *excellence. Nor does discount pricing make us top dog —by any metric.*

4

That Friday, Kris left the office precisely at 5 p.m. rather than lingering to wrap up even the noncritical leftover tasks on her to-do list, as she would have done any other day of the month.

By 5:30 p.m. she had set out wine glasses and appetizer plates after changing into a pair of jeans and a white hip-length tunic. Over the years, her work uniform of white tops and whatever pants and skirts were in style had spilled over into her casual wardrobe. It made one daily decision easier. For color and accent, she could grab whatever jewelry matched her mood or image *du jour*.

The doorbell rang and Susie Patel, carrying a platter of fragrant vegetable pakoras, let herself in. "Happy Friday! Can I re-crisp these in your oven?"

"As if you need to ask!" laughed Kris, opening the preheated oven for her petite friend.

"Hi!" Jo Garcia cried out as she arrived. "I am so ready for this!" She gave Kris and Susie a hug after setting her bowls of salsa and tortilla chips on the kitchen's expansive island.

"Not half as ready as I am!" sighed Diana as she followed Jo into the kitchen.

To an outsider, it might seem as if Susie and Jo were stereotypes, each bringing a food associated with their ethnic background. The reality was that if Susie didn't bring an Indian snack, and if Jo arrived with anything other than her homemade extra-hot salsa, they risked being kicked out of the G7.

That was the name the women had given themselves nearly two decades ago. It had been Sharon Burch's idea to adopt the shorthand of the international political group, whose number of nation states had varied over the years. Most of the women had met and bonded when they each had a child in preschool, but they didn't want to be a "mommies" group. From the start, they agreed that no kids were allowed at their bimonthly gatherings. They'd talk about the kids, of course, but their meetups were adult time. Somehow, even as doting young mothers, they sensed in each other an additional frequency that had nothing to do with being maternal. Not exactly ambition. More like kinetic curiosity.

Jo grooved on the idea that the G6, as they originally were called, could be the name of a girl band. She'd been in a garage band in high school, but early marriage and kids had pulled the plug on that dream.

Even as their children went off to college and lives of their own, the women continued to congregate every other month for an extended TGIF. Seven years ago, as their kids were becoming more independent and absorbing less conversational bandwidth, Kris asked if they could add Diana Delgado to the group. She and Diana had become mutual allies at work but didn't want to flaunt their friendliness in the office.

Diana had joined Klassik Eyewear six years before the business was sold to Roger. Within months of being hired, she'd slid into the role of customer service star, earning a quick promotion from receptionist to head of customer service, a role she handled from the front desk. Through nearly daily innuendo, Roger made it known that he thought Diana was a poor fit for receptionist because of her weight. She wasn't morbidly obese, but she was clinically overweight, and—aware of how others saw her—she was rigorous about her grooming. Her instincts about which styles would flatter her were spot on, and Kris envied her ability to draw a sharp eyeliner curve.

Despite his personal feelings about Diana, Roger left her in the position of receptionist because she clearly had the support of the entire staff and was a productive worker—and she hadn't asked for a raise in her modest salary. She could handle any and all customer or vendor inquiries and complaints. But Roger wasn't happy that Diana's was the first face he saw at work each day, and he'd fallen into a pattern of apparently offhand remarks that were clearly designed to make her feel ashamed of her weight. "Pancakes or burrito for breakfast today?" he might ask, even though she'd explained she usually ate oatmeal or scrambled eggs. "Good to see you eating healthy," he'd say if he saw her munching an apple for dessert at the staff picnic tables.

Diana had mastered the art of deflecting such petty attacks. At the front desk, she handled foot traffic, phone calls, email messages, and physical mail with unflappable competency. Though her body filled her office chair from arm to arm, she sat with a poise that proclaimed her self-worth. Kris had come to think of her as a female Buddha.

Though she didn't have kids of her own, Diana enjoyed children and didn't display boredom when G7 members launched into extended monologues about their offspring's latest crises.

Without explicitly framing their decision in economic terms, the group had agreed early on that each would contribute to the gatherings according to her budget and talents. Every couple of years they'd open discussion of renegotiated roles, but they'd end up where they'd settled in. So it was that Diana brought cute, seasonal, or snarky cocktail napkins; Susie, Jo, and Janice West—a chef who'd trained at the Culinary Institute of America in California's wine country —would bring nibbles; Sharon and Marie Serra would bring wine; and Kris would provide the venue and cleanup. After all, Kris explained, she had the biggest space for entertaining plus a cleaning woman scheduled to visit each Friday morning.

Once everyone had arrived, Kris invited them outside: "Grab a bottle or a plate and let's take advantage of this perfect fall afternoon!" ·

"Ugh," said Jo as the light breeze blew dark bangs over her eyes. "I'm overdue for a cut, but I can't find a time to go in."

"That's the price of success, dear!" said Sharon. "By the way, I should have you take a look at my toilet. It's been leaking sporadically, and I don't want to waste water."

"Sure. What's a good time?"

"Nearly anytime! That's the upside of unemployment," Sharon laughed.

"I'd hire you if you if I could," Jo empathized. "I cannot believe that a conscientious, experienced accountant can't get a job."

"It's that 'experienced' part that's the problem," Sharon's laughter carried a tinge of tannin. "I've been applying for jobs for five months, and all the postings either want someone who has just graduated or somebody with one to five years of experience—not forty. Nobody wants to hire a sixty-four-year-old."

"I guess I should be thankful I have a job, even though every day I feel like Sisyphus—trying to uphold our brand's reputation while management thrashes around cluelessly," Kris said.

"Why are you still there?" Jo asked. "You know you don't get the respect—or salary—you deserve."

"You're right, but I've got two decades of early mornings and late nights invested with Klassik. It's not just work friends; it's all the contacts I've made. It would be tough to start over in a new industry."

"Maybe, but you know what I've said since I was laid off at fifty-four and turned gray sending out job applications for two years," Marie warned, underscoring her point by dramatically gesturing to her hair. "The farther *uphill* you are from fifty, the farther *downhill* your employment prospects."

"I know …"

Despite her complaint about gray hair, Marie's hair remained predominantly dark brown. She stood five-six but made an impression more like five-ten because of her perfect posture and bright blue eyes that were hard to turn away from. She'd been a successful pharmaceutical company sales rep for nearly three decades, until one day four years ago. "The purge," as she and six other over-fifty colleagues around the country called it, was announced without warning. Each was contacted individually and told their job was being eliminated in a "reorganization" of territories and responsibilities. The manager in charge was new and located on the East Coast. Marie had never met him. She considered suing for age discrimination, but seriously, what chance did even a class-action lawsuit have against a deep-pocketed pharma giant? After two years of demoralizing job-hunting, she'd landed a spot as a patient advocate for a local hospital. It paid less than half her previous income, but at least she had employer-paid health insurance again. The irony was not lost on her.

"And don't forget, you're not leaving the company you joined twenty years ago, when Mr. Pearson ran things," Diana chimed in. "You've been miserable under Roger. It's almost as if anything you suggest, he'll do the opposite—unless he thinks he can take credit for it. That said, don't leave! I'd die without you there!"

"Well, Roger's not exactly evil, but his face does appear next to the entry for 'Shitty Boss.' Even so, there's something to be said for the devil you know. How many fabulous bosses have *you* run across?" Kris countered, looking at Marie.

"Point taken," Marie conceded.

"The only solution is to be your own boss—though Misha might argue he's my boss," Susie laughed. She and her husband owned a motel on old Route 66. Hospitality was a business that attracted many immigrant families from India and their American-born offspring, especially those with the surname Patel. It had become a good-humored inside joke that the Patel Motel Cartel owned roughly half of all motels in the United States. More-established families helped others get started, and it was a relatively low-risk business to get into. Susie and Misha hadn't taken the easy route, though. They had invested beyond the bare minimum in their property to play up its historic pedigree while modernizing rooms to appeal to both retiree and millennial road trippers. Their rooms came with free Wi-Fi, plenty of sockets and USB ports, a pillow menu, and water bowls in the pet-friendly rooms.

"Being the boss comes with its own worries," Jo added. She was five-seven and sturdy-strong. You wouldn't want to compete with her for the last cookie on the plate; she could muscle you out of the way with her hips, an arm—or a sideways shot of her brown eyes. "And when your job is a physical one, like mine, you worry about staying fit enough to do the job until you want to retire—which, for me, is never!" she laughed.

Jo hadn't gone to college. Instead, she married her high-school sweetheart, Manny, with whom she had four kids. She'd worked a hodgepodge of low-paying office jobs when the kids were younger. She wasn't unhappy, overall, but she'd always loved working with her hands more than sitting in a swivel chair. Friends and family had called her Mrs. Fixit for as long as she could remember, so when the last child started middle school, she went to Central New Mexico Community College to get her associate's degree in plumbing and gas fitting. After certification and licensing, she teamed up with a small firm whose owner, Juan, was about to retire. He and his wife had raised three girls, and though the daughters didn't want any part of his plumbing business, they'd been drawn to nontraditional work. His oldest was part owner of a moving company, the middle daughter was a police officer, and the youngest was working for the U.S. Forest Service.

Juan knew that, as a middle-aged woman, Jo would work harder and smarter than any young guy coming out of the community college. He took her on as a fourth daughter in an apprentice-to-ownership plan. Four years ago, Jo took sole control of the wrenches, augers, and everything else in the tool kit.

Jo's Plumbing, as it was now known, had created a unique niche. Having heard her friends, including the G7, complain about how they hated being home alone with male repairmen, she'd set up her business so each service call was responded to by a male-female team, upon request. Regardless of age, her crew's dress code was "No visible underwear. No butt cracks.

No boob cracks." Jo had an arrangement with the college to provide internships to newly graduated students, so she always had a fresh crop of trainees—mostly young men. The women were, for the most part, long-term employees, as few other plumbing companies welcomed them. Kris had volunteered her marketing expertise during the business transition, and the promotional strategies they'd developed were still bearing fruit.

"How are *you* saving your sanity during the job search?" Jo asked Janice. A year ago, Janice, fifty-two, had lost her job as a chef. She'd moved around from one kitchen to another when her daughter Amy was younger in order to keep hours more suitable to raising a child—a notoriously difficult trick in the restaurant industry. Now that she *could* work longer hours, she was of an age where she didn't like to spend more than one shift on her feet. Her latest restaurant had closed a year ago and Janice was finding no matches for her experience and salary needs, especially as newbies were willing to take grunt positions for far less than she required.

"I've been helping a couple of caterers and working on-call for commercial kitchens, but it makes for a fragmented, frantic schedule. And my boss is always changing. It helps me meet new people, but I never feel ownership of my work," Janice explained. "Though it gives me a way to prove I'm familiar with the latest local and national food trends."

"Like 'molecular gastronomy'?" Susie asked, pointing her nose in the air.

"Yes! In fact, it's even hit Albuquerque," Janice replied. "Such a farce. It's a way to create buzz and inflate prices by using what, honestly, are very simple techniques."

"Why is it that even when you maintain your professional credentials, you still have to go the extra mile to prove yourself?" Sharon asked rhetorically. "I'm tired of proving myself. I want to work for those who appreciate me, so I've been spending some volunteer hours offering personal finance assistance to the elderly at the senior center—checkbook balancing, tax preparation, that sort of thing. At least they're appreciative, I get to feel useful, and I can show prospective employers that I'm staying mentally active."

At five-foot-six, with just a hint of a muffin top and fewer wrinkles than one might expect on the face of someone who'd just turned sixty-four, Sharon was supremely ordinary looking until she smiled. Then her green eyes sparkled and you felt as though you'd been given a gift.

She'd been savoring Janice's contribution to the table: a Middle Eastern–inspired mix of spiced ground lamb, pine nuts, and dried apricot (all locally sourced) served on crostini. "I know you're trained as a chef, so anyone would expect you to cook well," Sharon said, raising her plate as if presenting evidence to a jury, "but you have a special talent for pulling flavors together in unforgettable ways!"

"Thank you!" Janice beamed. "I'm trying to use my unpaid free time to experiment again."

"Experiment," Sharon repeated, slowly. "For all the *talk* about reinvention and multiple careers being the new normal, when you hit middle age—especially if you're a woman—society seems to assume you're at the tail end of your useful life."

"No shit!" Janice jumped in. "It's as if you're wearing a stamp across your forehead that says, *Best by age 50,* which gives everyone an excuse to toss you out with the sour milk."

They all laughed at her analogy, but it was a bitter laughter.

"Maybe something more radical is called for, then," Sharon continued.

"*You*, radical?" Kris teased, but gently.

Appearing to not have heard Kris, Sharon continued, half to herself, "What if what we need at our *true* middle age—our forties through our sixties—is more experimentation? Like when we were in high school and college, imagining what we might do with our lives—before we settled into fulfilling expectations. All that potential."

5

Countless variations on familiar themes. That was Kris's assessment of the eyewear industry as she surveyed the vendor hall at the International Vision Expo in Las Vegas. It was her umpteenth year representing Klassik Eyewear at the show, and very little had changed in the industry, until recently. Most of the technical innovation and revenue growth was on the optics side of the business.

Granted, the digital revolution had enabled online direct-to-consumer eyewear sales; virtual reality had introduced online fittings; and now, 3D printing was promising greater customization—though materials and styles were limited.

Yet even with the recent innovation, Kris didn't see much that excited her. Sure, styles changed—or, rather, went through a predictable rotation of "contemporary" and "retro." Maybe that was because the vast majority of brands were owned and controlled by a handful of conglomerates. The few scrappy indie brands struggled to capture the spotlight, but at least a couple of them seemed to have some niche cachet.

Despite her daily frustrations with Roger, Kris loved her

job and the way it allowed her to express her creativity while serving a human need. And she appreciated that the industry had growth potential: Demand for glasses would only increase in the near term as the horde of baby boomers required reading glasses, progressives, and prescription sunglasses for those sunny retirement destinations. As she surveyed the competition, she took mental notes of new promotional approaches she might pitch.

She finished her circuit of the show floor just before the doors opened to attendees and returned to the Klassik booth. Frumpy. Cost-conscious. Nothing to see here, the booth proclaimed. The display setup hadn't changed in three years. Only one of the banners had been updated to show some new styles, but it was just more of the same.

Despite her unrelenting, clever efforts, Kris had been unable to get Roger to understand that optics count at an optical convention. He seemed to think the company could project a winning proposition just by having the sales team *say* Klassik frames were the best value. But value alone doesn't make the sale in the image business.

Even the name, Klassik Eyewear, was dated. In the right hands, her hands, it might have been used in the service of a retro-hip campaign, but Roger had dismissed that approach as dangerously edgy. As the financials became increasingly frightful, the CEO had retrenched. Instead of learning from what the rest of the industry was doing, he remained committed to cost-cutting. He professed to want innovation. (He must have been half awake in his business school classes.) He'd even used the buzz phrase "digital transformation" in one meeting recently. But Kris suspected that Roger feared anything he didn't understand, which was a lot, including digital transformation, which required investment rather than cost-cutting.

Another thing irked her—this year more than ever. Throughout the exhibition hall, she'd seen display after display featuring the flat, unlined faces of twenty-something models. Yet the end customers were predominantly middle-aged and older. Sure, younger adults (she refused to call them millennials) also bought glasses, sometimes as a pure fashion statement, but the dependable revenue was with the "mature" segment. Why was everyone so enthralled with young models? Did they really think a woman in her fifties, sixties, or seventies believed she'd look like the wrinkle-free waif modeling $450 frames? The only over-thirty faces belonged to the now-clichéd, scruffy-faced, salt-and-pepper-haired men channeling George Clooney from a decade ago.

As the traffic passed her booth all day—and it mostly passed rather than stopping—Kris kept projecting her friendly public face, saying hello to those she saw approaching the booth, greeting acquaintances by name. Unlike other booth staff, she never let herself be caught looking at her phone when a potential customer passed by. Always be engaging.

Even though her demeanor was on auto-pilot, it was draining.

Current and former buyers—when she could get them to stop—explained that they were looking for something new: eco, statement, eye-catching. When she gently pressed one former buyer for an explanation of why he no longer carried Klassik styles, he admitted he'd had too many customer complaints about poor quality, especially problems with the hinge screws. She made a mental note to talk with the production and sales teams about that.

. . .

This year, the show was more demoralizing than any she could recall. It felt as if Klassik were spiraling into oblivion. Nothing could pull them into competitive position if they stayed on their current course. The sales team had little to show for their efforts. They'd been forced to resort to arm twisting to fill the table at their customer-appreciation dinner on the Strip. The doldrums seemed to be affecting even perky Ashley; maybe she did have half a brain.

On the afternoon of the show's final day, Kris decided it was time to pull rank and leave Ashley to pack up the booth. She felt her shoulders and face relax as she exited the convention center for a quick sushi-and-cocktails meeting with a friend from a much larger eyewear brand.

Kris and Meredith Colvin had met a decade ago at Vision Expo when they happened to both arrive late at the fashion show. Standing together in the rear of the hall, they discovered they shared a similar take on the industry. They'd stayed in touch and now had a standing date for post-event cocktails.

Meredith waved as she saw Kris at the bar. Striding across the room in her two-inch platform shoes, she projected energy throughout her almost skeletal frame, from her toes to her boyishly short red hair. She was two years younger than Kris and had recently been promoted to senior vice president, according to her LinkedIn profile.

"Great to see you—you look terrific!" Meredith gushed as she gave Kris a quick embrace before sitting down.

"Well, as terrific as one can look after brutal booth duty," Kris laughed. "And you—you have that perennial California glow!"

"With a little help from my friends in jars," Meredith confided. "Tell me what's new in New Mexico."

"Nothing. That's the problem."

The two women had long ago recognized they were not direct competitors, which allowed them to safely support each other's careers. Meredith was Kris's most valued professional confidante, so Kris shared her concern that Klassik Eyewear was about to crumble under debt and a lack of leadership.

"I've said it before, but I'll say it again: You need to get out of there!" Meredith insisted, her hazel eyes flashing as she raised a martini to her lips. "In fact, you should come work with me."

"You mean *for* you."

"Maybe at first. Maybe according to the org chart, but we're growing and could really use your expertise. You know more about the industry than any other marketing executive I know. You have good instincts. You're wasting your talents in Albuquerque."

"Thanks. Your opinion means a lot. But I can't leave the state. My husband's job isn't transferable, and I can't really see us loving a long-distance relationship at this point in our lives —even with FaceTime. Plus, I don't think I'd have the patience for LA traffic."

"You get used to it. You sure?"

"Yes," Kris said slowly. "It's tempting. It really is. But I know in my heart it's not a realistic option. Anyhow, tell me all your latest adventures!"

6

An hour later, Kris opened the door to her hotel room, tossed her tote bag on the desk chair, kicked off her "comfortable" black pumps, and crawled under the covers, prepared to channel surf. Just as she picked up the TV remote, her phone rang.

"Kris? It's Sandy." The HR manager was calling from her work number, even though it was well past office hours.

"Is everything OK?"

"I'm glad I caught you. I have some news. Roger, who is here in the office with me, announced a reorganization today."

Kris's stomach fell as stress hormones pulsed through every vein. She knew this call could have only one narrative arc. She remained silent as Sandy continued.

"The market has been challenging, and revenues, as you know, have been falling, so we're merging your position with Sales. Mark will become vice president of Sales and Marketing. Your position is being eliminated. Your office is being packed up this evening, and your things should be delivered to your home before you return tomorrow."

Well, at least it was short and free of any false praise—not that Sandy was capable of genuine support or empathy.

Sandy continued with what was clearly a written script: "The severance paperwork will be emailed to your personal address. Please read the materials carefully before signing and returning them. You are being offered three months' severance pay. There will also be information about COBRA in the attachments. Please reach out to me if you have any questions as you're going through the materials."

Oh, I'd like to reach out and … she's not even worth it, Kris thought as she reined in her amygdala.

The call ended, and Kris laid her phone down next to the remote. The TV remained black. So like gutless Roger to announce a reorg when half the staff was out of the office.

Through the open blinds, she could see the garish lights that defined Las Vegas. All those colors flashing. All that glittering fool's gold. Fitting, she philosophized, that she should be let go while she was trapped on this island of artifice. Roger at least tried to act the part of a leader (though his performance was a flop); Sandy couldn't do even a passable impression of someone who cared about human resources. She hadn't asked how the show went, Kris realized. This had been in the cards for how long?

Clearly, she'd been far too naïve. Throughout her career she'd made a point to act with integrity. It was in her DNA. But she frequently gave others too much latitude to prove themselves fair players. Even when she suspected they had malicious motives, she interacted collegially with everyone. Look where that had gotten her.

Slowly, meditatively, she crawled out from beneath the bedding and walked over to the window. She realized she'd been holding her breath through most of the call. She took a long, deep inhalation. She wasn't prone to self-pity or anger. Her pragmatic streak ran through to the marrow. So, what now?

As if to answer, a ding announced a text message. She returned to the bedside and saw it was from Diana. *I just got laid off.*

Me too! Kris responded. *Just got a call from Sandy. U OK?*

Mad as hell they let U go! What the hell are they thinking?

They're not.

Right. Why should that change. [eye-roll emoji]

Let's talk next week. Come for lunch Mon. My place.

Kris was acutely aware that Diana lived, if not paycheck to paycheck, without a financial cushion to soften this blow. She'd inherited her parents' modest home when they passed, but Kris doubted there was much cash for unexpected expenses once essential monthly bills were paid.

Mike. How would he take the news? They'd always had a model marriage, an equitable partnership. They'd never squabbled about money. They didn't live extravagantly, but neither did they worry about small indulgences like new clothes or gear or vacations. Still trying to process what the news meant, Kris texted her husband.

Hey, hope you're still up. I just got some bad news. I got laid off. Diana too. "Reorg" puts Marketing under Mark. Now I get why Roger was so hot to hire cheap, chirpy Ashley. Yeah, I'm a little bitter. I'll get over it. But I can't talk or FaceTime tonight. Got to sort this out on my own first. I'll see you at dinner tomorrow. XO

Oh, K, I'm so sorry to hear that. But really, maybe it's for the best. They didn't treat you right, and you've been miserable for years. This could be an opportunity to do something new and better! It'll be OK. Safe trip home. XXOO

Don't tell Kate, OK?

Got it.

She'd text the rest of the G7 while waiting for her flight home the next day. She knew they'd offer support, be angry on her behalf, and check in with her over the weeks ahead. But Kate was another story.

They'd always been close. But unlike some mothers she knew, who tried to cultivate a best-friends relationship with their daughters, Kris had always respected Kate's boundaries. She didn't want to be the old, slow, spare tire when Kate and her pals got together. Nevertheless, she'd been her daughter's sounding board and role model. Now, with Kate nearly through college, Kris was neither an everyday mom nor a professional working woman.

She'd text Kate in the morning, as usual. She'd tell her about the show and sushi.

7

The last week of September was fuzzy around the edges. It was a work week, but Kris wasn't going to work. It didn't feel like vacation because Mike was at work. She wasn't home sick, yet she was home alone. She couldn't get together with friends mid-day because they were working. Even Diana had immediately taken a part-time volunteer position at the animal shelter, something she'd been wanting to do for years.

Her first order of business had been to review the severance documents. Klassik was offering three months' salary. Not great but not nothing, and she knew she'd need time to find something new that was worthy of her full attention.

There were strings attached to the money. Even though Klassik had terminated the relationship, they wanted to restrict her from working for a competitor while she was receiving severance. And then there was an odd nondisclosure agreement. If she took the severance, she was not to reveal whether or not she had received a payout. Her attorney had explained it was more like a payoff so she wouldn't sue for age discrimination. If she accepted the package, she was also forbidden from disparaging the company. Not that she would. She had too much professional integrity. But she found that clause off-putting. Standard provision, her attorney said. Take the money and good riddance, he counseled.

She wasn't the suing sort, so she signed.

Why? It's so unfair.

Yeah, life's unfair.

I've done an excellent job. Always said yes when asked to take on more work. I leaned in—even before Sheryl Sandberg told women to do what they were already doing. Even more since Kate's been away at college. This should be the pinnacle of my career; I've climbed the ladder, paid my dues, networked, and now I have more time than ever to focus on work.

The universe has an ironic sense of humor.

That, or the universe is sexist and ageist like Roger.

Like two evenly matched tennis players, the voices in her head battled for Kris's attention all week.

It was such a bad business decision.

And you're surprised by that?

I'll never get another job in the industry while I'm in Albuquerque—at least, not one I'd find as fulfilling.

Now there's a concept. Fulfilling. Most of Mom's generation didn't have the luxury of pursuing a fulfilling career. They did what was open to them if they wanted to work. Or if they had to work.

Well, I have to work. We can't support our current lifestyle on one salary.

Maybe not, but we won't be on the streets.

But that's not the point. I have as much right to a fulfilling and financially rewarding job as Mike does. And I like to work. Besides, what will Mom say when she learns I've been laid off?

Who cares? You're a grown woman. She had her life challenges; you have yours.

But she'll be disappointed.

But, but, but. Get off your butt and call her. Rip the bandage off and move on.

She had to plan that call. Pick the right time of day—after her mother would have had breakfast but before she left for whatever morning activity she had planned. That would give her the day to process the news so she wouldn't lose sleep over it.

But if she called and her father answered? Of course, he'd have to know, too, but her mother would want to know first—a mother's prerogative. Maybe an email would be better. Why hadn't she thought of that earlier? It would give her more time to choose her words.

Dear Mom and Dad,

For someone who was known as an effective communicator professionally, she couldn't find the next words.

Don't bury the lede. She'd read somewhere that journalists were taught to present the meat of the news story in the first paragraph. Though maybe that was old-school training? It seemed a lot of contemporary journalism read more like a mystery. Nevertheless, her no-nonsense mother wouldn't want anything but the facts, straight up. Her lawyer father might appreciate her setting the scene first, providing the circumstances before she presented the clincher. But it was her mother's imagined reaction that made her heart tighten.

She needed a second cup of coffee to get the words flowing.

I'm writing to let you both know that I was recently— Strike that. Even though contemporary usage had no problem with split infinitives, her parents were from a different era and might see one in print as evidence of shoddy work. And "recently" would be too vague for her father.

I'm writing to let you both know that I was laid off last week as a result of a Klassik "reorganization." I got the news the evening before I left Las Vegas, where I'd just wrapped the big annual trade show. My friend Diana Delgado, whom you've met, and a couple of sales reps were also let go. All of us are over fifty, but Diana and I are not suing, because these suits, as Dad knows, are rarely worth the time and money. In any case, we wouldn't want to return to work at Klassik under the current leadership.

I don't yet know what I'll do next. Mike is being very supportive and says I should take time figuring that out, but finding a new position at my age could take time, so I'll be dedicating "working hours" to that task.

I'm sorry to be sharing disappointing news by email, but I'm still processing this development myself and am not quite ready to talk about it.

I hope you are happy and well. I imagine the trees are beginning to turn there. Enjoy them for me. We'll talk soon.

Love,

Kris

Five minutes later, Kris had a reply:

Dear Kris,

Mom here. Your father and I just read your message and wanted to let you know right away that we are so sorry you lost your job. We know you loved the work but not the management, so maybe in the long run this will turn out for the best. Even so, we realize it prob-

ably doesn't feel that way at the moment. We are confident that some-
thing good is in your future.

Please let us know if there's anything we can do. We look forward
to a chat when you're up to it.

Much love,
Mom & Dad

Prompt. Efficient. Her mother as she'd always known her. Not overly effusive about her prospects, but encouraging.

As September reached its end, evening temperatures presaged fall. The cottonwoods in the bosque would soon turn their rich autumn gold.

"This year, you'll have more time to actually enjoy fall," Mike said, enviously, as he prepared chicken breasts for the grill. "You should take your bike along the river when the leaves turn," he added, as if reading her mind.

"I probably should," she agreed as she whisked the salad dressing.

"Have you told Kate yet?"

"No. Haven't figured out how to spin it."

"You don't have to spin anything. Shit happens. It wasn't your fault. You've got nothing to feel sorry about."

"In my head I know that's true, but I feel sick about it. My gut is a tangled ball of nerves."

"You've been sucker punched. It's a natural reaction."

"I don't want Kate to worry."

"She doesn't have to. We can support her through her last year of college. Then she's on her own. A little economizing will do her good. *We* managed on next to nothing when we were her age."

"I know, but I feel as if I'm letting her down. That I'm a failure for losing my job."

"I can't change how you *feel*," Mike said as he washed and dried his hands, "but what happened in no way means you're a failure. Even someone as organized and competent as you can't control everything and everyone. That's an important lesson for Kate to learn, too. You'll figure out a way through this," he said giving her a hug. As he drew her close, she became aware of her slight belly padding and his maddeningly flat stomach. For no good reason, she was unusually annoyed that he'd been able to keep his runner's physique while she'd had to start watching what she put into her mouth when she crossed into her fifties.

After dinner, Kris called Kate.

"Mom? Is everything OK?"

"Not really. But it will be."

8

A week after losing her job, Kris's alarm still went off at 6 a.m., but Mike had persuaded her to change the tone to a less-insistent one than the jangly Presto; she chose Slow Rise. He'd also pointed out that she could sleep in while he got ready for work, but she couldn't allow herself that indulgence. She still checked email immediately, but now the count was under ten messages each morning in just her personal account, and most of those were junk.

Roles in the morning mother-daughter text exchange had shifted just enough to unsettle Kris, who was used to being the one offering support and encouragement.

How are you doing, mom?

Fine. Spruced up my résumé yesterday and am hitting the job boards.

You'll find something perfect. I just know it.

Hope so. How bout U?

Good. Mia and I are planning to go to the game this weekend. Figured we should go once in 4 yrs! [laughter emoji]

Have fun!

As she set her phone down, Kris felt an unfamiliar emotion tugging at her chest. Envy? Maybe so. Not of her daughter's youth, but of Kate's confidence in the fact that her whole life and career stretched out before her. Her future held optionality. Kris wished she could believe the same was true for herself, but she was a realist. How to avoid realism devolving into pessimism or fatalism was the existential question staring back at her from the mirror.

The threat of those corrosive attitudes was new to Kris. Her entire career had been one lucky break after another—for which she had amply prepared, she reminded herself. Maybe she hadn't risen as high as she might have if she'd been able to relocate, but she'd always had a sense of job security. It's easy to feel optimistic and competent when you're benefitting from a positive feedback loop, she told herself. Even when Roger had been at his most frustrating, she'd always had the support of her closest colleagues and industry connections. But finding ways to face the day with genuine confidence when unemployed required conscious rerouting of the chaotic traffic in her head.

With no job to get to on time, she had no excuse for not exercising, yet it seemed harder to push herself through the full routine. Watching the local and national news as she worked out just made her more depressed. The federal Bureau of Labor Statistics reported that the unemployment rate had fallen the past three months and had dropped to 4.1% in October—but New Mexico's rate was 6.1%.

Online business news was no better. McKinsey & Company had just released a Women in the Workforce report that opened with this cheery finding: "Women remain underrepresented at every level in corporate America, despite earning more college degrees than men for 30 years and counting." It got better: "Many employees think women are well repre-sented in leadership when they see only a few."

"More like, *'Many male employees think ...,'*" Kris muttered to herself.

And then there was coverage of the gender pay gap, noting that, based on average male and female salaries, the average woman started working for free in mid-October.

But her age felt like the biggest obstacle. Fifty-five. Kris didn't need statisticians to tell her that, in addition to all the other numbers pushing against her, the date on her driver's license was probably the most powerful. Sure, economists claimed the over-fifty cohort would be needed in the work-force for the foreseeable future and that jobs would be there for them, but the examples they gave were part-time or low-salary positions. Grandma jobs, like museum docent or volunteer coordinator. She wanted to be immersed in business buzz. But what business?

Kris was determined not to let the odds defeat her. She was in better shape than anyone of any age at Klassik. She didn't feel old—at least not until the past week. When faced with projects and deadlines, her energy spiked. So why did she feel so drained?

And why was she suddenly focusing on how old she looked? Last Saturday, after a leisurely wakeup, Kris complained to Mike, who'd been shaving on his side of the vanity, "I've always relied more on my brains than my looks, and I'd never get a facelift, but I gotta say, it's a little annoying to see my face dissolve. I mean, how did that happen?"

"What do you mean, 'dissolve'?"

"You know how when you look at a young person's face,

it's clearly defined? You can outline it with an even stroke. Like when we're choosing frames for a face shape, it's round, square, or oval. But now, the outline of my face has these indentations and little droops, and ..."

"K, it happens to us all. Have you looked at my face lately?"

"I just gave it a good look, didn't I?" she grinned slyly.

"Well then, you should know by now that faces change as we age."

"I do know, but in the workplace—any place—the expectations for women are so much more unrealistic. Have you ever seen a man on TV who's obviously gotten facial injections to plump his lips?"

"Ouch."

"Gray in a man's hair makes him a 'graybeard,' someone experienced and distinguished and automatically recognized as an authority. But gray—or worse, wrinkles and sagging skin —just classify a woman as *old*."

"If that's how some people feel, if they can't see beyond those wisdom lines, then they don't deserve you."

"True, but there are a lot of people like that in the world, and they make it hard to land a job," she sighed as she smoothed sunscreen-enhanced moisturizer over her face and neck.

There had never been an age when Kris hadn't pictured herself as a working woman. A professional. A contributor to society. A provider for her family. It was the first time since high school she was without employment. Every previous job change had been of her volition. The odds had caught up with her.

During the first couple of unemployed weeks, she felt as if she were in a boat, drifting downstream without oars, with no control over the speed of the current and no knowledge of hazards ahead.

She'd never not known what to do—until now.

She wandered the house, thinking, daydreaming, worrying.

Just do something, she chastised herself. She cleaned drawers. Reorganized her closet. Made piles of clothes and shoes for Goodwill. Spent triple the time she normally would planning and cooking dinner. Paid bills. That cleared the mental fog.

Realizing she could face a two-year job search, as Marie had, she opened up a spreadsheet and began entering numbers. Nonnegotiable expenses like mortgage and gas got one color while second-tier expenses like the cable TV package got another. Third tier was everything nonessential to staying out of debt. Could wine really be nonessential?

Severance was a small cushion, and she was determined they wouldn't dip into retirement savings, so she disciplined herself to spend a forty-hour week on her job search. Scanning local and national job boards, reading the latest advice on how to craft a résumé when you're over fifty, how to lard a résumé with keywords mentioned in job postings, how to convey experience—but not too much experience. It was a full-time job.

At the end of her second week away from Klassik, she had scanned thousands of job postings, emailed ten applications, sent casually professional messages to three dozen acquaintances, and updated her LinkedIn profile.

Over Friday pre-dinner cocktails, Mike asked how she was feeling. "It's a new kind of exhaustion. I'm physically tired—though I shouldn't be. I'm trying not to be defeatist about the whole search process, but I've learned to read between the lines of job announcements. Even when the posters try to write nondiscriminatory descriptions, you can tell by the qualifications they're looking for someone well under fifty, even for management positions. I mean, who hires a marketing director for a firm of 2,000 people yet asks for 'two to five years' experience'? I look at those ads and know it's a waste of time to apply, especially when you have to tailor every cover letter and résumé so it contains all the essential keywords."

"You know, you don't have to spend all your time looking for another job immediately. We'll be OK."

"OK for a while, maybe, but I don't want us to live like college students again, so I need an income. Besides, I *like* to work."

"I know you do. And you've always been a terrific employee, but maybe you should take advantage of this unexpected break to enjoy the change of pace."

"But the pace is simultaneously boring and anxiety-inducing."

"Well, that's to be expected right now. You're still in shock. But seriously, give yourself some time to regroup. You've worked overtime for so long, and what appreciation did you get for that?"

"Nada."

"Right. So it's time to appreciate and value yourself. Invest in yourself for a while."

"How? Get an MBA? I'm so done with school. Besides, every MBA I know got the degree just to have the credentials. It didn't make them smarter or better managers, and at fifty-five, I doubt an MBA would be enough to clear the age hurdle."

"You don't have to get another degree. I mean, Bill Gates

and Mark Zuckerberg didn't even get undergrad degrees, and they've been successful in business. Let yourself be open to opportunities that may not seem obvious. You've always been the creative thinker in the family. And at Klassik you were always finding ways to improve the business—even if the dolt at the top wouldn't implement your ideas."

"So what should I do?"

"Give yourself permission to do nothing. At least for a couple of weeks. Ignore the job ads. I know you want to work, but don't box yourself in too early. Be patient."

"Not my strong suit."

"So work on that," he said, giving her a kiss on the cheek. "In the meantime, let's take in a bit of the Balloon Fiesta this weekend."

Albuquerque's International Balloon Fiesta was a big deal—the largest ballooning event in the world, in fact. The nine-day event in October reliably brought hundreds of thousands of tourists to town and in 2017 would have more than 173 million dollars' worth of economic impact. It was the most well-known annual event associated with the city. And no wonder. The images were hard to beat.

From the flames of propane burners just before sunrise ascensions to evening glow displays and fireworks, there was color, fire, and excitement all week. But the money shots were of masses of vibrantly colored balloons floating above the Rio Grande or of balloons with the Sandia Mountains behind them. Especially for those with professional photo equipment, there were endless opportunities for uniquely framed shots given the constant interplay of cobalt blue sky, puffy white clouds, and patterned balloons.

Mike and Kris had lived in the city long enough that they no longer made an effort to actively participate in the festivities. In fact, they made sure to avoid certain arteries during the event's framing weekends in particular. But this year, Mike insisted they enjoy the first Saturday's morning glow and mass ascension. They'd bike to the field to avoid traffic and parking headaches. That meant a very early morning alarm.

The thermometer registered forty-seven when they left the house wearing fleece jackets, but the chill felt good. Pumping blood to her muscles, elevating her heart rate, Kris was more alert, more herself, than she'd felt all week. When they reached Balloon Fiesta Park, though, her mood changed.

The field was covered with balloons in various stages of inflation, crews, visitors, and media. A festive, anticipatory buzz on the ground built until the first of the enormous balloons lifted off to exclamations and raised cameras. It was stunning. No denying that. So why was her mood dropping further with each ascent? What was holding her down?

It occurred to Kris that she'd never taken a hot air balloon ride. It wasn't on her bucket—or basket—list. Was that because someone else would be at the controls, putting her in a precariously high position from which she might drop unexpectedly? Well, she'd already been dropped, so no worries there. Ballooning was a passive activity for the passenger. Maybe that's why it didn't appeal. Still, the views would be unique. No, she'd rather look up to the air dance of colors.

Kris had never bothered much with self-reflection. Life was busy, full, and active. She knew what needed to be done as an employee, wife, mother, and friend. She'd never fretted long about any decision. If something didn't work out, she'd had the intellectual, emotional, and financial resources to change course. This was different. The buffeting winds of age were stronger. Balloonists wouldn't take off on a flight if the wind speeds were above ten miles per hour. A career liftoff was, she knew, rare for a woman over fifty.

When wind speeds prohibited ascent, balloonists hung around on the ground until conditions improved, even if that meant waiting for another day. Kris couldn't just wait around. Her prevailing wind speed was only increasing.

That evening, just as they'd finished cleaning up dinner dishes, her phone rang. It was Gerry Pearson, founder of Klassik Eyewear and her former boss. "This is Kris," she answered.

"What the hell?" Gerry exclaimed. She'd never heard him use even a marginal swear word in all the years she'd worked for him. "I just heard Roger laid you off. Is it true?"

"Yes, I'm afraid it's true."

"Well, that's just a shame. I'd heard rumors the business was in trouble, but why would he get rid of the strongest leader in the company?"

Kris, mindful of her NDA, remained silent.

"I guess we both know the answer to that," Gerry continued sarcastically.

They talked for another minute or two, and Kris explained she was diving into the job search.

"You be sure to let me know if there's anything I can do for you, OK? A reference or a phone call or whatever you need. Promise?"

"Promise. I really appreciate the call, Gerry. You were the best boss I've ever had."

9

Luna was the happiest creature in the park, enthusiastically sniffing everything to her left and right as she strained against Diana, who was holding the other end of the leash. It was a jewel-blue Sunday afternoon in mid-October—perfect for a walk around their favorite park.

Luna, a two-year-old yellow lab mix, had been overjoyed when Diana adopted her from the animal shelter as a pup. Though Diana had never had pets as a child because of her father's multiple allergies, she was now a besotted dog lover. Before allowing herself a visit to the shelter a decade ago, she'd borrowed every book on dog training from the library and visited every dog expert's website. After bringing home her first rescue dog, she enrolled them in dog-training classes. Luna was her second shelter pet.

Previously, on weekdays when she was working, Diana had had limited time for walks, so they simply circuited the block. But on weekends, she had always taken Luna to a public park to socialize her with other dogs and so she could learn how to play nicely with unfamiliar large and small humans. It had been an excuse to visit different neighborhoods as well, but since the layoff, she was more mindful of her gas budget and had become a regular at their closest public park.

It was the nicest and largest park in the northwest quadrant of the city. There were recreational options for every age, from kiddie playgrounds to ball diamonds and tennis courts for youth and adults. Walking paths connected the picnic shelter to the horseshoe pit and to all the other amenities. Luna's finest moment in this park had been catching an errant tennis ball after a single bounce on the path in front of them. The players had enjoyed the retriever's instincts and yelled over to Diana that her dog should keep the ball; this was going to be its last match anyhow.

Sometimes they stopped to visit with other dog walkers, and that always brought a smile to both their faces.

That afternoon in October, as Diana bent down to give Luna a drink from her travel bowl, she heard a growl behind her, turned her head, and came within two feet of a snarling rottweiler jaw. As she straightened up, she came face to face with Roger.

"Oh, it's you," his eyes widened. "I didn't know you had a dog. Good exercise for you, I'm sure. Well, we must finish our walk. Rex, come on, let's go," he said as he pulled on the snarling dog's leash.

The encounter, over in less than ten seconds, took them both by surprise. Roger, maybe embarrassed—was he capable of shame?—couldn't move along fast enough. But Rex had other plans. Just ten yards ahead, he took a dump beside a bench. As soon as Rex finished, Roger hurried him onward.

Diana and Luna had to pass the befouled bench and an older woman sitting in the middle of it. "He does that every week," the woman complained as she shook her head. "Never picks up after his brute of a dog. Just leaves the steaming pile of shit to smell up a nice afternoon." The woman was maybe eighty and had a cane braced at her side, but she sat with superb posture. Diana guessed that she lived in the nearby senior center. She was dressed as if she'd gone to church—or out to lunch—earlier in the day: black wool pants, flat but stylish black walking shoes, what looked like a cashmere camel-colored shell, and a belted black wind breaker. The juxtaposition of the woman's elegant outfit and the word "shit" coming out of her mouth made Diana chuckle.

"I'm sorry he stunk up your lovely rest stop. Let me take care of that for you," Diana said as she pulled a doggie bag from her pocket. "I wouldn't blame the dog, though. He's just doing his business."

"You're right, but I *do* blame his owner. And I saw his dog growling at you, so I still say he's a brute."

"It's all in the training," Diana explained. "Undisciplined and irresponsible humans tend to end up with ill-behaved pets. I see the difference training makes every day when I work with shelter animals and walk dogs for their owners."

"Well, that owner seems like a real piece of shit himself— pardon my language," the woman continued. "There are clear signs posted that dog owners are to pick up after their pets. How hard is it to bend down and collect the mess, as you just did? I swear, some people have no consideration for others." She shook her sleek bob of silver hair for emphasis. "I'd yell after him to pick up after his animal, but I'm worried the dog would take a bite out of me."

"Hm," Diana mused. "That might be wise. Do you walk here every Sunday, and is that dog here every Sunday afternoon?"

"I'm afraid so. We seem to be on the same schedule."

"How would you feel about meeting me and my dog at the parking lot next Sunday? We'll walk with you to your bench and deal with the mess so you can enjoy your afternoon."

"That would be lovely! I'm Sofia," she said, extending her right hand while letting Luna lick her left one.

As she walked on with Luna, Diana realized it had been an entire month since she'd seen Roger. A whole four weeks since she'd last heard a sideways remark about her weight—from anyone.

She'd been overweight her entire life and had been forced to develop antibodies against both innocently hurtful and intentionally cruel comments about her size. She was far from the stereotypical fat lady as portrayed on TV shows and in movies, but her pudginess was undeniable and impossible for many to ignore. In high school, she quickly learned she'd be the last chosen for teams and that the only prom invitations would come from third-rank boys—too short, too poor, or too aesthetically challenged to win the arm of more classically curvy girls.

An only child, she had stayed in Albuquerque after graduation to care for her parents, both of whom had struggled with chronic illnesses since she'd been in middle school. Though she'd dreamed of becoming a veterinarian, after high school she continued to live at home and took various receptionist and administrative assistant jobs until her mother died of kidney disease on Diana's fortieth birthday; her father passed just two months later of complications related to Parkinson's. They'd been loving parents and in love with each other. Their economic circumstances had been modest, but they'd managed to pay off the mortgage on their small ranch home, so Diana knew she'd have a roof over her head no matter what. But by the time she had the freedom to pursue a professional career, Diana had resigned herself to working jobs where her weight wouldn't draw attention.

Maybe it was the freedom from caring for ailing parents that gave her the courage to date, really for the first time, in her forties. Lord knows it took courage to entertain the idea of dating the sorts of guys who showed interest in her. The cute thirty-something busboy at the neighborhood diner turned out to be an undocumented immigrant hoping to marry his way to citizenship. Octavio, whom she'd met through one of her jobs, was more promising. He was about her age, worked for his father's construction business, and told her she had pretty eyes, which she did. He paid for their dates and didn't try to do much more than kiss her the first few times they were together, but soon he began commenting on what she ate when they went out. Clearly, he was looking for a trimmer Diana.

Before she died, Diana's mother had urged her daughter to start attending mass regularly. She wanted Diana to find "a good man." To honor her mother's wish, at least for a while, Diana began going to mass again. She'd taken to lighting a candle before she left the sanctuary, and one Sunday, shortly after her father died, she noticed a man watching her as she turned from the candles to leave the church. He was a few years older than her, dressed in crisp chinos, a button-down shirt, and a leather belt ornamented with an embossed silver tip. He introduced himself as Paul and said he'd known her father. He expressed sympathy for her loss and said he hoped she'd allow him to take her to lunch. Within a month, she was spending as much time in his home as in hers. She took his interest in spending time together as a sign that this might evolve into a mutually happy, long-term relationship. As the weeks went by, she realized they went out less and Paul was more frequently expecting her to cook for him. At first, she didn't mind. It was a change of routine cooking for someone who wasn't bedridden, someone who could help with the dishes. Until he didn't help.

She didn't notice the first time he headed off to watch TV while she tidied up. The second time, she teased him about it, but he snapped that she should be grateful he'd paid for the food, especially as he was feeding a fatty. The next meal they shared was less sociable. Paul ate but showed no interest when she tried to engage him in conversation. Realizing that she wouldn't be able to improve his mood that evening, she announced that she had to leave early. "Like hell you will!" he shouted as he unbuckled his belt. "You'll clean up the kitchen before you go or you'll get a taste of this." He whipped the belt against the table, the metal tip chipping off a piece of the soft pine. Frightened for her safety for the first time in her life, Diana did as she'd been ordered.

She never saw Paul again, and she never went back to church.

A year later, she read that Paul had beaten another woman within a breath of her life. But that wasn't what eventually landed him in jail. Only when he was found guilty of embezzling money from his employer did he do time.

In the meantime, Diana had decided that dogs made much better life partners than men.

10

Kris's November goal was to take a brisk walk every weekday. She knew the sun's Vitamin D was supposed to be good for one's mood, and it was free, so she laced up her cross-trainers and headed out the door at the first sign of self-doubt.

That unwelcome mindset usually surfaced early in the day, as she scanned half a dozen job boards. After her walk, she sent emails to every acquaintance she could think of. Each week, the list of people she hadn't reached out to shrank.

Hi, Tim,

It was great to see you in Vegas again this year. Your company's line is looking sharper than ever!

I'm no longer with Klassik and am exploring new options, preferably in the eyewear industry. Would you let me know if you hear of any positions that might be suitable? My experience includes sales, operations, and communications as well as marketing. Though I'd prefer to be based in New Mexico, I could travel as needed.

Thanks for keeping me in mind.

. . .

At the end of the day, Tim replied:

Kris,

Good to hear from you, but I'm sorry to hear you are no longer at Klassik. I'm afraid we don't have any openings right now, and everyone I interact with is still in belt-tightening mode. I wish you all the best in your job search.

Rae,

I enjoyed working with you on the committee to provide prescription glasses for low-income New Mexicans earlier this year and was really pleased with our results. I hope you'll consider inviting me to serve on that committee again.

In the meantime, if you become aware of any paid positions in your agency or other state agencies that might be a good fit for my customer-facing background, please let me know. I am no longer working at Klassik and am looking for a new position in northern New Mexico that would benefit from my managerial, organizational, and strategic skills.

Three days later, Rae responded:

Kris,

I'm sorry to hear you left Klassik. Unfortunately, I'm required to have someone currently in the industry serving in the role you had. Best of luck with your job search.

Jessica,

I know we haven't interacted much beyond the holiday parties for our spouses, but I've always enjoyed talking with you about your work in landscape design. I often thought that if I wasn't working in eyewear, I'd have been drawn to some other usefully creative field. Well, I'm no longer working in eyewear, as my position at Klassik was eliminated a couple of months ago. I don't know if your company is hiring these days, but I wanted to let you know I'm open to new industries and organizations in the region that could use my skill set —in marketing and business development perhaps? Would you let me know if you see an opportunity for me?

Jessica replied at noon:

Oh, Kris, I'm sorry to hear your news. I'd love to be able to say we have a position for you, but the scuttlebutt is that pink slips are being prepared here too. And, as someone about your age, I'm concerned I could be one of the ones whose position is eliminated in a "reorg." Those sorts of decisions tend to come down right before the holidays—to bolster year-end financials. That's why I'm responding from my personal email. Please stay in touch. I'll send leads for you and hope you'll do the same for me. I know I sound fatalistic, as if I've already lost my job, but the atmosphere has changed in my office lately, and it has nothing to do with the Thanksgiving decorations.

Dennis,

I was fascinated by how skillfully you pivoted from aerospace to electronics a couple of years ago. (Though I know Mike misses you at work!) Your comment about the skills being more important than the industry is reverberating with me now as I'm transitioning from the eyewear business to something new. I'm open to a variety of positions where I can deploy my abilities to quickly assess, strategize, organize, and manage projects and people. If you could let me know of any potential opportunities in your new firm, I'd be very appreciative.

Dennis replied:

Kris, good to hear from you. Any company would be lucky to have you on its payroll. Your drive and results speak for themselves. However, we're in a holding pattern here right now. I'll be sure to pass along any leads I hear about, though.

I was going to say, "Give my best to Mike," but I gave him my best for a decade! Seriously, I do miss working for him and hope you two are doing well.

Mara,

You asked me last year if I did any consulting. At the time, I said I was too busy with my job to take on side gigs. However, as of late September I am no longer at Klassik and am open to a variety of new engagements, including consulting. If your firm is still looking for full- or part-time consultants, I'd love to talk with the appropriate person.

Thanks for passing this news along. I hope to see you at next month's New Mexico Marketing Association lunch.

Mara, who was nearing forty, never responded.

Once she'd weeded through the job lists and sent as many emails to contacts near and far as she could stand for the day, what was left? She could thumb through general business and trade magazines that continued to appear in the mailbox, though that was easy enough to handle in the evening. What would she do if this were a business problem at work? She'd strategize after brainstorming, researching, and discussing options with others. Hm.

She picked up the pen and notepad she used for grocery lists. She started moving the pen in a circular pattern. It didn't feel right, and the pages were too small. Rummaging around in Kate's room, she found an unused spiral-bound notebook and a set of colored pencils. Setting them next to her computer on the granite island, she selected a navy pencil and put NEW PLAN at the top of the first page—and stopped.

Gazing out the window for inspiration, she began sketching an outline of the mountains in the distance. The Sandias' arch line was just uneven enough to be real. As if the wind had caught loose brow hairs above a mysterious dark eye. She drew an eye. Then the brow line. Flipping the page, she went back to circles. Then the curvature of Sandia's crest. Change the proportions. Angle the bottom. Duplicate. Add a bridge. What would its arms look like?

Absorbed, but not entirely aware of what she was doing, she was startled by the doorbell. Glancing at the page from a distance as she rose to get the door, she realized she'd drawn an unusual pair of glasses.

The UPS delivery man was waiting at the door for a signature on a box of wine. She'd forgotten to cancel their quarterly wine club membership. Oh well, one more shipment of premium bottles to enjoy over the holidays. She set the unopened box at the far end of the island and gave her sketch a second look. Not half bad. She'd forgotten she had a reasonably good hand for drawing.

In high school, art class had been one of her favorites. She earned As across the board nearly every semester, but she enjoyed art—especially sketching, whether with pencil or pastels. Though she didn't otherwise particularly enjoy visiting Boston's excellent museums, whenever her class took a field trip with sketchpads in hand to one of them, she came back with pages full of riffs on what she'd seen. Fortunately, her teacher had encouraged them to copy if they wished to or to interpret or reimagine what they were viewing. Kris always took the latter route.

Her favorite was the Isabella Stewart Gardner Museum. The eclectic art collection housed in Gardner's Venetian palazzo provided maximum variety in minimal space, but what truly engaged the young Kris was the space itself. Her sketchbook filled with the repeated pattern of the courtyard's archways. The secret garden atmosphere was mesmerizing— leaves and flowers of all sorts, season by season, set off against the Old World–inspired columns of multiple eras. Pattern, design, variety, yet cohesion. Intricate design grounded by straightforward geometry. Kris was entranced.

She might have pursued a career in some sort of art- or design-related field—architecture, landscape architecture, or graphic design. But by the time she was a junior, she was well aware that her mother saw the art path paved with, if not poverty, at least greater financial insecurity than a career in business, medicine, or law. Her brother had the law covered, and the sight of blood made her queasy, so business it was.

Another daughter might have rebelled against parental expectations. Kris wanted to please. Not exactly please; she wanted to make her mother proud. She wasn't sure why.

11

The November G7 gathering had always been held at noon on the Friday after Thanksgiving, regardless of extended family visits or travel plans. Whoever was in town gathered up Turkey Day leftovers, and the potluck turned into more fun than the official feast day.

Early that morning, Kate and her friends had headed north to Taos Ski Valley for a day spent in fresh, deep powder. Mike was out for a long, snowless, local hike with a work buddy.

At 11:45 a.m. the doorbell rang. "I know I'm early," Sharon apologized, "but I had to see how you're really doing before the rest got here and you put on your brave face."

They hugged and Kris admitted, "It's been a big adjustment. I'm still not sure where I'm headed, two months out. How are you? You look a little tired. Too much turkey yesterday?"

Sharon laughed and said, "No, it's just exhausting looking for a decent job when you're over sixty. And apologies for the bargain bottles, but my budget took a hit this month. At least there's a red and a white."

"Stop apologizing. I get it. I went into budget triage as soon as I realized what it meant to lose nearly half our income. I'm not complaining; I know we're lucky to still have one good salary, but ..."

Before she could finish her sentence, the doorbell rang again and Marie strode in with two bottles of red wine sticking out from her oversized Italian leather tote. "How are you? I've been dying to see you in the flesh. It was all I could do to not just barge in as soon as I heard the news."

"Well, I'm still standing, as you can see," Kris laughed. "You text me nearly every day, so you know what I've been up to. But seriously, I appreciate the support from someone who's been where I am."

"I just hope it doesn't take you as long to get back to work," Marie said, with a kiss on the cheek as Susie and Diana let themselves in.

Janice arrived last, carrying a covered casserole dish and a large Mason jar filled with a cranberry-red beverage. "What's that?" Marie asked. "Have you started making homemade wine?"

"Not exactly," Janice laughed as she set the jar on the island, where it caught the sun and cast a ruby shadow on the gold-toned granite. "I've been experimenting with nonalcoholic cocktails. This one's cranberry-based, of course, with a few accent flavors. You can drink it full strength on ice as an aperitif or add some sparkling water."

"I'll try it with bubbly water," Sharon offered, enthusiastically, opening the jar. "What made you think of creating a mocktail?"

"Is this a not-so-subtle hint that you think we drink too much?" asked Marie. "Because you *know* wine is the part of my cultural identity I take most seriously!" she laughed, raising her wine glass.

"I wouldn't dream of trying to separate you from a wine bottle!" Janice laughed. "The alcohol-free drink is about me, not you. November 15 was the one-year anniversary of losing my job, and I realized I'd been letting myself get a little sloppy. Not sloppy drunk, but sloppy about drinking whenever I felt like it. And I felt like it a lot. Aside from the empty calories I don't need, I didn't want to turn into an alcoholic. I've seen too many chefs slide down that road—even drinking on the job. As they get older, it's even more tempting because the booze dulls the pain of standing on your feet for hours on end. And I drank because I was angry—mad that there's such an obvious preference for younger kitchen staff, unless you own your own business, and there's no way I can finance that. So, I decided I wasn't going to let myself become the washed-up senior that employers seem to see when they look at this face." She laughed while the others protested her self-disparagement. Other than the permanent quotation marks between her brows and hints of softening in her cheeks, Janice bore few signs of being over fifty. "I decided to give up all liquor for a year—except for what I put in food, of course! You're my taste testers, so what do you say?"

"This is wonderful. It's got all sorts of things going on. Do I taste rosemary?" Jo asked. "And by the way, if fifty-two is considered 'senior,' then half a human life these days is as a senior. That's just crazy."

"Apparently, fifty is the new seventy as far as employers are concerned. Everyone let go at Klassik was fifty and over," Kris noted. "I can only take some small pleasure in knowing that one day, Sandy will find out for herself that there are only the old and the future old."

"And she's looking old before her time," Diana chimed in. "She sneaks cigarettes, and it's ruining her skin—that and sitting in the sun every day at lunch, cozying up to Roger."

"I hope they at least gave you two a decent severance package," Marie said vehemently.

"Define *decent*," Diana jumped in. "Besides, if Kris took a severance deal, she can't talk about it. But I can! They offered me one month's salary, but I turned it down because the terms required me not only to keep quiet about the money but to never say anything negative about the company or its officers and staff. I kept my mouth shut while I was there. I was the consummate professional, even when I had to take management's side in customer complaints, but no more. They can't buy my silence with one month's salary. Roger is an arrogant incompetent who is ruining everything that used to be good about the company."

"Not to mention that he was always needling you," Kris couldn't help adding.

Diana shrugged at the obvious truth and continued, "He never takes responsibility for his actions, always blames others for his bad decisions, and generally makes daily life miserable for those around him for no good reason. I just hope one day he gets what's coming to him!" It was a rare occasion when Diana dropped her cloak of calm to reveal the fierce defender of justice beneath.

"From your lips to God's ears!" Marie seconded.

"I'll admit I don't miss Roger and the squeeze he's been putting on the business and its employees, but I do miss working. How is it possible that more than half of us are unemployed?" Kris asked. "Has 'midlife layoff' become just another phase of life? Like that period of five years when it seemed everyone was getting married, or when all our friends were pregnant?"

"Well, I'm partially employed," Diana corrected her. "In fact, I'm as busy as I was working at Klassik, but now I'm running around everywhere instead of sitting in a chair all day."

"What are you doing?" Susie asked.

"I've been volunteering part-time at the animal shelter, and I've met several people who need help with their pets when they're at work or on vacation, so I started a doggie nanny service. It actually pays more per hour than what I was making at Klassik. You'd be surprised how much money some people spend on their pets. But, of course, there are no benefits, so I'm still on COBRA."

"Whoever named health insurance extension COBRA had a twisted sense of humor." Sharon grimaced.

"OK, so who's actively looking for a job?" Marie demanded, hands on hips. "Kris, Sharon, and Janice, right? Are you reviewing each others' résumés? Are you getting out there and networking? You've got to work twice as hard as a younger woman, you know."

"We know, Mrs. Bossypants!" Sharon laughed. "But it's not as simple as simply putting in the time—as you know. And some of us can't afford to take just any job. I'm not married, so I don't have insurance or a financial cushion through a spouse. Janice and Kris still have kids in college."

"I'm sorry. You're right. I know what it's like to be in application purgatory. It's just that I look at you all, and I *know* how capable you are, and it's a shame your talents are going to waste," Marie said, giving Sharon a shoulder hug, which elicited another, nearly imperceptible tightening of her lips.

"Application purgatory is one name for it; I have a few

others," Kris said. "I understand how all these AI-assisted screening services help employers, but in the end, I have to wonder if they don't screen out too many promising candidates. They're extremely literal about keywords, so if your résumé or cover letter doesn't contain enough of the terms mentioned in the job posting, then your name doesn't even get in front of human eyes."

"That's not the worst of it," Sharon jumped in, suddenly animated. "There have been positions that were great fits for me, but the only way to apply for them was through some résumé mill. You know the ones—you have to apply through a third-party site, the website where you have to upload all your documents or fill out personal information is *not* secure, and then, to add another layer of privacy violation, you end up getting spammed by 'job offers' from creeps who have scraped your résumé from those services."

"If there was ever any question before, there's no question now that the human element has disappeared from *human resources*," Janice added. "At least in hospitality there's a somewhat better chance of getting in front of the person who could hire you."

"And there's an automatic assumption that if you're over forty, your tech skills are weak. I remember one interview— one of the rare in-person interviews I was granted," Marie emphasized, "where I was interrogated about my computer skills. I wanted to tell the young woman from HR who was doing the initial screening, 'Listen here, *piccola ragazza*, you like to talk about digital natives, well, I'm one of the *original* digital natives. I used the first generation of computers. I remember floppy disks. I've learned more new applications and technologies than you have!' But of course, I held my tongue." The others chuckled. "I'd learned by then that these millennials like to believe they know it all, and they don't want older applicants to seem intimidating, even though our problem-solving skills can slice theirs to shreds."

"Yeah, some of the job descriptions don't even try to mask the fact that they're looking for young people. The language can be so blatant: *We're a team of energetic, young professionals ...* As if I'm not energetic just because I'm fifty-five," Kris shared. "The *difference* is that I don't need intravenous Red Bull to be energetic, and I get more done with less fuss than any twenty-something!"

"That's what I tell my boys," Susie laughed. "Just because I don't make a big show of being busy, I accomplish more—and faster than they do. They waste all their energy on their computers, on social media and YouTube, when they should be studying."

"OK, last call for the pity party!" Kris yelled. "Grab a glass of something red and take your food to the table. Everything's hot."

The round of hugs, words of encouragement, and laughter crescendoed and then dissolved into the aromas rising from Kris's turkey enchiladas, Jo's cornbread stuffing with red chile gravy, Janice's bourbon and maple syrup squash, and Susie's spiced green beans. "Mmm. Comfort food," Sharon cooed as she savored her first bite.

"I had to hide some of the stuffing and red chile at the back of the fridge or my boys would have eaten everything!" Jo laughed.

"It took me so long to learn how to cook for two again when Kate went off to college, but when she's home, we always seem to end up with half a dozen at the table, so I bought a huge turkey. It was as if the kids hadn't eaten all semester!"

By the time Diana brought out her pumpkin flan, the conversation had turned serious again.

"How are you all doing, really?" Susie ventured after they'd tasted and praised the dessert. "Thanksgiving is supposed to be about all the things we're thankful for, but I see most of you struggling. Is there anything I can do? I want to see all my friends happy."

"It's hard to be happy when I don't feel as if I'm doing anything worthwhile," Sharon explained. "Of course, I need an income, but I need more than that. I need a life worth living."

"Agreed. Mike has a good job, but that's not enough these days, especially with Kate still in school. I've gone into serious penny-pinching mode. But my wanting a job—needing a job—is also about agency. I *need* to be active, to help shape some small project in the world. But as I research the job market, the numbers are depressing. Did you know there are more women over fifty in this country now than at any other time? We're healthier and living longer, but at the same time, the Bureau of Labor Statistics says women over fifty have the hardest time getting a job—even when jobs are available."

"Maybe you need to start your own businesses, like Jo and Diana and me," Susie suggested, gesturing at Kris, Janice, and Sharon. "When you have your own business, nobody can fire you."

"True, but your customers or clients can decide they no longer want to do business with you," Jo pointed out. "And it takes money to start a business—unless you fall into a special arrangement like I did."

"I hear what you're saying, Susie, but I just don't want to take on everything that goes with starting a business at sixty-four. To be honest, even when I was younger I didn't want to be a business owner. We're not all cut out to be entrepreneurs. I just want to do good work in a worthwhile job for a fair salary," Sharon explained.

Janice had been quiet for a while. Finally, she spoke. "Since you asked how we're really doing, I've been looking at my personal balance sheet and have come to the unwelcome conclusion that I have to move. When Will and I split, I got the house, but I have to pay the mortgage, taxes, insurance, and maintenance, and I just don't have the cash flow for that while I'm not fully employed. Amy's sharing an apartment with a friend now, so I put the house up for sale last week. Maybe I'll rent for a while."

"You could rent from me," Diana offered enthusiastically. "If you help me repaint the second bedroom, it could be quite nice. There's good light. And though I don't have a chef's kitchen, it's got all the essentials, including a gas stove."

"Hm. I might just take you up on that. You're not worried people will think we're a couple?" Janice teased.

"So what if they do!"

"OK, *there's* something to be thankful for—helping each other navigate this maddening, midlife mess!" Sharon smiled, raising her glass.

12

As December descended, so did Kris's mood. The job search felt like a game of Pin the Tail on the Donkey. Even when she thought she had a decent chance at winning an interview, she sent applications into the ether and never received so much as an acknowledgment that her résumé had been received.

Though she forced herself to get out of the house daily, going for walks didn't fully lift the internal clouds. Fall's brief flash of yellow was long gone, replaced by a sere monochrome of tans stretching from their backyard to the Sandias.

She dreaded Christmas and the forced jollity she'd have to show at neighborhood cocktail hours and Mike's work team party. They'd gone to the latter every year for two decades, and though the affair was for his colleagues, she'd become close to several of Mike's workmates and their spouses. It wasn't as if she would normally have bought something new to wear to the party, but the fact that such a purchase was beyond consideration this year made her bitter—at least momentarily. "What am I complaining about?" she chastised herself. "I still have so much more than many. I should be grateful."

But "shoulds" are always relative. It wasn't just that Kris missed relatively guilt-free impulse purchases. She felt her stock diminished in public and at home. She had no stake in the economic life of her community. She had no fresh news or work gossip to share with Mike over dinner or with his colleagues at their holiday party.

When she was a kid, she learned that any complaint of boredom would be met by her mother's saying: "Smart young ladies don't *do* boredom; they do *something.*" So one morning after Mike had left for work, Kris took a look around her closet with a critical eye and selected a half-dozen work pieces. She hadn't worn them since her layoff, and she'd never really loved them. Time for consignment. It wouldn't be a windfall, but it would help finance some new threads when she really needed them. Grabbing a white silk shirt with a small hem stain, she headed to the dry cleaner.

When she walked in, Sylvie greeted her with a smile. "Hello, there! Nice to see you again."

In her working days, Kris had swung by the cleaners at least every other week, but now that her wardrobe was almost exclusively activewear, she had no need for their services. And because she had more time, she had stopped bringing Mike's shirts to the cleaner, opting to wash and iron them at home. Ironing, she was surprised to realize, was the closest to a meditative act as she was likely to engage in.

"Nice to see you, too, Sylvie," she said. "I just have one item for you today. I was laid off a few weeks ago." Kris had decided not to hide her status. Perhaps some random conversation about being unemployed might elicit a job lead. After all, dry cleaners know a lot of people.

"No! How is that possible?"

"It's possible because there is no justice in this world!" proclaimed a resonant baritone that Kris immediately recognized as belonging to Terry Wilkins.

She turned and laughed as he threw open his arms and cooed, "You need a hug, girl! Let me buy you lunch. Pizza down the street. We must talk."

Without giving Kris a chance to say no, he grabbed her arm and ushered her out of the shop while asking Sylvie to take good care of his favorite sweater. "I must look snappy for Papa Noel," he said with a wink.

As they settled in to their lunches, Terry asked Kris for "every little detail" about her post-Klassik life, promising that not a word would be leaked back at the office. After providing an executive summary of her job-hunting trials, she added, "The past couple months have been a lesson in taking nothing for granted. I'm back to budgeting like I did when I was Kate's age," she laughed. "Except that now, instead of maxing out student discounts, I'm maxing out senior discounts! Can you believe I qualify as a senior in many places, even though I'm not eligible for Social Security?"

"God, I can't imagine you retired," Terry rolled his eyes.

"Well, if this is a preview of retirement, I'm tired of it! But seriously, if I'm going to be classified as a senior citizen by employers, I might as well embrace AARP and all the perks I'm eligible for. Did you know," she said, holding up her iPhone, "that when you turn fifty-five, you and your partner are eligible for a two-device unlimited call, text, and data plan for $70 a month—if you have the right carrier? For an hour's worth of standing around in the store to switch our wireless plan, I saved us $80 a month going forward!"

"You always were a wizard when it came to budgeting."

"But I could never cut expenses deep enough for Roger. Oh, sorry! I promised myself I'd never speak his name again."

"Aren't you just a little bit curious about Roger's latest rampages?" Terry teased. "He's even gotten testy with 'Adorable Ashley' lately. With you and Diana and the older sales staff gone, he's had to pick new scapegoats. He even called her 'clueless' in a meeting last week when she couldn't immediately tell him how well the marketing initiatives were performing."

"Are you worried about your job? Are more layoffs in the works?"

"No, if they cut any more there'd be no company at all. Besides, they wouldn't dare get rid of me—I tick too many diversity boxes: veteran, black, gay! But there's more news, and I don't know if it will cheer you up or make you sad."

Taking Kris's cocked head as permission to continue, Terry began, "Mr. Rich Kid's dad cut off his allowance."

"Really?"

"Yes, ma'am! According to reliable inside sources, Roger's old man turned off the cash spigot the end of last month. Apparently, even he has lost patience with losing money. If Klassik weren't privately held, it would have hit the chopping block years ago. So now, Roger is making moves to sell the company."

Kris raised her eyebrows. "Who's he trying to sell to?"

"He's been contacting the conglomerates, but my guess is they'll ignore him. Klassik would bring no new market and no celebrity cachet to the big boys, so there's nothing in it for them. Yeah, I read the trades," he added in response to her look of surprise at his industry knowledge.

"So what's the current valuation?"

"Your guess is as good as mine, but it could be a fire sale."

. . .

As she drove home from lunch with Terry, Kris nearly missed a turn, so distracted was she by the cacophony in her skull. The internal dialogue she'd been having over the past several weeks about the job search and what she should do next with her life had been mezzo piano compared to today's riotous babble:

Finally, Roger has hit bottom. Wonder how he likes the feeling. All his prancing presumption of superiority simply because he'd been handed a CEO by daddy.

Never mind Roger. You can't control him. Focus on what this could mean for you.

Is it possible that a new owner might reassemble part of the old team? Could I really go back there? Too much history. New boss could be as bad or worse.

But you love the industry. You love the creative people. You've gotten job offers from others—just not where you want to live.

This whole transition could take months. Years. Can't expect anything. Got to find a place to land for myself.

So lean in and figure out how you can make this work for you.

To hell with the whole "lean in" movement. As if. Women have been leaning in forever; it doesn't guarantee success. Didn't for me.

But you know what guarantees failure? Sitting on your ass.

Well, I am applying for jobs.

And that has gotten you where?

It's only been two months.

And you're more miserable and frustrated than you've been in your entire life.

I couldn't possibly. I don't have the money, and who'd lend to a first-time entrepreneur my age?

You won't know if you don't try.

We could go into debt.

So figure out how to avoid financial ruin.

That evening, Mike noticed that Kris was quieter than usual. "What's on your mind?"

"I ran into Terry today, and we had lunch together—his treat."

"How was that?"

"He told me Roger has run out of options and is selling the company."

"Really?"

Though she didn't share her internal debate verbatim, Mike could read between the lines. "I think you know what you need to do, K."

"It's a long shot. There are no guarantees. It would mean I wouldn't have an income for longer than we'd expected."

"I know, but we can handle it. You'll always regret it if you don't take this chance. It's really the perfect opportunity for you."

"Scary."

"Scarier than marrying me and moving out to the desert of New Mexico?" he grinned.

"Way more!" she replied with a laugh. When they'd moved from the East Coast more than two decades ago, their families had made it clear they viewed this part of the Southwest as charming for a vacation but a hinterland for building a career.

As if someone had flipped a switch, Kris suddenly felt recharged. Getting up in the morning and onto the elliptical became something she looked forward to, even after a night spent lying awake thinking.

Day after December day unfolded in front of her computer, researching, writing, creating spreadsheets, messaging contacts with new requests.

Other than sharing daily updates with Mike, Kris kept her new activity to herself. When G7 friends asked how things were going, she told them she was exploring new options and would tell all when she had something worth talking about. She checked in with Diana, Janice, and Sharon weekly—if only to provide a virtual hug. When she learned that Diana, who no longer had dental insurance, had to have expensive crown work done, she was glad Janice's home had sold quickly and she had moved in with Diana. At least her rent would provide some dependable income for Diana.

Sharon had declined everyone's invitation to Christmas dinner, explaining that she had volunteered to help distribute gifts for kids at a homeless shelter. For some reason, Kris felt the need to actually talk to Sharon one afternoon, so she called instead of texting.

"I just wanted to hear your voice," Kris explained.

"How nice! So you have some new secret project?"

"I'm keeping it under wraps for now."

"Is there anything I can do to help? I'm feeling helpless, and the best way I know out of that funk is to do something— even something trivial."

"Why are you feeling helpless? The echo chamber of the job search?"

"That's part of it. Life is full of surprises. Some good; some you'd rather avoid," Sharon answered, cryptically.

"Funny you should say that." Over the years, Kris had learned that Sharon was the least judgmental of the G7. When she had something she needed to get off her chest, something to confide, a quandary to resolve, she'd gravitated toward the eldest member of the group. "I stumbled upon a surprise myself recently that has my head spinning. It's like I'm on a perpetual mental rollercoaster."

"So what's going on? You know I won't say a word to anyone."

"Well … OK. You know me so well, maybe you can tell me if I'm being audaciously gutsy or downright delusional!" As Kris launched into a mostly stream-of-consciousness explanation of what was going on with Klassik, what she'd decided to do in response, and how her rib cage was alternately exploding with excitement and crushing her heart with anxiety, she thought, *This must be what it feels like to go to confession if you're Catholic. Or maybe how people interact with a shrink. I know I'm rambling and not trying to hide my fears, and yet I'm not worried that I'll be judged as unprofessional or inadequate or crazy.*

"I get it," Sharon said after Kris had laid out her ideas in all their nakedness. "You're someone who always likes to be in control and take the prudent course of action, so I understand why this is frightening. But it also seems like what you were born to do." Though the words were affirming, Kris thought she heard a catch in Sharon's throat, almost as if she were fighting back tears.

"You doing OK?" Kris probed, genuinely concerned. "I know the holidays can be tough for you."

"Not completely OK, but I'm working things out," Sharon admitted. "I'm learning how to think out of the box," she laughed. "That's hard for an accountant, but I'm considering new options. Promise me that you'll keep working to make your plan come alive."

"Promise. See you in the new year."

. . .

Kris had no interest in Christmas preparations that December, especially as Kate had decided to stay in Boston for the holiday. At least their daughter would be able to spend a bit of time with the grandparents, and that would take the guilt-tripping from her parents and Mike's down a notch or two. Kate had proudly announced via text that she'd landed a weekend clerking job at a small boutique during the holiday season, and between Christmas and New Year's she'd be working as a live-in nanny for two preschoolers while their parents, who lived in a grand Chestnut Hill mansion, went on a Colorado ski vacation.

Instead of putting up and decorating their artificial Christmas tree, Kris bought a small rosemary bush that had been trimmed into the shape of a pine tree. She tucked a few dried New Mexican red chilis into the branches and called her decorating done.

13

It was the second Friday in January 2018. Two days earlier, everyone had received an email from Sharon, asking them to meet at Kris's house at 6 p.m. for a special announcement. That in itself was odd; Sharon never imposed on others, she usually texted, and it was a week before their scheduled G7 gathering. All she offered by way of explanation was that she'd supply the wine, and there would be a special guest named Dan.

Replies to her invitation went unanswered, which revved up the speculation engine.

Has she ever mentioned a Dan before? Kris texted the group.

Never, Jo replied. *But she hasn't seemed herself lately. Maybe he's the secret she's been keeping.*

What secret? Diana asked.

Well, I assumed something—or someone—was keeping her up late, cause she's seemed tired lately, Jo volleyed back. *But when I asked her about it last month, she just said she wasn't sleeping well. Nothing strange there for a woman her age.*

So, is this an engagement announcement? Marie wondered. *I'd love for her to be loved again. She's been so cautious with men since her divorce.*

Oh, I hope so! Susie typed. *Can I bring some snacks to go with the wine?*

Yes! Kris replied with a winking emoticon.

On Friday afternoon, Kris accepted delivery of four bottles of wine, each from a different wine-producing region in California. She lined them up on the kitchen island along with eight wine glasses, a stack of appetizer plates, and cocktail napkins left over from the previous G7.

As she studied the setup, she wondered what could be going on with Sharon. Mystery wasn't exactly her MO. Then again, what was normal for any of them these days?

Dan Riddle was the last to arrive, promptly at 6 p.m. Everyone else had been at least ten minutes early.

Dan had been called upon to handle some unusual requests, but this one topped them all. He was more than a little nervous about how the evening would go. He'd never met these women, though he'd heard a lot about them the past few weeks.

"Hello, I'm Dan Riddle," he said, extending his hand when Kris answered the door. "Sharon Burch asked me to be here."

"OK," Kris responded, looking beyond the conventionally gray-suited, middle-aged man with wire-rimmed glasses. "She said there'd be a special guest named Dan, but where's Sharon?"

"She couldn't be here, which is why she asked me to come. I'll explain as soon as everyone is here."

Marie jumped in impatiently, "Well, we're all here!"

"Good. May I set up my computer on your table?" he asked Kris.

"Sure. Right this way."

Though he was an experienced public speaker, Dan's hands were sweating lightly. He slowly pulled his notes and laptop out of a worn brown leather briefcase and set them on one end of the table. "I think this might work best if you all take a seat," he began, running a hand through thick, wavy dark hair that was past due for a cut.

"I don't like the sound of this," Marie muttered. Jo pursed her lips off to the side in the gesture the rest had learned was her "I'm seriously skeptical" face.

The dining table sat eight. The chair facing Dan at the opposite end remained empty.

"Sharon couldn't be here today, so she asked me to come on her behalf as her attorney."

"Attorney? Is she in trouble?" Kris interjected.

"Not really, but her situation is a bit complicated. There are three parts to what she asked me to share with you: a brief overview, reading a short official notice, and playing a video."

"This is very weird," Diana muttered.

"I still want to know why she can't be here," Susie said. "I made her favorite pakora."

"Is this some sort of hoax? I've had it with fake news," Jo blurted.

"It will all make sense momentarily, if you let me explain," Dan said in what he hoped was his most soothing yet authoritative voice.

"I have been serving as Sharon's estate attorney and have helped her organize her legal and financial affairs. I have *not*, however, been privy to her latest plans. She did ask me to keep today's date open, but she wouldn't tell me why. Earlier this morning, I received an email that contained several attachments and a link to the video I mentioned."

"First, the overview, and," he cleared his throat, "there's no easy way to say this, but Sharon is no longer with us."

"*What?*"

"Are you saying she's dead?"

"What the hell?"

"Who the hell are you?"

"Is this some kind of sick joke?"

"I'm calling the cops."

"Please, ladies, let me explain. I assure you this is no joke. Sharon asked me to begin by reading the obituary she wrote and that she has asked me to place in the paper tomorrow."

"This is crazy!" Marie exclaimed.

"Yes, it is, but let's hear him out," Kris counseled.

"Thank you," Dan said, giving Kris a grateful glance before he began reading. "Sharon May Burch ended her life on January 12 at the age of sixty-four."

Gasps, closed eyes, clasped hands, and sighs fluttered around the table as the women finally acknowledged what all the signs had to add up to, yet the shock was so strong it held back their tears.

"She was born in Denver, Colorado, to Eleanor and Thomas Burch. The family moved to Albuquerque when Sharon was six and her brother Michael was fifteen. She attended public schools and then studied accounting at the University of New Mexico. After earning her CPA certification, she took a series of jobs in banking before landing a job with a consulting firm. She held progressively more responsible positions for twenty-one years before she was laid off five months ago in what was called a 'division reorganization.'

"The summer she turned twenty, Sharon married William Sena. Three years later, they had a son, Gabe, whom she adored. Sharon and William divorced when Gabe was twelve; William moved to Seattle and died of a heart attack the following year. Gabe was a talented musician and a competitive biker. He was killed by a drunk driver while riding his racing bike along a frontage road two weeks before his seventeenth birthday.

"Sharon loved to teach and served as a Saturday morning math tutor for disadvantaged students for the past decade. She enjoyed good food and wine.

"Sharon leaves no immediate family but is survived by a group of long-time friends whom she considered family. She requests no formal services."

"Whoa!"

"But why?"

"That was raw."

"Honest. She never should have lost her job, but was she *depressed* about that?"

"I had no idea she tutored."

"I know she was frustrated with not being able to get another job, but why suicide?"

"She told her own story. Good for her."

Diana sat silently.

"Ladies, I know you have lots of questions, and I think this video Sharon made may answer at least some of them. If you'll allow me, I'd like to turn my computer around as soon as I've connected to the video so you can all see it," Dan explained as he clicked on a link in Sharon's email message.

When the screen faced down the table, there was Sharon,

frozen in the still frame. Her short, wavy hair was familiar, but her face was slightly less round, her cheeks a bit gaunt. She'd stopped coloring her hair several weeks ago, and her roots were now half gray, half auburn. She wore mascara and lip gloss. Heavy bags under her eyes gave witness to lack of sleep. Dan clicked the play icon.

"Hi!" Sharon smiled. "Thanks for getting together on short notice (at least, I'm assuming you're all there). I know you must have a million questions, and I'll try to answer as many of them as best I can.

"I've always been better with numbers than words, but numbers tell stories, too, and so this is a story, I guess, of what numbers told me recently.

"But before I get into that, the most important things I have to tell you, in no particular order, are:

"I love you all. Even though I've known some of you longer than others, I still love the old-timers! And I love that, whatever interruptions there are—she winked—I'll get to fully speak my piece!

"There is *nothing* you could have said or done that would have made me change my mind about what I did yesterday.

"Exactly what I did is not important.

"I don't want you to feel sorry for me *or* to blame me.

"I'm counting on each of you to do something big or small that you've wanted to take on but were too afraid to. More on that later.

"OK, so as I record this, I am of sound mind—body, not so much.

"As you might have guessed, I've been fighting something recently: the Big C. But that's not the full story of why I decided to end my life.

"Let me be clear: I am *not* depressed. I can't speak for others who decide to end their lives, but I am not suffering from any kind of mental illness. I'm actually feeling quite happy, knowing that I can do some small good with my last acts.

"I am not a 'public health issue,' as the media and health industries like to label people who end their lives; we're not all the same. That said, I agree that those who consider suicide because they suffer from depression should receive the best healthcare possible.

"I guess this is as good a place as any to tell you how I *really* feel about what's commonly called suicide.

"The word 'suicide' has so much religious and cultural baggage that most people can't think straight about the decision to end one's life. We need a new word! Seriously, people get all bent out of shape about what I did, but it's one of the most personal decisions—not one that a church or the state should have any say in judging."

Marie and Jo glanced at each other, as if to say, "She's talking about us Catholics."

"By the way, there are whole cultures and whole countries, like Switzerland, where suicide is legal. The Swiss even have an organization, called Exit—I love that!—dedicated to helping people exercise their 'right to self-determination.' They have lots of safeguards in place to ensure the person isn't cavalier about the decision, but they understand that providing an unpaid assistant is actually a way of preventing suicide—the more conventional kinds, which can be more dangerous for everyone.

"That unpaid part is important, because the Swiss don't want anyone to benefit financially from someone else's decision to end their life. On the other hand, ask yourself who benefits when people are forced to 'live' to whatever long and bitter end they may face. Profit is a powerful reason for the healthcare and financial systems to oppose any sort of choice about a self-expiration date."

Kris and Jo couldn't suppress a quiet chuckle.

"Think about this: Why do we allow—and in some places, encourage—people to make babies, to start a life, without church or state approval and without lengthy psychological evaluations, but when someone wants to end their own life, the assumption is that they are depressed and should be medicated out of their decision? Or others will try to guilt them out of their decision by saying they're committing a sin. All I'm asking is that you think for yourselves.

"My decision to end things on my own terms is a totally sane and rational one.

"The CliffsNotes version of the story is that I learned I had stage four lung cancer seven months ago."

Gasps all around.

"I went to the doctor because I was sick of coping with that persistent shoulder pain. He couldn't find any obvious reason for what I was feeling, so he ordered an X-ray, thinking I might have cracked a rib that was radiating pain. What they found was cancer that had metastasized.

"The weird thing is that I haven't had any of the usual symptoms—maybe other than shortness of breath, which I chalked up to cancelling my gym membership!

"I can just hear you complaining, 'Why didn't you *tell* us?' Well, you've all got your own problems, and I needed to sit with mine for a while by myself. Maybe it's because I'm an introvert, but I needed to think this through before I shared it with anyone.

"Fast forward through multiple visits to specialists, proposed treatment plans—there is no cure—and a prognosis that didn't look great regardless of what the healthcare system did to me.

"In the midst of those clinical visits, I got laid off. That was bad enough on its own, but the timing couldn't have been worse. As you know, I'm a year shy of Medicare eligibility, and COBRA really is only a partial solution: Even with coverage of pre-existing conditions, the cost is crazy, especially when you factor in all the out-of-pocket expenses. Not to mention that I wouldn't be able to work if I underwent any of the grueling, recommended treatment plans, so no incoming funds. But that's a moot point because, as you know, my job search has been fruitless.

"The day after I got the boot at work, I started calling up medical offices and asking for costs. How much for each oncologist visit? How much for each chemo treatment? How much for the drug regimen Dr. Loser recommended (I could tell from the way he spoke that even he didn't believe the drugs he wanted to prescribe would help)? How much for home healthcare?

"Here's where I entered the Twilight Zone. At every office I called, nobody could tell me how much the treatments and medications would cost. It all depends on your insurance plan —what they bill the insurance company and what the insurer decides to pay, so you never know how much you'll be stuck with.

"After weeks of phone calls and office visits and online research, I tallied up my projections. Depending on the variable healthcare costs and my life expectancy—which I was told would be somewhere between six and eighteen months—my savings would be sucked dry either just as I gasp for my last breath or long before.

"Speaking of that last breath, it's a desperate, ugly one for those of us with lung cancer. I saw what my cousin Beth went through. Even with the best care and support, it's murder on family and friends. Damn those chain-smoking parents we both had!

"I don't need to worry about what my family would go through, because I don't have any more real family. And no, my decision isn't rooted in some depression about Gabe's death. I made peace with that a long time ago.

"But what my friends would go through, that I do care about. This is going to hurt one way or another. I'd rather the pain be sharp and short than heavy and prolonged. Maybe I'm being selfish, but you are, too, if you wish I had "toughed it out till the *natural end*." There's nothing natural about the way cancer is treated, and there's nothing natural about the way the healthcare system operates.

"My decision to schedule my exit is not just about avoiding prolonged physical suffering and eventual wasting away, though I'd be lying if I didn't admit that's part of it. It's more about control.

"OK, now, enough with the knowing glances! I have fully copped to being a control freak, and I know that it goes beyond being a number cruncher.

"The bottom line: I'm going to hit zero soon, whether it's on my terms or the cancer's terms.

"So, I decided that, rather than let the healthcare and insurance systems get rich off my dying, I wanted my friends to benefit from my passing. Before you get too excited, I can assure you that I cannot make you rich. But I want my remaining resources to do some good for the people I care about—not the insane medical-insurance complex.

"Dan—who, by the way, knew nothing of my exit plan, so don't give him a hard time—Dan has helped me set up my financial and estate affairs. He helped me liquidate all my accounts. All that's left is the house, which will pay final bills and then go to the charities I've selected. Dan will have a check for each of you within the week. I want you to think of it as seed money. Each of you may decide to plant one large seed or lots of smaller seeds. That's up to you, though I have a pretty good idea of how some of you might decide to use your gift.

"Use the money to take a gamble—not at a casino, but on yourself! I don't care if the gamble pays off, and I don't want you to care about the outcome either. I just want you to have the freedom to *make* the bet.

"We've all been responsible adults for so long that I think we've forgotten the point of life is to live. We followed the rules and paid our dues, but that hasn't always guaranteed success.

"Virginia Woolf wrote that a woman needs a room of one's own—yes, even finance majors read novels in college! But I say a woman needs an *inheritance* of her own. Most of you aren't in a position to enjoy an inheritance from family, so I want to provide a small one. Besides, with extended life expectancies, whatever you *do* inherit is likely to come too late for you to do anything really fun with it!

"One last thing: I have had more fun, and experienced more joy, in the past weeks as I have been planning this surprise than I have felt since Gabe was a baby.

"I love you! Group hug!" She concluded with a puckered smile as she extended her arms out and around her laptop's screen.

. . .

"What the hell!" Marie exclaimed. "I mean, she's not totally wrong about the healthcare business, but I could have helped her."

"Could you have cured her?" Jo asked.

"Well, maybe not, but I could have helped her negotiate the treatment path. I know she didn't have a husband to be by her side through it all, but we would all have helped."

"I think she was saying she didn't want that kind of help. It wouldn't have kept her alive," Kris added.

"I need a drink," Janice declared, rising from the table, "and not a mocktail." The others followed her into the kitchen, where she reached for a bottle of red Paso Robles Rhone blend. "Sharon always did have good taste in wine!"

"Hey, I think we need a toast," Kris said, reaching for a wine glass. The rest slowly moved toward the island, as if sleepwalking. One by one, they filled their glasses. Dan took the change of venue as an opportunity to wave a discreet goodbye to Kris before letting himself out the front door.

"Who wants to go first?" Kris asked.

"I don't want to toast this at all. I want Sharon back," sniffed Diana.

"We all do, but she was a realist. She wouldn't want us wasting time wishing the impossible," Kris said as she put her arm around Diana's shoulder.

"I'll go first," Susie said. "Sharon was my favorite person to cook for outside of my family. I'm not a particularly religious person, but without food, we cannot live. Sharon treated food with reverence." She paused and then raised her glass. "I will pray for you each time I sit down to a meal, dear friend."

"I was raised to believe that suicide is a mortal sin," Marie began. "But honestly, after all the sins I've seen in my own church, I find it hard to believe in eternal punishment for someone as sweet as Sharon. Even so, what she did *does* make me uncomfortable—both the way she ended her life and her 'seed money.' It feels like such an obligation ..."

"But I think her point was that it shouldn't be an obligation; it's mad money, love money, to take a chance with, to live with," Janice interrupted.

"Maybe," Marie said slowly. Then she raised her glass and said in a strong voice, *"Fino alla morte ogni coglione ci arriva.* That's something I heard my grandmother say a thousand times. It means, 'Until we die, anything and everything can happen.' "

Janice stepped forward next. "I share your feelings about suicide, Marie, and I'm even less observant than you, but if there's one time I would have wished for the assistance of every saint and angel out there, this is it. Sharon," she said as she raised her glass and looked to the ceiling, "may angels carry you to safety and solace."

Diana spoke next, slowly and quietly. "Sharon was the most generous person I've known—and I'm not talking about whatever money she left us. Did you know she took out a second mortgage on her home so she could pay for her mother's end-of-life care three years ago?"

"I didn't know," Kris said, surprised. "Why didn't she say anything to the rest of us?"

"She didn't want anyone's pity; she wasn't looking for attention," Diana explained. "She only told me when I was thinking about a second mortgage on my place. She advised against it and spent a whole weekend helping me figure out how to keep the house, afford a reliable used car to get to work, and not go into debt. With this last act, she was generous to a fault—and I do think taking her own life was wrong—but I don't want to speak ill of the dead, so my toast is, To the woman who worked magic with numbers for me—I wish I had a magic wand that could have cured your cancer!"

"Jo?" Kris felt she should go last.

"I'm pissed that she's gone," Jo began, unable to even say Sharon's name. "She was so much more than most people saw. She had a way of making each of us feel we were her BFF and that she would hold our confidences. It wasn't like keeping a secret from the rest; it was more like she was Mother Confessor, I guess. She's the only person besides Manny I ever told about my miscarriage."

"What?" Marie interjected, as the others registered surprise.

"It was an unexpected, perimenopausal pregnancy, and an early-term loss—just a month after Gabe passed. At first I didn't tell her, because I knew she was in her own private pain, but she knew something was off and insisted I talk. So, yeah, I'm angry that she's gone, but I'm also so grateful to have known her." As Jo raised her glass, she began, "The Prayer of Saint Francis includes the line, 'For it is in giving that we receive.' Sharon showed us how to give!"

Kris was silent for a moment and then took a deep breath. "I have two toasts. One's for Sharon; the other's for us. My heart aches," she began, as she struggled to hold back tears. "I don't think anyone's feelings will be hurt if I say that, as much as we all love each other, Sharon was our rock. She never overreacted when we brought a problem to her. She never told us what to do, exactly. She really was like the best teachers: She had a way of asking probing questions that helped you figure things out for yourself. That's a rare talent. She probably should have been a psychiatrist!" She eked out a small laugh. "To Sharon, who made us all stronger than we knew we could be. And, for all of us, *To life!*"

"To life!"

14

Despite their toast to life, all the G7 members could think about in the following weeks was that Sharon was gone. They'd never see her again. Never be able to confide in her. Never enjoy the cozy-sweater comfort of being around her.

For the first week, they mostly mourned alone, in silence. Once the promised checks arrived, the texts flew.

Susie: *Are you all as shocked as I am at the size of Sharon's check??*

Jo: *OK, I'll go public: $50,000.*

Marie: *Same here & yes it's a lot!*

Janice: *How did she come up with so much to give away?*

Kris: *I think she cashed out all her retirement savings, even though she'd have had to pay a penalty.*

Diana: *I feel bad taking her money.*

Kris: *You shouldn't. She called it seed money. I admit it's unusual, but she wanted us to have it.*

Janice: *But how to use it in a way that honors her?*

Jo: *I think she wanted us to figure out how it can help *us* live more deeply—not thinking about how she would have used it.*

Marie: *So how are you all going to use your "mad money"?*

There was a long pause before the next responses.

Kris: *I think I know the sort of project mine will go to, but I'm not ready to share yet.*

Marie: *You and your secret!*

Kris: *Well, what about the rest of you?*

Marie: *This is more money than I'll probably inherit from my parents when they pass, so I'll have to give it some thought.*

Janice: *The timing is good for me, but I don't want to waste this gift on basic expenses.*

Jo: *Seems we should do something we wouldn't otherwise have done.*

Diana: *Agreed.*

Susie: *I know we are now a group of six, but can we still call ourselves the G7 — to include Sharon?*

Her motion passed by acclamation.

By the end of January, Kris and Mike were eating every meal at the kitchen island. They had no choice, as Kris had turned the dining table into her office. Dog-eared trade magazines covered the far left corner. On the far right, a Nature Conservancy calendar was open to January, which featured a photograph of a coyote. Underneath it was a hand-drawn twelve-month calendar with a large star on September and a red Sharpie-drawn exclamation point on May. To the right of her laptop was a spiral notebook with several sticky note tabs; to the left was a multipage budget spreadsheet and her phone.

Each morning, as soon as Mike left for work, Kris created her to-do list. One item at a time, she worked through the items, diving into the virtual world to research or to ask questions, then picking up her phone.

When she left the house for quick errands, she found herself doing an informal survey of all the eyewear she saw. Albuquerque wasn't the most fashion-forward place in the country, or even the West, but there had to be something to learn. Whenever a man, woman, or child wearing glasses stood in line behind her at the grocery store, she posed her survey questions: How long have you worn glasses? What do you like and dislike about this pair? What features would make you love your frames? What would make your glasses feel special, unique?

15

It was one thing to commit to the idea of buying Klassik Eyewear from Roger. Actually pulling it off would require skills Kris had rarely employed and behaviors she found alien —like secrecy.

If Roger had the slightest suspicion she was attempting to buy Klassik, he'd block her offer even if it meant financial ruin for himself. Of that much, she was certain. It wasn't in her nature to lie or dissemble, but the situation called for discretion, which in this case required concealment.

That posed problems for the entire acquisition process, starting with the formation of her own company. She'd come up with a name and confirmed it was available for use. But in registering that name, she'd have to reveal the LLC's owner, and Roger's business broker would surely discover and share that intel. On a whim, she Googled, "Can you keep a business owner anonymous in New Mexico?"

"Holy shit!" she exclaimed aloud to no one else in the house. She had just discovered that her state was one of fewer than a handful where it's possible to form an LLC in such a way that the owner is anonymous. "If that's not a good sign, I don't know what is," she said, aloud again, as she put her hands together and raised them in silent thanks to Sharon, whom she imagined cheering her on.

As of February 2, Kris had registered K&S Enterprises, LLC with the state through a registered agent. The next conundrum: making herself known as a potential buyer without making herself known.

She knew Roger had engaged a business broker who was hunting for a buyer. Obviously, she couldn't directly approach him. She considered hiring her own broker. There had to be a sort of "buyer's agent" as there was in real estate, she reasoned. But when she began investigating how business brokers worked, she quickly learned the situation was more complicated and opaque. You never realize the full complexity of an endeavor until you're deep within it, she reflected, whether it's parenting, mountain climbing, or starting a business. Fortunately, she had always been a stellar student and loved to research. But Google had its limits. At some point, she knew she'd need other humans on her team. But whom could she trust to speak for her? The registered agent had served a purpose but wasn't the best choice to serve as her purchasing agent.

She'd conducted as much due diligence as she could on her own over the weekend. On Monday morning, after two cups of coffee and an hour of mental chess, she committed to making the next, critical move. She picked up her phone and dialed. One ring. Two.

"This is Chuck!" The voice on the other end was borderline gruff.

"Hello, I'm calling to get some information about the services you offer to *buyers*—whether you provide specific services hourly, whether you have ever shared a commission with the seller's broker, that sort of thing."

"Is this for a local business, out of state, or international?"

"Local."

"Then I prefer to meet with the client first and provide that information in person. I'm free tomorrow at 11 a.m. if that works for you. What's your name?"

"K."

Whatever the outcome with the broker, Kris knew she'd need a business attorney eventually, so her next calls were to a short list of business law firms.

The next morning, Kris arrived on the other side of town at a small office park built in the local faux-adobe style. The one-story, tan stuccoed complex housed everything from a podiatrist to a private eye. Southwest Success Business Brokers sat at one end of the interior courtyard. Kris opened the door and found herself face to face with Charles Stein. Rising from behind a large oak desk, he hurried to greet her with a handshake. "You must be Kay. I'm Chuck. Have a seat," he said, gesturing to the three matching leather chairs arranged across the desk from his own Herman Miller chair. A printer and file cabinet stood in one corner. The only thing on the expansive desk was Chuck's laptop. Chuck himself appeared to be kissing sixty and had the weather-worn skin of someone who spent every non-working hour outdoors.

"So, what can I do for you? You mentioned an interest in finding a buyer's representative."

"That's correct."

"Have we met?" he asked, looking at her intently. "You look familiar."

"Maybe. But first, I need to be sure that whatever we discuss remains confidential."

"Of course."

"The reason I called you is that you know the business I want to acquire. You were the seller's broker about five years ago, when Gerry Pearson sold Klassik Eyewear."

"Of course! That's where we crossed paths."

"Well, the business is up for sale again, but the owner—the CEO—wouldn't sell to me if he knew I was interested."

"Wait. Are you still employed there?"

"No. I was let go last September with a couple other employees in one of CEO's cost-cutting rounds."

"I see …"

"I don't need all of the traditional broker services because I know the business from the inside, but I do need someone who can represent me and protect my anonymity throughout the negotiation process. Is there a legal way to do that? Can you use my business name only?"

"It's unusual, but there is a way. Do you have an attorney?"

"Yes, and I would put you two in touch with each other, but honestly, I need to ensure I'm getting the best price, which is why I'm talking to you. You know this business and how to negotiate a sale better than an attorney," she said, not averse to using a little flattery to plead her case. "And because I don't need a full-service broker—especially as I don't need your services to find a business—I was hoping we could negotiate some sort of reduced-fee plan. Perhaps a fixed fee for a defined set of services rather than your usual minimum or a percentage of the selling price."

"As you say, since I'm not *finding* a business, and as I'm familiar with Klassik, I think we can work something out. As a matter of fact, I'd be more than happy to help you negotiate a favorable deal!" he said, slapping the desk.

Suddenly speaking more animatedly, he continued, "As it happens, the current owner, Mr. Kohl, approached me to represent Klassik when he first considered listing the business. I took an initial meeting with him, but I quickly saw that his expectations were out of scale with the realities of the current business. He thought he could sell for close to what he paid five years ago, but the trend lines didn't warrant the multiple he had in mind. I tried to reason with him, but he kept rambling on about how the 'brand equity' was the most valuable asset. Then he tried to negotiate a commission that was half my usual rate, and that put the kibosh on our potential working relationship. Deals like that, with an unreasonable seller, they're time hogs."

"So, what would you charge for representing my company in this process?"

"I could put that together later today and email you a contract, but I have to ask you about one critical matter before we go any further. Do you have the cash or financing to close the deal?"

"I have some but not all. I was hoping we could structure the purchase as a down payment and installments. My business plan explains how I plan to make the company more competitive and profitable," she added, handing him a printout of her slide deck.

"That's a possibility," he said slowly. "Especially in this case, where I sense Mr. Kohl wants to get out of the business as quickly as possible, but with as sweet a sale price as he can squeeze out of a buyer. You'll have to show you have a substantial down payment."

"How much?"

The dollar range he offered represented a 2x to 3x multiple of the company's estimated EBITA. "If you can't demonstrate that you've got the financing to do the deal, you won't even be considered a serious suitor," Chuck concluded.

"Understood. You send me your contract. I'll send you information about my current resources, and I'll let you know as soon as I secure the balance."

Kris had, in fact, heard the same warning from the attorneys she'd spoken with, so after leaving Chuck's office, she headed to the bank, where she set up an account for K&S Enterprises, LLC and deposited Sharon's $50,000. The rest she'd have to work on.

16

The house Diana inherited from her parents was in a small, older, residential neighborhood that had become nearly invisible with the addition several decades ago of adjacent residential and commercial developments. The proximity of Klassik's office in the latter had been the main reason she applied for the receptionist position, as she could easily drive home at lunch to check on her ailing parents. After they passed, she needed a new mid-day routine.

When she started at Klassik, she had carried her lunch to work and, in good weather, would eat it at the picnic tables beside their office building. It was nice to get outside for a bit. But after Roger bought the business, even if she avoided sitting at his table, he always seemed to shoot some unwelcome remark her way. If it wasn't an assessment of her lunch's caloric content, it was a barb disguised as small talk. "Got a hot date for the weekend?" he might ask, with a shit-eating grin. The subtext, she knew, was that no man would be interested in dating her, let alone a hot one. How any woman could have married Roger was a puzzle. Maybe his wife was attracted to the family's money, she speculated.

Even though her coworkers tried to soften the impact of Roger's comments by privately calling him insensitive—or worse—Diana tired of being in the line of fire when she was supposed to be enjoying her work break. About a month after Roger arrived, she changed her mid-day routine. She'd always been curious about yoga, so she enrolled in a class at a studio in the adjacent strip mall. Promptly at noon, she pulled her yoga mat from beneath her desk and walked past the Klassik picnic tables en route to her 12:15 p.m. class. An hour later, she was back at her desk, sipping a protein shake for a late lunch.

Yoga was a refuge for Diana. Though she was one of the heavier women in the class, her mat mates included women of all ages and shapes, plus a couple of men. Her cohort was clearly the highly scheduled lunch crowd, squeezing in a workout between job and family responsibilities. Far different, she'd heard, from the mid-afternoon Retiree Roundup of socializers and the morning Lithe Leisure Yogis, modeling the latest perfect-body-hugging apparel.

For thirty minutes during class, Diana was encouraged to do the best she could, without self-judgment. "Keep your spine extended. Be aware of your body," the instructor told the class as she modeled a series of standing poses. Diana had never been unaware of her body, but in class, she drew confidence from it for the first time. She was surprised to discover she had an affinity for the practice. Perhaps because she'd learned how to carefully carry the edges of her body through the world, she had a refined awareness of her center of gravity. Her favorite pose was brave warrior, for its full-body stretch and the way its openness pushed the morning's stress out past her fingertips. The slow, controlled transitions from one pose into another suited her patient approach to most activities. Focusing on breath and posture banished all quotidian worries. Whatever crap landed on her desk after class wouldn't perturb her. She could even ignore Roger's double entendres more easily in the afternoons.

Post-layoff, Diana's daily routine was once more in disarray. Without required working hours, she could go to the yoga studio at any time, but after trying out different classes, she reverted to the lunch-hour one. She needed something familiar and consistent in her life, so she rearranged her dog-walking schedule to protect the noon hour.

Lunch-hour errand-runners crammed the central parking lot that served both the shopping mall and office park, so Diana often found the only empty spaces were near the Klassik office. On those days, as she walked past her former coworkers at lunch, some would wave and say hi. Diana, one hand balancing her yoga mat bag on her shoulder, might wave or just nod her head in acknowledgment. Roger would pretend to not see her or would suddenly engage in animated conversation with Sandy.

That avoidance behavior didn't surprise Diana. What she did find baffling was that Roger had not varied his dog-walking schedule, even after her layoff, and even after he had to have noticed that she sat with Sophia each Sunday, even in the chill of winter. As Rex and Roger neared the two women, Roger would look in the other direction or far ahead in the distance to avoid eye contact. When Rex reached his favorite dumping ground next to their bench, Roger would walk ahead a few paces without glancing back. Then the man and his dog would continue down the path as if there were nothing and no one worth stopping for.

17

Armed with a printout of her business plan and a PowerPoint pitch deck on her laptop, Kris walked into her bank and asked to see a loan officer. It was a local branch of a large national bank, where she and Mike had been customers for over two decades. She'd dressed in her work uniform—a white cotton shirt, black wool trousers, black pumps, and a three-quarter-length camel hair coat she'd picked up on sale during a trip to Boston the previous winter.

"Hello, I'm Robert. I understand you want to talk about a business loan," said the man who approached her in the reception area. He wore a blue shirt and black tie with pleated chinos. Mid-thirties tops, she estimated.

"Yes, I'm Kris Wright," she said, extending her hand and giving his a practiced, firm shake as she caught a glimpse of a tattoo on his right forearm that was just barely concealed when he dropped his arm and led her into his office.

Sitting on the front of the chair to ensure good posture, she explained why she was seeking a loan. After passing the business plan to Robert, she went through the main points she had rehearsed, closing with the dollar amount.

"I see," Roger responded after listening silently. "And what were you planning to use as collateral?"

"Our house. We have 80% equity, and your bank holds the mortgage, so you can see we have a spotless repayment record."

"Before I can move forward with any application for a loan using your home as collateral, I'll need your husband's signature as well."

"That won't be a problem."

"But what might be a problem is the size of the loan you're requesting, which far exceeds the value of your home."

"Does your bank also offer Small Business Administration 504 loans?" She knew they did. "I understand they max out at $5.5 million."

"Yes, but SBA loans take more time to process and, as you've noted, the business you're planning to purchase carries a lot of debt, so ..."

"What if I applied for the maximum SBA loan your bank would approve and secured the rest of the funding elsewhere?"

"That would be fine, but we'd need to know the source of the other funds to ensure your ability to repay. Since 2008, lenders have been under increased scrutiny, so we need to be sure the loans we write can be repaid."

That night over dinner, Kris recounted her meeting with the banker, concluding, "It feels like a catch-22. If you need money, you don't qualify for it, but if you have it, no problem!"

"You knew this process wouldn't be easy," Mike reminded her, "but this is just the first lender you've talked to."

"I know, but the premise—which he as much as said applies to all lenders—is that they won't loan you money if you don't have a guaranteed way to repay. I won't use my 401k as collateral, but the thought has crossed my mind. I do have that small emergency cash account that I've been building since college. I suppose this would be a good time to put that to use. The birthday and Christmas cash always went into that account, along with bonuses—back in the days when I got them."

"How much do you have in that account now?"

"As of yesterday, just shy of $80,000."

Mike whistled. "Not bad for ad hoc deposits."

"The power of compounding. It helped that CD interest rates were over 10% when I started saving. Still, it's a laughable amount to a bank, considering the total I need."

"But it might help if you could show you're putting extra skin in the game."

Three days later, after more research and a handful of tweaks to her pitch, Kris ventured out again, this time to a business bank.

The loan officer, in his early forties, she guessed, wore a white shirt and red tie but no jacket. He gave her a hearty welcome and invited her to his desk. After an introductory exchange, she handed him her business plan. He flipped through it quickly, his face betraying no hint of reaction. He was either the fastest speed reader or had predetermined that the details were not worth his attention.

With his right index finger resting on the page detailing key personnel, he said, "I see you have some middle management experience but no prior business ownership and no senior management experience. Do you have a succession plan in place for the business should you acquire it?"

Now that's a new twist on ageist bias! Kris thought to herself. "Not yet," she replied. "I plan to work for well over a decade, by which time I'll be able to identify any internal, as well as external, candidates for CEO."

"I can process an application and send it up the chain, but from what I've seen with similar cases, I don't want to get your hopes up."

With that kind of attitude, Kris knew there was no point in jumping through the next set of hoops.

"I even explained that I'd be increasing the headcount and bringing good jobs to the city," Kris told Mike over dinner that night. "You'd think a business bank would be interested in growing the business community, but apparently not. Or maybe it was just that he didn't believe I could execute the plan."

"What about online lenders?"

"They're mostly involved in microloans. I need a macro loan to finance purchase, expansion, and working capital. There are a couple of entities that say they offer larger loans, but the terms aren't great."

"Why don't you check them out, just in case? You don't have to accept the offer if you don't like the terms."

"Point taken."

Kris was surprised when she landed a meeting with a local

venture capital firm, especially on relatively short notice. She'd chosen ABQ Ven because it had a history of investing not just in startups but also in business expansions. She figured a business acquisition that included expansion plans should qualify for consideration. She had researched the enterprises previously chosen by these money men (and they were all men, according to their website), and though they were mostly science and technology focused, there was more variety than was typical for VC firms.

Having never met a venture capitalist in the flesh, she decided to wear what she hoped would look sufficiently hip yet age-appropriate—whatever that meant these days: black skinny jeans, black pima turtleneck, black leather jacket, and slightly oversized squarish black tortoise acetate frames.

Her meeting was with John Mosley, identified on the website as a managing director. He met her at the door when she arrived exactly a minute before her 9 a.m. appointment and led her into his office. Broad-shouldered and hovering just above forty, he looked as if he'd probably played football in high school—maybe even college. He wore a brown leather western sport coat over a button-down blue dress shirt. Expensive Southwest casual. "You're looking for a large sum here," he remarked after perusing the business plan.

Kris was determined to not assume his opening comment was sexist; she had to be careful how she responded. "As we've all heard and seen," she began, hoping to demonstrate her business knowledge while establishing a point of agreement with her potential investor, "one of the most common reasons for business failure—whether it's a new enterprise or expansion—is underfunding. I know the eyewear business, and I know that this company needs a cash infusion to literally retool its processes and make it competitive again. The current owner's cost-cutting measures have led to loss of market share and brand value, which is why I am planning the top-to-bottom reorganization described in my business plan."

"Yes, I see. To be honest, we're used to investing in startups and turnarounds with more of a new technology edge."

"And that's why I was interested in meeting with you," Kris said, being sure to smile. "I realize that eyewear isn't a new, disruptive industry, but what I plan to do with Klassik leverages the latest technology in the space to give the firm a fresh start."

"That's great," John said, "but I'm just not seeing the high-growth potential here that we look for."

And so, after a few more desultory remarks, that interview concluded.

February was the longest month Kris had ever endured. One rejection after another seemed designed to make her accept that her combination of gender, age, and experience was a losing package for any financier.

Was she deluding herself? Who was she to think she could take over a struggling company and make it a success? Mind you, it was a relatively small business. People bought small businesses all the time and made them their own.

Was she too emotionally involved? Was she trying to recreate the past? No! Her vision was sharply focused on the future—new markets, new staff, new technologies.

Was she pursuing this purchase for the wrong reasons? Was it all about revenge against Roger? No. He wasn't worth this much effort—though proving she could make the business thrive where he failed would be a lagniappe.

So why was it so hard to get her hands on the one essential

thing—money—that she needed to put her plan into action? Well, she'd never asked for money before. Doing anything for the first time was bound to be hard. But this hard? Especially considering the amount of money handed to failing banks after the 2007 financial debacle, what she needed was a pittance. But the male bankers with their hands held out wore bespoke suits and had been using other people's money to get rich their entire lives. Maybe that was her problem. She'd been raised to believe that hard work, personal integrity, and kindness to others was the way to live. Not, apparently, if you wanted to succeed in business.

Was she being punished for being ambitious? Get real! A man would never ask that question.

On February 28, her heart skipped a beat when she saw an email from an online lender. Uttering a silent prayer to Whomever, she opened the message.

Dear Mrs. Wright,

This message is in regards to your online application for a business loan dated February 15. We regret that we are unable to approve your loan at this time. ...

18

Thermometers were forecast to reach seventy degrees on the third Wednesday of March. With Albuquerque's sunny skies, it would feel downright balmy. Though Diana knew the spring tease wouldn't last, she was determined to make the most of it.

The previous weekend, she had been shopping at Walmart when she noticed summer yard and entertainment merchandise already on display. She and Janice had been working on plans to turn the backyard into an aromatics garden to supply Janice's budding beverage business. They'd begun ripping out the small lawn and other long-neglected vegetation. Next would come soil amendments, plants, and seeds. The jumbo pack of rubber-palmed gardening gloves would surely be worth getting.

Even kiddie pools and water toys had already been stocked. She had enjoyed a backyard inflatable splash pool when she was a cute, pudgy toddler, if family photos were to be believed, but she'd never had all the extras—the water guns, float toys, and pool balls. *Lord, this water gun says it reaches thirty feet! That could be artillery for a neighborhood water fight. Luna would love it.*

Wednesday noon, Diana headed to her yoga class as usual, mat bag slung over her left shoulder. As she'd expected, several Klassik employees were just sitting down to enjoy lunch outside on the unseasonably warm day. Walking along the sidewalk, she stopped when she came directly across from the table where Roger, Sandy, and Ashley sat, casually ignoring her as usual. She lowered her mat bag to the sidewalk, unzipped it, pulled out the bazooka, and fired, emptying the reservoir on Roger and his lunch. The sequence of smooth motions took no more than five seconds.

"ACK!" Sandy screamed as she leapt up from the table, vainly trying to shake the wet mess from her clothes.

Ashley, who hadn't been in the direct line of fire, nonetheless suffered a few dark splatters. "Eew! Are you crazy?" she asked, looking at Diana for the first time since she'd been laid off.

Moans were all Roger dared utter, as his face was dripping with a sticky dark substance that surely announced its composition to his nostrils.

"What the hell?" Sandy yelled over at Diana, who had left the bazooka on the ground, zipped her bag shut, and thrown it back over her shoulder.

"Shit happens," Diana yelled back, matter-of-factly. "I was just returning Rex's excrement to his owner."

As she turned and headed toward the yoga studio, she noticed her other former workmates at another table, unsure how to react. Liz and Terry quickly replaced their initial gape-mouthed glee with poker faces and headed inside the building, saying they'd get some paper towels.

"I'm calling the cops!" Sandy yelled, while Roger just

moaned and wriggled in an attempt to shake off the sopping foulness.

How long they stood there in stink before venturing inside to the restrooms, Diana didn't know. She took her place on her mat as usual.

When she left the studio after class, a couple of police officers were waiting for her. "Diana Delgado?" the female officer asked.

"Yes," Diana replied.

19

News of Diana's escapade ricocheted via text from Terry to Kris and then across the G7. Despite all attempts to get Diana to comment, her only message was, *Details when we meet Fri!*

Two days after the headline-worthy event (which never did make the papers), Janice and Diana were the last to arrive at Kris's house, armed with three new mocktail flavors and a package of napkins that read *Grammar: The difference between knowing your shit and knowing you're shit.* Immediately, Diana was assaulted with a chorus of questions.

"Did you spend the night in jail?"

"What did they charge you with?"

"Did you get him right in his filthy mouth?"

"Will you have a record now?"

"How'd you get the dog shit into the gun?"

"I'll tell you the whole story after I have a glass of wine in my hands—sorry, Janice," Diana mock-apologized.

As Kris, Marie, Susie, and Jo crushed her with hugs, high fives, and congratulations, Diana basked in the hero's welcome.

"I recognize that what I did wasn't in keeping with my calm, yogi demeanor," Diana began, as the women broke into a second raucous wave of laughter. "But it was *before* class."

"How did you ever come up with the idea of using a water gun, and how did you get the poop to go through the chamber?" Jo, familiar with piping and pluggages, wanted technical details.

"Well, the plan came together in stages. That first day, I picked up Rex's poop in a separate doggie bag, but when I dropped Luna's bag in the park trash can, something held me back from depositing Rex's bag."

"Who knew there was a devilish Diana!" Marie interjected approvingly.

"I took it home and put it in a recycled plastic container and froze it in the garage fridge—the one my dad used for beer. I hadn't plugged it in for years, but we put it back into service when Janice started all her experimenting. Don't worry," she rushed to clarify, "there was nothing else in the freezer compartment!"

"Whew, I was just going to sniff for any hint of poo," said Jo, who had poured herself a taste of Janice's latest—a black carrot–based, buzz-free beverage.

"After picking up Rex's steaming pile for a couple of weeks while visiting with Sophia—who's an amazing lady, by the way—I decided the dog waste shouldn't go to waste, so I started taking it home each week and freezing it. I didn't know exactly how I'd dispose of it, but I knew it needed to be deposited with Roger somehow."

"He always seemed like a nasty boss whenever you two talked about him," said Susie, who rarely spoke ill of anyone and still couldn't bring herself to use the S word. "I knew you two were tough professional women, but when you spoke about his behavior, I could tell he had a cruel streak."

"Cruel but careful," added Kris, at this point not giving a shit about her NDA. "The thing about Roger is that he uses his little personal jabs as a way to belittle anyone who doesn't totally suck up to him. Individually, they might seem minor, and he's careful to never cross any obvious harassment line, but the barbs add up, and they either hurt you or piss you off until—"

"Until, if you're sure-shot Diana, you give him what he has coming!" Janice jumped in.

"But what about the water blaster?" Jo insisted.

"When I saw the soaker at Walmart, just before we were to get a temperature spike—which I knew would draw Roger outside at lunch—I suddenly put all the pieces together."

"Timing is everything, in cooking and life!" Susie nodded.

"I thawed some of the frozen stock, added water, and did a few test fires in the backyard, which is a total mess right now anyhow. When I had the right proportions, I mixed up a larger batch."

"Nobody saw you getting ready to fire?" Jo asked.

"Nobody at Roger's table. They always pretend to not see me. Terry and Liz were sitting farther away, and they wouldn't have stopped me anyhow!"

"Too bad no one was there to catch it all on video," Marie lamented. "Next time you come up with such a poetically just plan, I'm riding shotgun!"

"To be clear," Diana emphasized, "the toy doesn't look anything like a real firearm, and it was bright yellow."

"So, did they arrest you? Terry saw the police drive you off in a squad car," Kris reported.

"Roger was going to press charges; he wanted to see me

spend time in jail. But they couldn't even get me for misdemeanor trespassing on private property, because I stayed on the sidewalk, and there was no permanent property damage, so he tried to get his lawyer to go for disorderly conduct.

"Anyhow, I was sitting in the police station before Roger's lawyer arrived, and as I'm giving my statement to the officers, I can tell everyone else is eavesdropping. The other officers and a couple of residents who are in making reports all have one ear lifted in my direction. I'm explaining how Roger never picks up after his dog in this lovely public park, where little kids are running around and where seniors are walking and trying to enjoy the day—next to a smelly pile of poop. And I hear an officer at the next desk whisper to his partner, 'My neighbor lets his dog do his business right in front of our mailbox every morning. Never picks it up. I wish this story would make the paper so I could wave it in his face as a warning!'

"Finally, Roger's lawyer shows up and talks to the officers and reads my statement. Long story short, they end up not charging me with anything, especially as I have no priors. It seems the attorney figured out he'd have a hard time making even the disorderly conduct charge stick given my history as a model citizen and the fact that I have a corroborating witness to Roger's perpetual failure to pick up after Rex. I overheard him telling the cops that it would be better if there were no record of the event because it wouldn't look good for the company—which is up for sale, by the way."

"Really?" asked Marie and Jo in unison, looking at Kris.

"... if word got out that a 'disgruntled former employee' had 'attacked' the CEO."

"Now I know why you wouldn't take your severance package!" Kris laughed. "They couldn't even hold that over you.

Did you say anything about how Roger has belittled you for years?"

"No. I thought about it, but that sort of behavior is so common that we're all just expected to put up with it, especially when there's nothing obvious enough to serve as a smoking gun. Plus, I figured if I was dealing with male cops and lawyers, they'd be less inclined to see Roger's comments as a mitigating circumstance."

"Smart!" Marie agreed. "How many times have we all wished we could serve up that sort of response to the assholes we encounter?"

"Just about daily! You should have been a fly on the wall in some of the kitchens I worked." Janice picked up her nonalcoholic libation. "It was enough to push some women to drink or drugs."

"A toast," Kris proposed. "To Diana, our own Annie Oakley, settling scores for scores of women!"

Cheers and laughter filled the kitchen, accompanied by a few tears. "I haven't laughed this hard since before Sharon …" Susie couldn't bring herself to finish the sentence.

"You know, it was Sharon's spirit—her demand for self-determination—that gave me the cojones to pull it off," Diana explained. "Her example—her bravery in doing something socially unacceptable that was right for her—was a bigger gift than the money. And, honestly, I thought I might have to draw on that gift to make bail!"

20

"Hello!"

"Gerry, this is ..." Kris began.

"Kris!" the enthusiastic bass voice interrupted.

"How have you been?"

"Just dandy, now that I've relaxed into full retirement. It only took me five years. Now I'm busier than ever, but I don't take meetings! What's up?"

"If you could find time in your unscheduled schedule, I'd love to meet you for coffee and a chat."

"How about the country club, tomorrow morning?"

"Actually, it's a private conversation."

"OK, then. Come over to the house. I can make coffee, and Anna just pulled a batch of cookies out of the oven. You can save me from myself by eating a couple. In an hour?"

"I'll be there!"

An hour later, Gerry opened the door. He'd grown a full beard since Kris had seen him last—maybe eighteen months ago. Like the wavy hair on his head, his facial hair was off-white and neatly cropped. Instead of the sport coat and gray wool pants she was, used to seeing him wear when he'd been her boss, he wore a green polo shirt and khakis. He looked relaxed and happy. "Come in!"

"Thanks for seeing me."

"Thanks for *calling.* I've been wanting to catch up with you, but I wasn't sure you'd want any reminder of your old life."

"It's true," Anna confirmed, as she waved Kris into the kitchen. "He's always said you were his best hire—executive material. Too bad that rat Roger couldn't see it."

"Oh, I think he saw it and was intimidated," Gerry huffed. "But enough about Roger. How are you?"

"Excited, anxious, frustrated," she began before launching into a condensed narrative of her due diligence, funding challenges, and her vision for how the company could evolve.

"I didn't want to bother you with this until I was certain I wanted to go forward with a purchase," she concluded.

"Sounds like a stealth takeover!" Gerry grinned. "I love it!"

"I know it probably sounds crazy, because I've never run a company and I don't even have an MBA, but you started Klassik Eyewear without a business degree, and you made it a very profitable business."

"Precisely. You don't get senior management experience until someone gives you the opportunity—or until you make your own opportunities. Besides, the title does not make the man, or woman. Leadership ability is a matter of character and skills, not titles."

"There are still a couple of strong people around with finance and operations expertise," Kris continued, "as well as institutional memory of prouder days. I'm confident that with a few additional strategic hires and new partnerships, I can steer the enterprise in the right direction. I was hoping, with your knowledge of the business and the industry, that you could suggest some other financing options I might not have considered. I want to keep the company private, because I don't want to be pushed by investor demands for a quick return.

"I've even talked with staff at the state Economic Development Department about what I'd have to do to qualify for a Local Economic Development Act grant. I thought that since my plans include making capital investments and adding a new production facility—which entails adding and training staff—I might have a chance to secure some funds from the state. They were actually quite encouraging, but that grant money—they said I could qualify for as much as a million—is contingent upon having additional, private sector financing, which so far has eluded me."

Gerry, who had been attentive but quiet as she spoke, looked over at Anna, who was wearing a grin, and sighed, "I'm so glad you told me this. I've been sad and angry and annoyed since Klassik started losing its way. When I sold to Roger's father, I never suspected he was just buying the business to give his loser son something to do with his time. It's been embarrassing to see good people let go just because the CEO is inept.

"It took me a long time to stop thinking about the business every day, wondering what was going on. Things seemed OK at the start, but then I began catching wind of problems when I ran into former employees. There's no way *I* should be part of that company anymore, but I want to help *you* find a way to lead it. Give us a couple of days to talk about this and to make a few calls," Gerry said as he looked at Anna. "But don't worry; we'll figure something out."

"Of course! Take all the time you need. I'm grateful for

whatever advice you have. You know how to reach me," Kris said as she stood to leave.

Precisely two days later, her phone rang. These days, she was more likely to get text pings, so she knew before looking at the screen that it was Gerry. "Can you come over this afternoon?" he asked. "We have a proposition for you."

It was nearly four when she pulled into their driveway. She wasn't sure if she was apprehensive or excited. She gave her hair and makeup a quick check in the rearview mirror and then opened the car door. Gerry was waiting for her at the open front door. "Come in! We're set up in my office."

Gerry had specified a home office when they built their house in 1980. It looked out over the backyard's trees—apple, apricot, and native piñon. Though he left work promptly at five so his employees wouldn't feel compelled to stay late, during the years he owned Klassik, he routinely carried a briefcase full of work and product samples home for after-hours attention.

On his desk were two short stacks of paper. Instead of sitting behind the desk, Gerry claimed one of three chairs arranged in a semicircle in front of it. Anna sat in the middle, and Kris took the remaining seat. "After you left the other day, the two of us talked," Gerry began. "Then we called the kids." The couple had twins, neither of whom had been interested in running the family business. The son had gone into civil engineering and moved to California, while their daughter was practicing medicine in Taos. "Tom and Sarah are fully supportive of what we're proposing, so we had my old business attorney draw up a simple agreement."

Kris noticed how, although Anna had not played a visible

role in the business, Gerry spoke inclusively, as if he and his wife were equal business partners.

"The document spells out all the legal details," Anna said, "but the bottom line is that we want to invest in you and the business. We've managed to save a nice chunk of money, but the kids have their own careers and don't need to count on inheriting anything from us. Of course, we do believe you will make the business profitable, so in the end they could inherit far more!" she laughed, and Kris remembered that Anna had earned an accounting degree when the twins were in grade school. She probably had been a more active silent partner than anyone realized.

"The executive summary is that we're providing the balance of what you need for the acquisition plus two years of operating expenses," Gerry said. "And there's a little incentive if you bring the firm back to profitability in under two years. You'll be making quarterly reports to the two of us, and you can pick our brains—what's left of them—any time you want, even if we're on a cruise! I want you to have your attorney look this over before you sign," Gerry said, rising, "but assuming this is compatible with your vision, do we have a deal?"

"Yes! I can't thank you enough for even considering this," Kris said, her left hand over her chest as she found herself getting uncharacteristically emotional. As she shook Gerry's hand, Anna took a phone photo.

"It's a little premature for celebratory champagne, and I don't want to jinx this," Gerry admitted, "but I think a finger of Scotch is in order—if you still like whisky."

"I would love a Scotch!"

21

Was she a fool to think she could pull this off? She finally had the financial puzzle piece in place, but a dozen other critical pieces remained missing.

Self-doubt hit Kris most frequently after lunch—when she forgot to eat. If she stopped to think about the timing (which she seldom did when she was in the flow of planning), she'd realize her mood nose-dive was at least partly related to low blood sugar. Then she'd grab whatever she found in the fridge and take it back to the table. She'd have to break that habit when she moved back to the office. Wouldn't set a good example to eat at her desk. She wanted her staff to be productive but not chained to their chairs all day. Made for bad morale.

But people weren't her focus this week. Machines were. Multiple precision-engineered machines for the new production facility were at the top of her shopping list. She'd been researching the options for months and had two top vendors, both in Italy. She'd have loved a buying trip to Italy in her past life, on someone else's expense account, but neither budget nor schedule would allow that now. Instead, she polished her draft email messages and attached her request for proposals. To show some cultural attentiveness, she added a greeting (*Gentile ...*) and closing (*Cordali Saluti*) in Italian. And, just in case the businesses were old-school formal, she'd send a copy of the letter and RFP via airmail.

Yikes! She hadn't printed letterhead yet. She couldn't remember the last time she'd used corporate letterhead. At least she had a logo. Her printer could turn the job in a day if she uploaded files tonight.

One week later, she still hadn't heard a word from Italy. She knew the email addresses were correct. This wasn't a major vacation period, though Easter had been April 1. *Did they take the whole week off? Could they be blowing me off because I'm a woman? Did they not need the business? Maybe I should call. Let's hope someone there speaks English.*

Thirty minutes later, Kris ended a call with her first-choice vendor. She'd caught them just before the end of their day, and the international business manager was all apologies. Profusely, gallantly apologetic about the Easter break. About the busy time of year. About how dearly they wanted to work with more North American customers, so of course they wanted her business. He understood the time urgency. Yes, they had set up their machines for specialty materials and could accommodate whatever proprietary ones her company developed. Yes, they provided training—in person, online, and remotely via video headset. Yes, he had a Skype handle, and they could meet via video chat next time—or any time she had questions.

· · ·

She'd been promised an emailed bid in response to her RFP by close of business the following day. Instead, it was three days later. Well, maybe someone had to work extra hard on reviewing the English, which was remarkably well-phrased. In the meantime, she'd gotten an email response from her second-choice equipment manufacturer. They were so sorry that they would have to decline the RFP. They were in the midst of a six-month "cease of manufacturing" while they retooled their own production facility. At least her first choice had come through. She could buy the machines outright for an eye-popping number of euros or lease them with an option to purchase. Clearly, the latter was the only feasible choice. The promised delivery date wasn't as soon as she had requested, but it might just allow for enough production to take orders in Las Vegas come September.

But before she made one of her two biggest financial commitments, she wanted a second opinion.

"This is Gerry. How are you, Kris? Has your head stopped spinning yet?"

"Not yet. In fact, that's why I'm calling. I don't want to spin out of orbit on a critical deal and was hoping you could take a look at it with me."

"Sure thing."

"I'm forwarding an email as we speak. It's a contract for frame-making machinery from what I believe is the best manufacturer for our needs."

"Got it. Give me a moment."

Kris remained quiet as Gerry read. She had always hated when someone asked her to read something but then talked at her the whole time she was reading. It's not that she couldn't multitask. Instead, it was more that the talker rarely added anything useful—like analysis or critical backstory—to the document she was reading. Plus, she still believed it was impolite to interrupt—especially a boss or financial backer—in a business setting.

"This looks about as I'd expect it to," Gerry began. "Given the small number of respected vendors, they've got everyone over a barrel on pricing. I assume you're considering the lease option?"

"Correct. I can't afford to burn through your cash too fast!"

"Well, then, my only two concerns are the delivery date and the maintenance contract. You're going to be pushing it with your September roll-out."

"I know. I don't like their counter-offer on delivery date any more than you do, but I don't really have a choice. The also-ran isn't taking any new orders for six months."

"Then, I'd see if you can get them to whittle down the maintenance contract fee a bit."

"Will do."

"And it might not hurt to offer up a prayer to some Italian saint or other!" Gerry joked.

"Not really into that, but I do appreciate your considering all the angles! I'll also have the attorney review this before I sign. And I promise I won't pester you too often."

"You're not bothering me at all. In fact, it's nice to feel needed—not that you really need my opinion. You're more in tune with the industry than I am these days."

"Thanks for that latest vote of confidence!"

Kris was in overdrive. She'd reached a deal with the Italian equipment firm. She was closing in on a lease for a production facility.

It was getting real really fast. Sandia Design was going to happen.

In addition to her office on the dining room table, she had notebooks on the bedside table and in the car. In February, she'd begun making audio notes to herself on her phone while walking. In March, she'd learned how to use a new cloud-based productivity/project management app. Now she started setting it up for team use. Trouble was, she didn't yet have a team to assign tasks to, so everything was a Kris to-do item—with a few exceptions for Kate and Mike, whom she'd added to the team as soon as she signed with Gerry.

She realized she could no longer handle everything herself, yet who could she trust to help who wouldn't leak the secret to the Klassik folks? Then it hit her. Time to partially lift the veil of secrecy. She sent a text.

Diana, can you swing by my place sometime in the next couple of days? I need help, and you're the only one who can provide the help I need!!

Sure. How about lunch tomorrow? I'll bring takeout. OK if I have Luna and another dog with me?

Perfect!

Once the dogs were settled in the backyard, the two women headed inside. As Kris held the patio door open, she asked, "I hope you don't think I'm being too personal, but it looks as if you've lost weight. I was going to say something when the G7 met last month, but I didn't want to put you on the spot—especially when we were celebrating your revenge on Roger!"

"Yeah," Diana laughed. "These past few months have been good for something at least. It's not so much what I eat as everything else I do. More time dog-walking has helped, I'm sure, but I no longer feel I have to stress-eat when I get home because I no longer have a stress-inducing boss. And with Janice around, I'm eating healthier meals in general because there's someone to cook with and eat with. I'm even sleeping better than I have in ages, just knowing there's another person in the house with me, and according to the latest experts, lack of sleep can contribute to weight gain. Still, it's not much. Less than ten pounds. But I feel better, and that's what matters to me."

"Totally agree. But that raises a related question: If you're enjoying self-employment, and it's been so good for your health, would you consider returning to an office job?" After outlining her purchase plan and a new job description for Diana, Kris asked, "What do you think? Would you be willing to return to the old office?"

"Working for you? Absolutely! It wasn't the work stress, it was the boss stress. And now that I've had some reset time, I really miss being in the midst of the daily buzz—instead of just the daily bark! And let's not forget the benefits. Even with the latest reforms, healthcare costs are always a looming threat if you don't have employer-provided insurance."

Over chicken Caesar salads, the two former colleagues speed-talked about Kris's business plans. And laughed. "Who'd ever have imagined you'd take over Klassik from Roger? If that's not the supreme revenge for his firing you—"

"Actually, revenge has never been my motivation. The timing was just right, and I can't seem to get this industry out of my bloodstream."

"OK. If you say so. But you won't judge if *I* take some pleasure in thinking of this as a little revenge plot for my part in the takeover?"

"Of course not!"

It was a relief to tell Diana her plans. It was one thing to talk about the company with Mike and Kate, but they had their own responsibilities and deadlines. They were supportive, but not emotionally invested. Diana, on the other hand, got it. She glowed with anticipation and shared Kris's vision.

"So, what you're going for is a complete reboot, right?"

"Yes, in terms of business plan, product mix, target market, supply chain, branding. But we won't be giving the boot to all the remaining staff."

"Just Roger?"

"Also Sandy and Ashley. And there are a couple of maybes who may not be happy under new leadership. Remember, this is in total confidence. Please don't share details—especially personnel information—with anyone. Not even Janice, though I understand you'll want to tell her that you'll be working with me in some capacity again in the near future."

"Got it. So what can I do to help in the meantime?"

"Honestly, it's been such a relief to just talk with you about all of this. But if you have some free time, there *are* a few tasks I'd love to hand off. I can't compensate you via payroll yet, so how about I prepay for a year at the yoga studio? I can expense it as a business gift."

"Perfect!"

Without Kris's financial responsibilities for the outcome, Diana could focus solely on excitement and execution. She was positively ebullient. Her attitude lightened Kris's mood for the first time in weeks.

And Diana was a lifesaver: a quick learner, eager to play around with the new software, diplomatic with potential vendors and business associates, and discreet. It suddenly occurred to Kris that Diana had become her new personal and professional confidante—her new Sharon. Almost.

. . .

The tasks to check, people to contact, documents to sign, and invoices to pay—already!—seemed to increase rather than decrease as Kris crossed off the days on her desktop calendar.

So immersed was she in details that one morning she forgot to text Kate. Around noon Eastern time, Kris's phone pinged.

You OK mom? You didn't text this am

Sorry! Been paddling as fast as I can to keep up with everything. What's up w U?

I've got an interview this afternoon with a consulting firm out of Austin. Psyched and scared!

You'll do great, sweetie! Good luck! [heart emojis]

If Kate got the job—this one or any other—would they want her to start right after graduation? Then she couldn't help out at the office this summer as they'd planned. Kris had been counting on Kate to be her personal assistant, and she seemed excited about getting exposure to every department in the business. It would be essentially a startup experience. If she went straight to Austin, who would be her right hand during the critical transition period?

Seriously? You'd wish bad luck on your own daughter? You'll figure it out. Don't borrow trouble. Just focus on the next step.

22

"Have you bought plane tickets yet for Kate's graduation?"

Kris had always been the family travel and vacation planner, but she could only plan so many things at once. "No, sorry. I've been focused on work. I can do it this evening." They were eating grocery-store frozen entrees for the third time that week. "Given the timing, I'll only be able to go out for the weekend."

Mike waited a beat and then said, "I'd like to take a week's vacation before graduation. Spend some time on the South Shore with my folks. I don't know how much longer they'll be able to stay in the house. I know they'd love to see you too."

"I'd love to go with you. It would be heavenly to spend some lazy days with them—and you—but there's no way I can be away that long right after the takeover. Even getting there in time for graduation will be a stretch. I wish the timing were different, but you'll have to go without me."

"OK. Why don't I make the reservations, then, since we have different itineraries? I'll fly back with Kate. I'll make her reservation too."

"Thanks!"

She felt a twinge, just a small one, at Mike handling a responsibility she usually enjoyed. *I've got to get better at delegating at home, not just at work*, she thought. *Too bad he isn't as proactive with housework.*

Between the two of them, they managed to keep the kitchen relatively clean, but the rest of the house had been neglected. Though they had both worked their entire marriage, they'd fallen into mostly traditional domestic roles. Mike took care of yard work, car service appointments, and paid their joint monthly bills. Kris did laundry and meal planning, shopping, and cooking. Until her layoff, someone else had done the weekly top-to-bottom housecleaning. Afterward, she'd had time to take over, but since securing final financing, dusty furniture and water-spotted mirrors hadn't seemed important.

"By the way," Mike ventured, "Are you doing laundry tonight? I'm down to my last underwear."

"Um, sure. Give me five to finish this RFP." Kris had begun multitasking during meals and had moved her laptop to the kitchen island during dinner the past couple of nights. "Or," she ventured into uncharted territory, suggesting, "you could throw in a load of whites. Just set it for hot and cotton."

"OK. Just thought I should ask first, as you often have special care conditions for certain items."

"Right now I'm not wearing 'office whites,' so I don't have any special fabrics in the white bin."

"Got it."

The following evening, as they were eating pre-marinated lamb kabobs Mike had picked up at the grocery on the way home, he suggested, "Let's take the weekend off and squeeze in a mini-vacation before you become CEO. That will give you two more weekends to cram before the big day. I was thinking maybe we could fly up to Denver, visit a museum, catch a show, get a massage."

"Ahh, a massage sounds heavenly, but I wouldn't be good company. I've got so much to do. Besides, can our budget handle a weekend away right now? Especially as we're going to Boston next month?"

"Well, it won't put us into bankruptcy," Mike tried to joke. "I just thought you could use a break before you go public and life gets even more hectic."

"Point taken, but I'd just be stressing about what I'm not doing if we go away now."

"OK, but promise me you'll get a massage one day soon. You need to schedule some relaxation too."

"Promise." Kris hadn't had a massage in years. She wouldn't know where to book. That would be more research time she should be spending on final prep.

23

On a brilliant Monday morning, the first in May, Kris was ready to go public as the new CEO of Sandia Design, formerly Klassik Eyewear. The closing and transition had been executed with military precision through the K&S Enterprises attorney, broker, and HR consultant. Finally, Kris could let the sun shine on her identity.

Over the weekend, her professional representatives had ensured that all locks and passwords were changed, that anything Roger had left behind was boxed up, and that an invitation to an all-hands meeting at 9 a.m. on Monday awaited employees when they returned to work.

Kris pulled into the loading zone in front of Klassik's office building at 7 a.m. and opened the Subaru's hatchback. Nobody else was around yet, so she left the front door propped open as she made several trips from her car to the office. One box was deposited on the receptionist's desk, one in her office, and another in the conference room. Then she moved her car to the middle of the parking lot.

She was singing Patti LaBelle's "New Attitude" as she

unpacked the conference room box. Then she turned to Roger's beloved "Attitude is Everything" poster. The frame was still in good shape, so she decided to recycle just the poster. In its place she hung a new photo in a new frame. "Thanks, Gerry!" she said to the picture that Anna had taken of the two of them shaking hands on their deal.

Early the previous week, as soon as the parties had reached agreement on a sale, Kris had asked her HR consultant to send each current employee—except for Roger—a questionnaire. It was presented as part employee survey and part job application. They were told that only the new CEO would see the materials and that the goal was to retain as many existing employees as possible while reorganizing the firm and positioning it for greater success.

The instructions read, "In answering the following questions, be honest, fair, and forward-thinking. Do not assume that the way things were is the way things have to be. The goal is to ensure that all employees play the roles that are best suited to their talents and professional goals as well as the company's needs. Responses are due by the close of business on Friday, before the new owner takes over."

Kris knew many of the answers existing staff would give, but she wanted to uncover any hidden talents or grudges before finalizing the reconfigured org chart. More importantly, she wanted everyone to reinvest in their jobs.

QUESTIONNAIRE

The following questions relate to your position and the company as it operated prior to the recent sale. Please be specific.

What has been the most professionally satisfying aspect of working at Klassik Eyewear over the past five years?

What has been the most professionally frustrating aspect of working at Klassik Eyewear over the past five years?

What has been the most important factor in your not leaving the company?

Can you continue to work in this company while leaving behind prior dissatisfactions and personal rivalries?

The following questions relate to your employment with the company going forward.

What adjustments to your current position would make you more enthusiastic about your job?

What personal or professional development changes would you need to make to achieve the next level of success with Klassik Eyewear 2.0?

Do you consider yourself a risk-taker or risk-averse on the job? Give an example.

What organizational, process, and/or personnel changes would improve the company's success and why?

What would it take (excluding a bump in salary) to increase your pride in your job and the company you work for?

Ignoring salary considerations, if you could apply for a different position in the company (one that currently exists or one that you think should be created), what would that be and why?

Over the weekend, Kris had printed up the completed questionnaires and arranged them on the table like a puzzle. With each one, she circled, underlined, and annotated, sometimes cross-referencing another set of responses. By Sunday afternoon, her org chart had just a couple of question marks and open boxes.

She had anticipated everyone's responses fairly accurately, so she hadn't made many changes to job title–people pairings, though there were a couple of surprises.

One recent IT hire—probably added to be groomed as a cheaper Terry—answered with the brashness of youth. This was Lee Martinez's first professional job, and he took the injunction to be "honest, fair, and forward-thinking" at face value. He dispensed with any sugar-coating when complaining that the website design was dated, that the former CEO had no clue how e-commerce, customer tracking, and dynamic content worked—even when he and Terry had repeatedly, carefully explained these easy-to-add functionalities. He did praise Terry for being a decent boss and for having good ideas, even though the CEO never provided approval or funding to implement them. He wanted to be involved in "bringing the website into the 21st century." Ouch. So, he was a risk-taker and rough around the edges, but he seemed to get along with Terry, who could use help in the new order.

And Eugene Pullman showed a lot more promise than he'd ever been allowed to display under Roger's rule. That was a shock. All Kris remembered was the constant bickering between Eugene and Mark. But Eugene's answers to her questions were practically college application essays, replete with pertinent details, sound business insights, and great ideas. His suggestions for improvement—use higher-quality materials and production facilities (while keeping the manufacturing process in China, where 90% of frames were made)—weren't as radical as what she had planned, but with the right assistance, he had the potential to take charge of a critical scope of work.

At 8 a.m. that Monday, Roger pulled his silver Range Rover into the parking lot. Last fall, after his final round of layoffs, he'd traded in his three-year-old Jeep Grand Cherokee for the more luxurious vehicle, more than double the price. He had to have an SUV for Rex. He needed the V6 engine and off-road capability for … well, he never really drove off road, but he imagined others envisioned him skillfully navigating gnarly mountain and desert 4x4 trails. New Mexicans loved the outdoors, and their vehicles showed it, with dirt and dents and sun-faded license plates. Roger felt his wheels should fit in with the local vibe yet convey sophistication; hence the appeal of the British brand associated with everything from African safaris to royal hunts. Not that he'd been on either. But he could bask in the status his Range Rover conveyed.

He parked in the spot closest to the door, as usual, and headed for the front door. Official office hours at Klassik were 8:30 a.m. to 5:30 p.m., but the receptionist had always arrived a half-hour early, and 8 a.m. was the time the new owner had given for a meeting. Finally, he'd learn who had bought his company. It was all very odd, he thought, that the buyer wished to remain anonymous. He'd made repeated inquiries, but the buyer's broker and lawyer wouldn't let a hint slip. Probably some famous person in the industry wanting to keep a low profile, he had speculated during final negotiations. He'd been curious, but that wasn't going to stop him from closing the deal. He was tired of leading a failing company and coping with loser employees. Maybe a move would refresh his business prospects. He'd always been drawn to Las Vegas, and people were constantly coming and going there—fresh blood. Could be just the change he needed.

During the closing, Roger had insisted on a meeting with the buyer himself. The buyer's broker said Monday morning would work. Roger's broker suggested taking over a nice bottle of French champagne as a thank you, in celebration of the successful transaction. Roger wasn't much of a wine connoisseur, let alone a sparkling wine aficionado, but he did pay attention to prices. Wandering the aisles in the liquor store that afternoon, his eyelids rose as the clerk suggested various French bottlings ranging in price from $25 to $80 and up. "But if it's a big deal you're celebrating, you may want to consider some of our vintage champagnes." Roger declined, said he'd look around some more, and stopped at a display of domestic sparkling wine. He recognized some of the names on the bottles, and they were cheaper than the least-expensive French champagne, so he picked one up.

Holding the bubbly in his left hand, he opened Klassik's front door with his right and nearly lost his grip on the gift. Sitting at the receptionist's desk was Diana Delgado. She looked up at him as if nothing was out of the ordinary—but also as if she'd never seen him before. "Good morning. You can go on up to the conference room at the top of the stairs," she instructed.

It took Roger a split second to process what she'd said. For the first time when face to face with Diana, he was speechless. Slowly, then more quickly, he moved toward the stairs, pausing halfway up the flight to glance back at Diana, as if he still couldn't believe his eyes. Diana was back at work on her computer.

As he entered the conference room, he saw the back of a woman placing a stack of orientation packets on the table. The cover read, "Klassik Eyewear is now Sandia Design." The woman turned and Roger nearly lost his grip on the bottle for the second time in a minute.

"What are *you* doing here?" he gasped.

"I'm the new owner," Kris responded, extending her hand for a shake.

Roger either was too flummoxed to see her hand or chose to ignore it. "You? Seriously?"

"Yes."

"But how … Why …?"

"When I heard the business was for sale, I started looking into the possibility of buying it. I had," she emphasized the past tense, "always loved working here, and I believe in the prospects for a refocused and rebranded enterprise. I suspected that if you knew I was interested in acquiring the company, you'd have rejected my offer."

"You're right about that," Roger snapped, his kohl-black eyes narrowing. "First Diana's assault, and now this," Roger whined. "Why are you women out to make my life a living nightmare?"

"It's not about you," Kris explained, with Zen-like calmness she might have borrowed from Diana. "It's just business. You were selling the company, and I bought it."

Roger, who clearly had never been so soundly bested, was apoplectic. A volcano was roiling in his chest, but somehow he couldn't find the words to release the emotions creating that burning sensation. How could this woman, who had reported to *him*, have turned the tables? Conspiracy theories writhed in his brain. There had to be someone to blame for this turn of events. Otherwise, there was only his shame and embarrassment.

Nobody likes to be shamed, but a certain type of insecure

man likes it least of all. Kris knew Roger was one of the tribe that particularly hated losing to a woman. That hadn't been her goal. She'd never been out to shame Roger. It's just that he left her no choice. And it's not as if she were doing it publicly, in front of the rest of the company.

"I wish you the best in your future endeavors," she said, extending her hand once again. When it was met by air, she continued, "If you'll excuse me, I have to prepare for a meeting."

Roger, as unresponsive as a fighter down for the count, stood there a full two seconds. Finally, he turned to exit the room and saw the new photo. "So, looks like you found your sugar daddy!" he mocked, turning toward her once again.

Ignoring the innuendo, Kris responded, "Gerry knows a good investment opportunity when he sees it." Then, because Roger had failed to rise to the occasion in any way, she considered allowing herself to retort, "I understand *your* daddy cut your allowance." But she held her tongue. Truth-telling would serve no purpose and could push him past the boiling point. Who knows, he might lob that bottle of bubbly at her head.

Unable to generate a follow-up insult, Roger harrumphed, turned tail, and with the bottle in danger of being shattered by his grip, ran down the stairs.

Kris took a deep cleansing breath and slowly released it. Then she closed the door and got back to work.

The staff weren't used to seeing the conference room door closed before a meeting; they waited impatiently until it opened at 9 a.m., revealing Kris, who welcomed them in. The sleek, uncurled shoulder-length cut she'd adopted in the new year seemed to signal the shift in her new level of authority even though she wore a familiar white shirt under a burnt orange linen jacket and skinny black jeans.

"Are *you* the new owner?" Liz, the controller, gasped, enfolding Kris's proffered right hand in both of hers.

"Yes, I am!" Kris laughed, as the rest of the staff jockeyed to be next in line to congratulate her. The pre-Roger cohort was the most enthusiastic, but even Roger's hires wore the broadest smiles she'd seen.

"I know you're the boss now, but can I give you a hug?" Terry asked without waiting for an answer. "You can sue me later! I'm just so relieved it's you!"

Once the initial shock subsided, Kris had everyone take a seat. "I know you've got questions, and I'll answer some of them now, but you'll find more detail in the rebranding plan.

"I want to start by talking about people—those of you who are here and some who are not. I appreciate the thoughtfulness with which you responded to the survey. Your comments confirmed that there's more talent and passion in this group than has been drawn on previously. To breathe new life into this company, I'll be calling on you all to bring every ounce of skill and energy to your jobs—starting today! You'll notice that a couple of familiar faces are missing …"

"No Roger!" Terry's exclamation was met by *sotto voce* cheers around the table.

"And that's to help us focus on the future rather than past grievances," Kris continued. "Sandy and Ashley are no longer with the company. We'll be outsourcing most HR tasks to a professional vendor, and our new VP of Marketing will be Meredith Colvin, who is moving here from LA, where she has been VP of Marketing for a larger brand you're all familiar with. I'll also be bringing on a new, local design consultant who will work with Eugene to launch a whole new line of eyewear, while Terry will be in charge of overseeing our enhanced digital presence." At that announcement, Terry made a joyous fist pump but managed to remain silent.

"And, even though we'll be making investments to retool this operation from top to bottom, we also have to manage expenses tightly, so that means I'll be bringing in a couple of minimum-wage-earning interns for the summer months. One of those is my daughter Kate, who is looking forward to working across departments in whatever capacity she's needed.

"Probably the most obvious change beyond the org chart is the corporate rebranding. It has to happen quickly but smoothly, so you all need to read the plan in front of you, cover to cover, right after this meeting. We'll be working out many of the details along the way, but today we bid farewell to Klassik Eyewear and say hello to Sandia Design.

"With Sandia Design we're leaving behind the mass market and the race to the bottom for what's usually called the luxury market, but instead of using that nomenclature, we're marketing Sandia Design as 'Handcrafted in the USA.' " Her announcement was met by audible gasps. Everyone immediately knew what Kris's Made in America message meant: No more Chinese production partners. What they didn't understand was how the company would manage to move manufacturing to the U.S. But Kris was barreling ahead with more new initiatives.

"We're also leaving the door open to brand extensions beyond eyewear, but for the foreseeable future, the goal is to build a fresh, distinctive brand that appeals to customers tired of both predictable and outlandish design trends.

"We're capitalizing on the popularity of products with local roots, but we believe that in doing so, by drawing on the rich, evolving culture and popularity of the Southwest—without resorting to stereotypes—we can produce frames that appeal to eyewear connoisseurs worldwide. I know that sounds ambitious, and it's going to require time, but even though we're starting with a focus on the North American market, I believe we can create a brand differentiator that will make Sandia Design internationally popular."

"Whoa!" Kris heard Eugene exclaim under his breath.

"Whoa, indeed!" she echoed. "Your department is going to get a complete makeover. We'll be assembling an actual production staff—right here in Albuquerque. No more outsourcing to China. The learning curve will be steep, but if you're willing to collaborate with a new manufacturing floor supervisor and our new head of design, I think it could evolve into your dream job."

"I think I'd like that." Eugene's face lit up.

"Good!" Turning to Mark, she addressed the new org chart that was part of everyone's packet. "Mark, we can discuss details in my office after this meeting if you like, but I hope you will stay on with the team even though your short-term VP of Sales and Marketing title has been changed to VP of Sales and Customer Support. I'm confident that with your skills and the new product line, you'll find the Sales leadership position more interesting and lucrative than it's been since you joined Klassik. We're aligning Sales with Customer Support to ensure that we're listening to customer needs and feedback. And there will be a new incentive plan for sales reps that puts a premium on customer retention rather than just sales commissions."

"No problem. I'm not hung up on titles as long as I see room for career growth."

"Good to hear. And yes, you will have room for growth. In

the near term, I have three critical tasks for you." As Mark picked up his phone to take notes, Kris enumerated his marching orders.

"First, by the end of this week, we need you and your sales staff to contact all our existing accounts, share the corporate brand change, and let them know there will be a four-month hiatus on product delivery. They may not be happy about that —at least those who were actually still selling Klassik frames— but reassure them that, come September, we'll be introducing a whole new line of distinctive product. We'll miss out on the summer back-to-school sales, but our new market just barely overlaps with the student sector, so we don't need to worry about that." Kris naturally used the plural when speaking of corporate initiatives and team work, but now more than ever she intentionally used "we." She hoped to convey the need for unity and to avoid sounding like an order-issuing despotic boss.

"Second, though we can't force them to comply, encourage existing distributors to clear out all remaining Klassik inventory by the end of this month. Whatever inventory we have stateside or in China, have it sent here immediately. Then, as soon as she arrives next Monday, I want you to work with Meredith to start distributing the leftovers to a couple of New Mexico organizations that provide free or subsidized vision care. That will give Meredith a good hook for her rebranding publicity blitz.

"Third, new clients. I don't need to tell you that the premium optical shops haven't given us a second look for years. Well, those retailers are our new primary target. From now until our new product launch in September, your job is to build excitement for the new line. That means you'll have to work collaboratively with Design, Production, and Marketing so everyone builds the same body of new knowledge and can speak about it in the same terms. You'll all have your areas of expertise and responsibility, of course, but we have no margin for error in this quick pivot. Everyone has to push in the same direction. No territorialism. No ego plays. That goes for everyone—sorry if it seemed I was singling you out, there, Mark!"

"Understood," Mark smiled. "I'm eager to help make this business profitable again."

"Terry, you'll be working with a contract graphic designer to completely rebuild our website. I'll send you some Coming Soon placeholder content later today. You'll also be working with Meredith and one of our summer interns to update the site weekly with new teaser content to build anticipation for the new product. And, to answer the question I know you're dying to ask, we *will* be adding virtual frame fittings on the site, but we'll wait to fully roll that out until after the fall show."

"Excellent!" Terry cheered.

"Liz, you and I will put our heads together after this meeting to review a number of changes. I've set up appointments later this week for us both to meet with the attorney and our HR vendor. And tomorrow, we'll meet with Eugene and Diana to finalize the leasing of a production facility here in Albuquerque and expedite the process of getting our hands on all the equipment we'll need there—as soon as possible!

"As you all can see, Diana's role is evolving. She'll be our new director of Facilities and Operations. Her first task will be hiring a new front office specialist. Her real job, regardless of title, is to ensure that everything runs smoothly day to day."

"Diana always has been the one person who knew what

was going on everywhere and with everyone!" Liz couldn't help interjecting.

Kris smiled. "Now let's get to work! We've got to sprint all the way to the fall show. We only get one chance to make an unforgettable first impression."

24

"Who's the heart-throb in the conference room?" Liz asked Diana in a whisper. She was inquiring about a strikingly handsome man, young for this office, whose posture and gait, as he walked from the table to the white board and back, signaled self-assurance but not a whiff of arrogance. He stood five-eight and was perfectly proportioned, as could be inferred from the fit of his skinny denim jeans and what looked like an expensive Italian white dress shirt, collar open to highlight the patterned placket. Thick, straight, nearly shoulder-length hair framed his dark-tan face. Like many New Mexicans, he looked as if he might have Native American and Spanish ancestors, though it was hard to pinpoint his ethnic background definitively. At the same time, something about how he dressed didn't quite look local.

Diana, who had ushered said heart-throb to the conference room, just grinned and replied, "Kris will introduce him at nine."

All the senior staff were in their seats before 9 a.m. for the second weekly meeting of Sandia Design, eager to share week-one feedback, problems, and plans.

"OK, everyone," Kris began as she walked into the conference room with an unfamiliar woman about her age. "I know we have a lot to report from our first week under the new banner, but I'm going to ask you to hold weekly reports and questions until after we introduce our new design plan. We have two new key members of the team joining us today, and I want to start with Meredith Colvin.

"Meredith comes to us from that mega-LA eyewear brand we used to envy, where she led their marketing department for over a decade. She's also held marketing roles for a prestige LA jeweler and a manufacturer of high-end industrial measurement devices. I met her a few years ago at Vision Expo and have been impressed by her career achievements. I'm excited to see the new ideas she'll bring to our refreshed company. Meredith grew up Arizona, went to college in Texas, and has visited New Mexico countless times, so she understands the Southwest, which is central to our brand identity. Would you like to say a few words, Meredith?" She turned to Meredith, wearing a sleeveless, waist-cinched dress in a vibrant pattern of lime green and white that perfectly set off her bright red hair.

"I'd love to. First, you all should know that less than a year ago, I tried to lure Kris to 'that mega-LA eyewear brand'! I knew her talents were being squandered at Klassik, and I had deep respect for her unique combination of talents, professional integrity, and competitive drive. We have been communicating regularly over the past several months, and I mentioned that, although I had a great job, I was hungry to work in more of a startup environment where I could feel my contributions were having a direct and immediate effect. When she called to say she was buying Klassik and completely re-envisioning it, I told her I'd take any job she needed to fill. I'm so grateful for this dream-come-true opportunity, and I'm looking forward to working with all of you."

"Thanks, Meredith. The second new face belongs to Paolo Vitale, our new design consultant. Although he'll be on premises nearly full time through the end of the year as we get up to full production speed, he also has a couple of other interests. Before Paolo says a few words, I want to explain why I hired him.

"Paolo, too, comes to us from California, but he's actually coming home. He was born and raised right here in Albuquerque. I read a profile of him and his work last year that, for no good reason at the time, I bookmarked. The article's main focus was Paolo's work with a famous industrial and consumer products design firm. It talked about how he was using principles of biomimicry—using lessons from natural systems to solve complex design problems. Something about that approach—as well as the products showcased—resonated with me. When I began looking for someone to lead our new design effort, I remembered that in the interview, Paolo kept coming back to influences from his childhood in New Mexico. He'd already worked with so many different media in both commercial and fine art realms, I wondered if he might be interested in eyewear. By the end of our first phone conversation, not only did he seem interested in eyewear, he also was very interested in moving back to New Mexico, so here he is!"

"Thank you, Kris," Paolo began as he pulled a wayward strand of hair behind his right ear. The relaxed movement hinted that he was used to being noticed but wasn't vain about his good looks. "For the record, I'm twenty-eight, but though I'm the youngest on your senior team, I've been working in various art and design disciplines since I was a kid, and I've been earning money as an artist since I was in middle school.

"My names come from my father's side of the family. My father, Antonio, came to New Mexico from Italy when he was in his early thirties. His training and expertise was in art restoration—especially plasterwork, but he had the travel bug, so when he was just hitting his stride, he took a break. He'd been fascinated by the American West since he was a child, so he used his interest in natural building and decorating materials as an excuse to apply for a sabbatical of sorts to study adobe brick-making and traditional earthen clay plastering. Not long after he arrived in Albuquerque, he met a talented Acoma potter, Alice, who would become my mother. I'm sharing all of this not to be long-winded about my genealogy but so you understand the roots of my design sensibilities and how, like many New Mexicans, I treasure my rich, diverse, and complex cultural and artistic heritage.

"From my mother, I learned to make halfway decent pots, though I was never patient enough to match her precision and exquisite detail. I earned a degree in studio arts from the Institute of American Indian Arts in Santa Fe, and then, instead of riding that local horse, I got on a bird and flew to Italy for a year. My father still has family and many professional connections there, so I did some traveling to visit relatives, took some art workshops, and even worked for a couple of months under the same restoration master as my father had. I'd gotten really interested in digital arts at IAIA, so while I was still in Italy, I applied for positions where I could acquire some cred in that world. As Kris mentioned, I was fortunate to land a job with a design firm in Silicon Valley and gained a lot of valuable experience. But Silicon Valley isn't the Rio Grande Valley, and I'd been missing New Mexico, so when Kris called, it was easy to say yes."

"What Paolo hasn't mentioned is that he also has produced and sold dozens of mixed media conceptual art pieces over the past few years and just had one piece accepted for the Smithsonian Institution's National Museum of the American Indian." Kris wanted to be sure that, even if Paolo wouldn't brag on himself, the rest of the team should know exactly the caliber of design professional they would be working with.

"Wow!"

"Impressive!"

"Congratulations!"

"And because he wants to continue developing his own pieces, we have Paolo as a part-time but long-term consultant," Kris continued. "Could you talk a little bit about the design vision, Paolo?"

"Sure. And to be clear, though I have the designer title, the original and sustaining vision is Kris's. If I didn't feel comfortable with what she sketched out, I wouldn't have signed on. And by the way, Kris sketched the original concept for the logo, and as we've been trading preliminary sketches, I've learned that she's a very talented artist herself."

"Kris?"

"Who knew?"

"Amazing!"

"You've been hiding more than one talent for years!"

Paolo's praise and her staff's reactions brought an unfamiliar rush of red to Kris's cheeks.

As the buzz decrescendoed, Paolo continued. "The first issue Kris raised when we began talking about this position was her concern that what we produce not be interpreted as cultural appropriation. I know everyone has a different take on that controversial topic, and there will always be someone who complains, but I feel really comfortable—and excited—about where we both see Sandia Design going. All of the designs and color palettes will have some reference point in the Southwest, especially New Mexico. Many will take their inspiration from the natural world and some from the cultural traditions. Let me give you an example.

"I mentioned Acoma pottery, which is part of my heritage. We're not so much reproducing Acoma designs as bringing that tradition's attention to precision and detail to the craft of eyewear design. So you may see black and white geometric patterns that are *evocative* of Acoma designs, but they'll be transformed in some way. Or take the black-on-black designs you know from Santa Clara potters or the carved, embossed technique. Those vocabularies could provide the building blocks for a new type of pattern that would be expressed in a unique frame style that celebrates New Mexican cultures without appropriating or disrespecting them."

"There's another element of traditional design we're using as a guiding star," Kris interjected. "Like traditional Acoma pottery, our new lines will be designed to be both lightweight and durable. Though not made entirely of clay, the hand feel of one of our materials, a proprietary composite that includes actual New Mexico clay, is like that of a treasured decorative pot that also gets daily use."

"We're also drawing on my Italian heritage," Paolo transitioned. "Because, after all"—he opened his arms to the room, palms uplifted—"you can't suppress an Italian!"

Everyone laughed as Kris picked up the brush again. "The more Paolo and I traded ideas and embellished each other's concepts, the more obvious the connection became: Italy and New Mexico share a color palette, a love of nature, and a respect for tradition that somehow also encourages innovation —at least in art and design!"

"Our color schemes and style names will be inspired by New Mexico," Paolo explained. "Did you ever notice that, although we have countless shades of 'earth tones,' it's rare to find anything in nature that's a standard crayon brown? So many of our colors—in New Mexico and Italy—are shifty. They depend on the angle and quality of light. We want to bring that complexity, that depth of color experience to our frames."

"Now, the idea isn't to make the designs so unusual that they detract from the person's face," Kris clarified. "We'll have a range of options for those who want their frames to blend in to their face—whatever its hue—and those who want their eyewear to stand out. One of my favorites in the latter category is one we're calling Blanket Flower; this color scheme pulls deep rusty orange from the native wildflower's center for the primary color and accents it with orange and yellow from the petals. It's for the confident person who doesn't mind being seen!"

"Sign me up!" Terry raised his hand.

"You won't find a standard, square black plastic frame in the lineup—ever," Kris promised.

"Instead, for those who want to make a more subdued fashion statement, we'll have a dark gray color scheme called Tuff that evokes the state's volcanic stone. We'll even embed tiny particles of tuff in the temple pieces," the designer explained, the fingers of his right hand fluttering as if depositing volcanic dust on the table.

"One of my favorites," Kris said, grinning, "is our alternative to the ubiquitous tortoiseshell plastic frame. Rather than take our name and color palette from a turtle, our mottled pattern will take its inspiration and name from our New Mexico Horny Toad!"

"Love it!"

"Cheeky!"

"Can't wait to see it."

As Paolo and Kris traded strokes of the new design vision, they put the rest of the team at ease. These two, despite their difference in age and backgrounds, made an impressive pair. They spoke the same language and saw the same potential.

"All of Paolo's brilliant design work will be pointless if we don't execute brilliantly." Kris, a bit taken away herself by their summary of the new design vision, knew it was time to loop in the rest of the group with some practicalities. "In the process of developing these new designs, we'll be testing some new materials and working with high-quality acetate in new ways, as you've heard. I've engaged a materials scientist to do some free consulting for us on that aspect."

"Uh, would that be your husband?" Terry probed.

"Yes, in fact, Mike has agreed to spend some time with Paolo and Eugene to get our material sourcing and manufacturing processes customized so we can turn vision into reality. While we're getting the chemistry, physics, and tooling details locked down, I'll be working with Eugene to set up all the Italian-made machinery we need for the production operation. We've got a signed contract with the most respected equipment vendor, but now we have to speed up those Italians and get some serious decisions made.

"Everything we produce will be driven by the vision you've heard outlined today, which is encapsulated in our new tag line: Elevated eyewear rooted in the Southwest."

25

"That was fun!" Kris laughed as she rolled off of Mike. The queen bed took up half the space in Kris's childhood bedroom. Her parents had replaced her twin bed after she'd married so it could be a guest room. Her desk had been replaced by a brightly upholstered reading chair beside the window.

"Been awhile!" Mike grinned. "I've missed you."

"It hasn't been *that* long," Kris protested.

"I don't mean this. I mean just spending time with you. Tonight was nice. It's the first time in ages I've had you all to myself."

Kris had arrived in Boston late Saturday afternoon, and after dinner at home, her parents had left for a bridge tournament, so Kris and Mike strolled around the leafy Newton neighborhood, marveling at broad, lush lawns. Typically, when they walked together, they'd match each other's gait. That night, Kris—legs moving as fast as her brain had been spinning in recent months—kept looking back for Mike, who lagged by a full stride thanks to a week of vacation and walking the dog with his father.

"Let's get ice cream!" Mike proposed.

"Remember, they closed Steve's decades ago. There's nothing quite as good anymore, and I know you don't like frozen yogurt."

"You're right. I guess being here just makes me want to relive my youth."

"Besides, you already had dessert."

"I know, but I'm on vacation, and calories don't count when you're on vacation."

"How about a nightcap on the back veranda instead?"

"OK."

"Everything's so *green* here!" Kris sighed as they turned into the driveway. The basketball hoop to which she and Kevin had devoted endless hours still hung on the garage, sun-bleached but sturdy. "They don't make hoops to last like that any more."

"Are we made to last?" Mike asked.

"Let's find out. I'll race you to my room!"

Kris and Mike had been married for thirty years but together for thirty-four. They'd met while running the Boston Marathon when they were both college juniors, Mike at MIT and Kris at Boston College.

Mike had taken up running later than Kris, but he'd gotten serious about it in college when he realized that going for a run was an excellent way to break the stress of hunching over lab tables and text books for hours on end. He'd just managed to qualify for the marathon and only hoped to finish it. Kris, who had grown up surrounded by the hoopla of the famous marathon, had decided the day she was admitted to BC that, before graduating, she would run the race, whose course passed right along the edge of campus. She knew other runners, but nobody in her immediate circle had run the marathon, not even her brother Kevin.

To train, both Kris and Mike had run portions of the course, but usually they had to settle for more immediately accessible routes. Neither had run a full twenty-six miles in a single day.

On the day of the race, Kris had just conquered Heartbreak Hill—the last but hardest, given that it came after more than twenty miles—and had just received a boost of energy from her cheering classmates lining Commonwealth Avenue as she passed the BC campus when she tripped. It should have been easy going at that point, downhill at a slight grade. In retrospect, she decided she'd gotten sloppy, looked sideways at the wrong moment, and stumbled on little more than a pebble. She fell, but only suffered a hand abrasion. But she was down. A bit stunned. And then, crouching beside her was a young man with wavy, sandy hair dripping sweat onto his shoulders —and her knee. "Are you OK?" he asked, and she looked up to see warm hazel eyes. A bit embarrassed, she assured him she was and quickly stood up to continue. "Do you mind if I run with you—or try to—the rest of the way?" he asked. "Sure," she answered, and for the last four miles, they ran side by side, exchanging no more than a dozen words.

By the end of the day they had traded names and phone numbers. By the end of the month they had met for coffee twice and talked on the phone half a dozen times. By the end of the school year they had contrived a way to both get summer jobs in Cambridge so they could meet for lunch every day. By the time they graduated, they'd decided to move in together.

Mike had the intellect of an MIT geek (to whom that designation was a badge of honor) and the looks of a Hollywood star. But it was his personality that sucked Kris in so deep she never wanted to date another guy. He was easygoing socially but laser focused academically. That was a rare combination, she'd learn, among the scientist set. In later years, Kris credited his mother for that balance. She'd insisted that Mike take summer jobs working with the public throughout high school and college—lifeguard, waiter, gopher at the local hospital—to balance his natural bookishness. He'd always be an introvert, but he could work a cocktail party with ease.

Around Kris, he was relaxed. Self-confident but not cocky —unlike far too many of the young men attending Bay Area colleges who either traded on their family's name and money, their own intellect (which they frequently overestimated, in her opinion), or both.

Though they'd both grown up near Boston in quiet suburbs, they first experienced urban life together. As young professionals working their starter jobs—Mike as a researcher at a new MIT spin-off and Kris as marketing assistant for a local clothing brand—they rented a one-bedroom apartment in a Somerville triple-decker. When they had time off together, they ran together. Every weekend they'd celebrate with ice cream at the original Steve's in Somerville.

"I can't believe you're working," Mike chided. Midday Monday, they were sitting in the parents' section at graduation and Kris had pulled out her phone to make a couple of notes to herself.

"Everyone has their phones out. I'm just making a quick

note. It is a workday, after all. Besides, I need my phone at the ready when Kate walks up."

The cloudless, powder-blue sky above the stadium made for perfect photos of the grads, many of whom wore sunglasses—an occasional accessory in Boston rather than the everyday necessity they were in Albuquerque. Kris took note of the styles. Mostly classic aviators on the male graduates. Tortoiseshell, aviators, miscellaneous dark plastic squares, and a few round frames on the women. Overall, pretty conventional.

Both sets of grandparents, sitting beside Mike, had joined them for the ceremony and were catching up with each other. Kris could just hear her mother's voice. She smiled as she realized her mother was trying not to let on to Mike's mother how often Kate had stopped by their house over her four years at BC. Well, it wasn't favoritism as much as accessibility. Her parents were just a T stop away—though Kate had confessed she never turned down an invitation for Sunday pot roast and brownies.

One more thing. As her thumbs danced on her phone screen, she glanced sideways, apologetically, at Mike.

Riding the T to the airport by herself late that afternoon, Kris gave way to a few minutes of self-pity. She'd always enjoyed the vibe of Boston's public transportation (except when stuck on a stalled train), but today it irked her that she couldn't work while hanging on to a strap, suitcase braced between her legs.

After a weekend surrounded by those she loved, who loved her, she was all alone. The visit had been so easy. Her mother played hostess as smoothly as she remembered. They'd taken dozens of three-generation selfies—in the Public

Garden, eating chowder, with Kate in her black graduation cap and gown. The days had been full of revisiting familiar places, seeing them through Kate's eyes, which were already nostalgic. Evenings were one long party of food, drink, and stories retold from Kate's childhood, and hers. Laughter. She couldn't remember the last time she'd laughed so much.

They'd agreed it made most sense for her to catch the B line right from the college after the ceremony. Mike carried her suitcase from the car to the Green Line stop and gave her a kiss goodbye. Then he was off, walking faster, to join in more celebrations and a final day of vacation.

She admitted to being envious of his week off. What she wouldn't give for a week lazing around, book in one hand, gin and tonic in the other. Maybe with an ocean view for a couple of days. But this is what she wanted. What she'd been working so hard for since December. With Kate's graduation, she'd closed one book of responsibilities and opened another. This time, she was responsible for many more people's livelihoods and well-being.

26

"God, I missed this place! Well, not exactly *this place.* New Mexico generally." Kate was unpacking and settling back into her old bedroom for the summer. "I mean, I love Boston, but the weather sucks for all but a couple of months, and those are ones when I had to be indoors, studying."

"It's mostly the effect of humidity," her mother empathized.

"Right? In summer you sweat so much you need three showers—something I'd feel guilty about here. In winter the damp seeps through to your bones. I never understood how anyone could wear a wool sweater until I tried to get through my first winter with just fleece."

Kris laughed and hugged her daughter. "I guess you're a desert girl at heart. I'm happy to have you home—at least for a bit."

Kate was the same height as her mother and shared her slim but moderately muscular build. Kris sported the soft buff prelude to a summer tan, while Kate still wore her winter white. Catching the two of them in the mirror, both in jeans and tee shirts, Kate noticed the difference. "God, I'm pasty, aren't I? The very vision of the cloistered scholar who never sees the sun. Time to work on that! I think I'll ride to work most days, if you'll let me borrow your bike."

"Of course, though I might want to use it occasionally on the weekends."

Kate glanced sideways at her mother. "Seriously? I mean, it's your bike, and you can use it whenever you want, but Dad says you haven't had it out since last fall."

"I guess it has been awhile. I've taken to speed walking for exercise. It's easier to record voice memos on my phone when I think of something I need to do for the business. Speaking of which, everyone is eager to have you join the team for the summer. You know some of the old-timers—Diana, Terry, Liz. And I think the other intern, Robert Sena, was in a couple of your high-school AP classes."

"Yeah, I remember Rob. He was into the sciences more than I was—much to Dad's chagrin."

"He still is, but he said he wants to round out his background more and is eager to learn how a consumer products business operates. He'll be spending most of his time with Eugene, setting up the production facility."

"What scope of work do you have planned for me?"

"Well, I took you at your word when we first talked about this, and you're going to be what in your grandmother's era was called a Girl Friday!"

"Does that mean I only work Fridays?"

"That would not qualify you for a full-time paycheck—even if it is only minimum wage."

"At least I get free room and board, right?"

"Of course. Though you will have to pick up after yourself, do your own laundry, and help out with cooking and dishes."

"After living off-campus with slobs this year, that will be a breeze!"

"So at Sandia, starting tomorrow, you'll officially report to me, but most of the time you'll be working with and reporting in to Diana. She's always been the one who kept all the balls in the air, so she'll be a great resource and can answer most of your questions. You'll have longer-term projects that you are responsible for and we'll adjust your short-term responsibilities week by week. The majority of your time will be spent helping various department leaders prepare for our official launch. I've got you down to help Mark strategize how to deploy our CRM software now that we're targeting a different market. We don't want to destroy all the old records, but most of our previous clients won't be our future ones. Mark has some thoughts on that, but I want you to bring fresh eyes to the transition. After all, I'm sure you'll encounter Salesforce at some point in your career, so this will get your feet wet."

"Sounds good. Any new tech skills I can add will save me onboarding time later."

"You said you wanted exposure to finance and marketing, so you'll be helping Liz set up some new processes. She's a pro, so even if she has you doing something as mundane as data entry, you'll learn how all the pieces fit together in AP and AR. And Meredith is as savvy as they come in the eyewear marketing world ..."

"Better than you?"

"I hope so! My goal was to hire people who are smarter and more effective than I am at each of the critical functions. Meredith has even more industry connections than I do—partly because she worked for a much larger firm and lived in LA, where there were dozens more networking opportunities. She's a connection queen—knows exactly how and when to touch base with the right people, without being a nuisance. That's a harder skill to finesse than you might think—especially in this social media era."

"I'm looking forward to meeting Meredith. You've always spoken so highly of her. Think she'll take *me* out for sushi and cocktails?"

"Don't push your luck! There's one more thing I'd like to ask of you."

"Name it."

"Be my second set of eyes and ears as you work across departments. Let me know if you see anything that seems off, or if it seems someone is struggling to do their job, or if certain staff members aren't getting along for some reason. I think we've got everyone on the same page, but sometimes it's hard to completely put old grievances aside. I'm not asking you to spy so much as I'm asking you to start seeing yourself as the business consultant you'll be in the fall. That goes for me too. If you see me approaching a problem or task in a way you think could be done better—faster, cheaper, more effectively— speak up. And speak up sooner rather than later. Everyone's projects are on a fast track, so we need immediate course corrections before any element or person goes off the rails. I know that's a rather amorphous goal, but …"

"No, I get it. You nailed it when you described it as a consulting assignment. I'll be on the lookout for process, project, and personnel adjustments that would benefit the schedule and the bottom line."

The next morning, Kris tacked on a short all-hands meeting

before the leadership team meeting. "Good morning everyone, and welcome to our first monthly stand-up, standing meeting! The first Monday of each month we'll have a 'standing meeting,' a quick update for everyone in this office. If you have specific issues you'd like to hear addressed, please submit them to me via email by close of business the previous Friday. And it's a stand-up meeting to ensure we keep it within fifteen minutes—and because we don't have room for everyone to sit.

"The primary agenda item today is to introduce our two new interns, Robert Sena and Kate Wright." After the two gave a wave and accepted applause, Kris continued. "Though we're calling these two young professionals interns because of their temporary employment with us, they are anything but inexperienced. Both have previously held part-time or summer jobs in their fields—chemistry for Rob and business for Kate—and both will be leaving us in September for full-time positions. Rob will be going to work at Sandia Laboratories here in town, while Kate will be working for a consulting firm in Austin. Rob will mostly be working with Eugene to get the production facility on the south end of town up and running, while Kate will be based in this office and will report to me but will be working with every department under this roof. She wants to learn as much as possible about how a small business operates, so throw your toughest problems her way!"

As Kris was introducing Rob and Kate, she noticed Paolo give Kate a soft smile. They hadn't yet met or worked together, but they would be the two youngest staffers in the headquarters office. It was probably just a friendly smile for the boss's daughter. Still, they couldn't avoid noticing each other. Where Paolo was all dark, cool masculinity, Kate was his polar opposite. Every inch, from her long, wavy strawberry-blond hair and blue eyes to her narrow ankles sparkled with feminine, athletic energy.

"I realize everyone is being asked to handle old tasks in new ways as well as completely new responsibilities. I know that can be stressful, but I hope it's also invigorating. If you feel you might be headed toward trouble with a deadline, *please* speak with your supervisor right away to resolve the issue. The project goals and deadlines in Sales are connected to those in Marketing, which are connected to those in Production, and so on. We've got three months to fine-tune those interdependencies, so let's get them right as quickly as possible.

"Now, since you didn't have a chance to submit any issues for discussion at this first stand-up meeting, does anyone have concerns or comments of general interest?"

After four long seconds of silence, Kris wrapped up. "OK, then, if there's nothing else, let's get back to creating the strongest indie eyewear brand this century!"

After the leadership meeting, Diana requested a word with Kris before they headed back to their offices. "What's on your mind?" Kris asked.

"I didn't want to bring this up during your open comment period because I worried it was too personal, but I think you should know that there's some chatter about your not spending any casual time with the staff. The monthly all-hands, stand-up meetings are a great idea, but that's still pretty formal. Even those who have known you for a long time are complaining they don't have a chance to just shoot the breeze with you. And they've noticed you haven't yet joined them for lunch outside."

"Hm. I guess I have been eating at my desk a lot. I didn't intend to. It's just that there's so much to do ..."

"I get it, but even if you ate outside a couple days a week, they'd appreciate it. You wouldn't even have to spend the whole lunch break out there; just be more visibly available."

"So, do staff not feel comfortable stopping by my office? My door is always open, unless I'm on a confidential call."

"I think they're worried about interrupting you. They know you're busy."

"Do I seem aloof?"

"I don't think it's exactly aloof, but everyone is trying to figure out how to interact with you now that you're the boss rather than a colleague. You give clear direction and leadership, but it's the softer part of management, which I know you're good at, that's maybe getting a bit lost in the rush to the September deadlines."

"That's a very delicate way of saying I'm all spreadsheet and no people culture. I appreciate your frankness, Diana. And you're right. I have spent too much time in my office. I'll make a point of circulating more. And at lunch, I'll be sure to sit at a different table every day. I don't want to encourage the sort of cliques we had when Roger sat in this office."

The next day, Kris set an alert on her phone to ensure she wouldn't forget to take lunch outside. She'd brought a colorful salad of leftover grilled chicken on greens with grated carrots, sliced grapes, pistachios, and a side of sesame dressing. Kate had offered to make weekday lunches for the family over the summer and had suggested that her parents take turns, week by week, planning and shopping for meals with her. It was a brilliant plan—one she and Mike should have adopted ages ago, but having Kate as a prep partner made it fun as well as practical. Though Kris had always enjoyed family meal shopping and cooking, she wondered now if she had stunted Mike's domestic skills in that realm. Kate had taken the lead that first week with her dad, but Kris could see his tastes playing a role in the attempt to minimize carbs and increase protein portions—plus the heavier hand on chile, cumin, and oregano. It was all good. Honestly, it was a relief to not think about making dinner on the way home from work every day.

By the time she reached the picnic tables, there was only one spot left. "Have a seat!" Mark invited as he saw her approaching.

It was already ninety degrees, but the building, trees, and umbrellas provided just enough shade that it was worth getting out of the climate-controlled building for a few minutes. She took a seat beside Mark and across from Terry and Kate. "When did it get so hot at noon?"

"Oh, it's been sneaking up on ninety since the end of May," Terry answered. "You've just been chillin' in your office all day every day, so you haven't noticed."

"True. And I'm going to tear myself away from the desk more often. Though if it gets much hotter … Actually, it feels kind of good, almost therapeutic—at least for a while." Kris chewed slowly, appreciating the heat penetrating and slowly relaxing her tight shoulder muscles.

"At least we don't have Boston's humidity," Kate added, appreciatively. "It's hard to look like a polished professional for on-campus interviews when you've walked half a mile in 90% humidity while wearing a skirt suit and pantyhose. I'm so glad Sandia is business casual."

"What about your new consulting firm?" Kris asked.

"They have a dress code, but it's more relaxed than what

we were coached to wear for interviews. Austin is a bit more laid back, so panty hose aren't required. The general rule is to avoid having your clothes or exposed skin draw attention."

Kris didn't add further comment, but she couldn't help thinking that her daughter would draw attention regardless of what she wore. Her china-smooth skin needed no makeup. Her sleekly wavy veil of glossy hair set off her fair complexion and jewel-blue eyes. But what Kris always noticed first was Kate's lips. Funny, perhaps, for a mother to focus on that feature, but Kate's lips at rest somehow conveyed that she was comfortable in her own skin and open to others. Not in a seductive way, but in an I'm-ready-to-explore-the-world-and-hear-your-story way. There always seemed to be a slight upturn to the corners of her mouth, as if she were about to smile. And when Kate did smile, she made everyone around her smile as well.

It was fascinating, too, to see how her employees—it still sounded odd to call them hers—interacted with Kate. Some had met her a few times over the years, but this was the first time they'd spent time with her since she'd left for college. Kris knew Liz and Diana would be no-nonsense about their assignments and management of Kate; being the boss's daughter wouldn't gain her preferential treatment with those two. Meredith she wasn't sure of; though she knew her as a business friend, she didn't yet know much about how she operated in the workplace day to day. Mark and Eugene were used to almost all-male direct reports, but they were young enough to have worked in companies before Sandia where women were their peers. As for Terry, he treated everyone irreverently while never sliding into insubordination. And he got results. He knew how to cajole others into compliance and how to hold his assistant, Lee Martinez—fresh out of community college—accountable for milestones.

As she excused herself from the lunch table, Kris realized everyone seemed to be treating Kate as just another young professional. Which she was. It occurred to her that she was seeing her grown-up daughter in a completely new light. She'd simply been daughter and student for so long. Now she was a working woman.

Later that week, Kris made a point to get outside earlier so she could sit with a different group. Lee, Robert, and Eugene were deep in rapid-fire conversation about the pros and cons of automation. "Glad to have you join us," Eugene said. "I could use someone with a little more perspective on my side of the argument."

"What exactly is the argument?"

"Our two recent graduates are all-in on all forms of automation and artificial intelligence, including autonomous vehicles. My view is that we shouldn't move so fast on mission-critical systems or those where personal safety is involved. There are always unintended consequences of new technologies, and the sooner we can understand them, the better we can mitigate them before an entire sector is so locked in to the new algorithm overlords that we lose our ability to think for ourselves."

"Of course, we have to be careful about implementation," Lee tsk-tsked, "but we can't lose the economic edge that automation provides."

"Take, for example, the equipment we'll be using on the production line," Robert jumped in. "From what I've read, we can program almost infinite variations and then set the machines to do the work—far more consistently and reliably than any human could."

"Yes, but even there," Eugene emphasized, "we humans are in control of the programming and can make manual adjustments on the fly if we see something that's not right. What I'm worried about is too little skilled human oversight of systems we depend on for everything from power to banking to healthcare—right, Kris?"

"Oh, I'm not going to pick sides here," Kris laughed. "Though I am glad you're having this conversation. In fact, it's one I wish more companies, and more people—especially across generations—would have." Looking across the table at the two young men, she added, "I hope you see that this company is committed to leveraging automation and digitization wherever it's likely to give us an edge. Like the coding you're doing for our virtual frame fittings, Lee."

"That's the sort of thing I was hoping for when I applied for this job. I didn't want a basic, boring network support position, though that's what it was until you arrived—excuse me, *returned*."

"I'm glad to hear you're finding your work engaging. But even while we're providing that digital tool you're creating, we're also providing the human element in the transaction, because for eyewear at our price point, buyers want to know that an experienced professional optician is ensuring they get the right fit and specifications for their needs. I think it's more a matter of finding the right balance of automation, self-service, and human problem-solving." Kris let Eugene take up the balance baton again as she focused on her flatbread, hummus, and tomato sandwich.

The battle between the tech-fearless and tech-cautious men

raged on. They barely paused to say goodbye to Kris as she rose to leave.

Meredith, Paolo, Diana, and Kate had been seated at another table when she arrived. Now, as she turned to head back inside, Kris noticed that just Paolo and Kate were left, facing each other. Laughing softly. Flirting?

27

"Do you have a minute, Kris?" Kate stood in the doorway awaiting a reply. Kris had asked her daughter not to call her "Mom" at work. She didn't want to display any hint of favoritism, and she thought having Kate address her the same way everyone else did would help her daughter take her summer job more professionally—not that she seemed to have any problem shifting between family and work modes.

"Yes, come in." Kris was preparing for her first quarterly report to Gerry and Anna, but this was the first time Kate had requested a one-on-one, so it must be important.

"May I close the door?"

"Sure." Now Kris was worried. Kate had been working at Sandia Design roughly three weeks now. Was she hating it? She hadn't hinted at any problems when they talked at home.

"Remember our conversation the day before I started, when you asked me to keep my eyes and ears open—in consultant assessment mode?"

"Yes, of course."

"Well, I think we may have a potentially significant problem brewing between Meredith and Mike."

Now Kate had her full attention. She moved her laptop aside and asked Kate to sit. "What exactly seems to be the problem?"

"I've been spending some time working with Meredith on the marketing plan that runs through the end of the year, and Mark is opposed to the basic premise of that plan as well as to many of the individual components." Kris marveled at her daughter's ability to cut to the chase. No hesitation phrases. No qualifiers. No ad hominem digs either.

"Go on."

"You had asked Meredith and Mark to convene for weekly updates to help Sales and Marketing collaborate more closely, to ensure everyone was speaking the same Sandia language. This morning I sat in on their second meeting. Meredith asked Mark to start by discussing the progress he'd made on the Sales side. He said he'd had a contract sales guy threaten to quit because he was upset about the four-month hiatus in sales activity. Meredith pointed out that this contractor is also working an additional sales job covering other parts of the optical business and would be making more commission on eyewear after the relaunch, so it was in his best interest to remain engaged.

"Then Meredith shared a rough draft of her marketing plan —the dual-pronged distributor- and consumer-directed strategy, some specific tactics, general schedule, but not budget. Mark took a quick look and asked about budget. Meredith said specific budget numbers weren't ready to be shared but that you had allocated more than usual for Marketing through year-end because a new brand launch requires it. I try not to assume too much about other people's emotions, but Mark was getting red in the face and practically spitting out his words as he attacked the inclusion of consumer advertising—something Klassik had never done, he said (or at least not while he'd been with Klassik). He thought everything in Meredith's plan was a waste of time and money—from the social media blitz to the influencers promo to the ad campaign.

"Meredith explained that, under the new brand, the company is pivoting from an emphasis on price to a focus on distinctive style, unique qualities, and new markets, so it stands to reason that the marketing and sales approach also needs to pivot. Mark insisted that all he really needed was a glossy brochure and a price list to be ready by the show.

"Toward the end of the meeting, Mark was actually yelling at Meredith: 'I've been here five years. I know what our sales staff needs to close a deal!'"

Kris sighed and said, "Part of Mark's pushback may be a result of what he sees as a demotion. When I was laid off, he was made VP of Sales and Marketing. Now Meredith heads Marketing, she's his peer, and Mark has been asked to recon-figure the salesforce, their sales approach, and their target client list. That's a lot to swallow all at once, and his ego may be a bit bruised. Just be aware of that."

"Understood."

"If this were a consulting engagement—which it effectively is—how would you handle the situation?"

"Well …" It was the first time Kate had hesitated at all. She continued, speaking slowly and choosing her words carefully, "There may be personality and authority issues that could be exacerbating disagreements over the work plan. Something Mark said at lunch one day gave me the impression he'd never had a female supervisor before. Now he has a female super-visor—you—and a female peer he's being asked to collaborate with. I'd expect someone in his mid-thirties to be more adept at handling workplace gender dynamics, but I'd want to avoid drawing attention to that. I would look for a way to let Mark know how important his role is—without drawing attention to what he may see as a demotion. I'd emphasize that everything Design, Production, and Marketing do is wasted effort if Mark and his team don't complete the loop by closing the deal. All the new elements—from the updated website to the broader marketing efforts—are designed to make his job easier. I'd remind him that he'll be making fewer client visits but enjoying a higher potential ROI on those visits. That will enable his sales team to spend more time customizing their pitches, which will make their clients feel more valued. And I'd suggest that over the next few months, everyone will be in testing, feedback, and adjustment mode, so his reports back to Meredith on how the new marketing efforts are being received will be critical—his feedback will be essential."

Impressive, Kris thought. "That sounds like a well-reasoned approach that allows both parties to save face. Do you feel comfortable playing consultant mediator with those two? At least as an initial effort? Normally, I'd jump right in and handle this sort of thing myself—after all, I've known Mark longer than you or Meredith—but I don't want to get in the way of your opportunity to learn. Besides, if I get involved immediately, it could undermine Meredith's authority."

"Sure. Do you have any particular dos or don'ts?"

"The next time you meet, ask if you can have a few minutes before the three of you start with the planned agenda—but give Meredith a heads-up that I've asked you to make some observations about the challenges that come with a major rebranding and change in personnel. Remind them that I've asked you to be Sandia's roving consultant this summer and that you're speaking in that role—a role that in three months you'll be billing companies over $200 an hour for! Then share the observations and suggestions you just articulated. Invite them to look at the company and their roles as if Sandia Design were a startup, which it is. That's a positive way of conveying to Mark that what he did under the Klassik name is largely irrelevant. If it seems they're ignoring you or you're not getting through to them, let me know and I'll get involved after they've cooled off for a day."

"Will do," Kate agreed as she left the CEO's office.

28

"This is terrific progress for any first quarter of a new business —and remarkable under the circumstances!" Gerry's face opened up into a broad smile that also conveyed relief. Kris had just presented her first quarterly report on Sandia Design. Gerry had suggested bumping the delivery date up to the end of June so Kris would have less on her plate while she was racing to the Vision Expo deadline. The second quarterly report, due right after the event, would tell the story of how well she and the newly configured team had executed on her plan.

"Thank you." Kris resisted the urge to lead with self-deprecation. "Everyone has stepped up to the challenge, and though most of us are putting in some overtime, we're making sure to keep weekends work-free—or at least the rest of them are! There's still way too much going on for me to keep official office hours."

"That is a great temptation." Anna's comment was brief but weighted.

The three of them were sitting in Gerry's home office. The

open windows admitted the sound of crickets, a light wind, and distant street traffic. "Do you see those trees out there?" Gerry asked, pointing to the apple, apricot, and piñon in their backyard. "We planted them when we built this house, and they all have different purposes. The apple we hoped would bear some fruit, which it has. We knew that, given the climate, the apricot might struggle to produce a crop, but we knew it would reliably provide shade and spectacular spring flowers. And the piñon provides evergreen color as well as nuts to feed the birds. They all have their purpose, and we'd be foolish to expect them to all play the same role. Over the years, those trees reminded me that I couldn't do everything on my own— at least not all at once. I had to rely on others who were specialists in their areas to deliver the fruit and nuts, if you will. What I'm getting at is that you can't do it all alone either. You've made good staffing decisions, so now concentrate on helping those people maximize their potential—rather than trying to do their jobs in addition to yours."

"You're saying I need to delegate more?"

"Delegate, yes, but also trust that Liz has a keen eye for the financials and that all the other department heads have the skills and temperament to keep their realms of responsibility humming along. You have weekly leadership meetings, right?"

"Yes."

"Use those to push and praise each of your leaders so they all know that you both appreciate what they've done and believe they can achieve even more—within reason, of course."

"Understood. I do set stretch goals, but I'm mindful of not pushing so hard that the best people want to leave."

"They won't leave if they also know you see and appreciate

their work. If you'll allow me another analogy, there's something else those trees taught me over the years. They didn't grow to their current size overnight—not even in a year or a couple of years. Now I realize the analogy to Sandia Design isn't perfect, but I want you to think about your big goals and then break them down into smaller ones—growth spurts, if you will. I think you've done a pretty good job with the designs themselves, rolling out a limited number in year one so you can assess the market's response. But you might be banking on a too-aggressive schedule for actually getting those first new frames to market."

"Where exactly do you see the challenges?" Kris asked. The second Gerry commented on her "too-aggressive schedule," her stomach sank. Success at their first public launch in September depended on that schedule.

"Two places. First, your equipment vendor. Now, I know *you* always make extraordinary efforts to meet all your contractual and other commitments in business, but you're going to encounter those who aren't as reliable as you. I don't know this particular firm, but I do know that vendors don't always meet their delivery dates. You may need a Plan B in case the equipment doesn't show up as promised. Second, your new local production staff will need time to train on the equipment. They won't turn out perfect product right from the start, and as a perfectionist, that may frustrate you, so be prepared. You don't need to make this part of the production schedule public, but mentally add in at least a couple of weeks for trial and error. Don't be too harsh on Eugene and his staff when the first units aren't up to spec."

"You're right. I've been so focused on having product ready to ship right after we take orders at the show that I didn't add wiggle room for the onboarding process. Do you think it's reasonable to have at least two polished units of each design by show time?"

"That should be doable, but having a backlog of orders is preferable to shipping out inferior product."

"Agreed."

"There's another element to these quarterly reports that isn't in the formal presentation you gave." Anna, who had been quietly taking in the exchange between her husband and Kris now spoke up. "How are *you* doing? How are you handling the stress of a much larger role and all the extra time I know you're putting into this business?"

"You're right about the time! But it's also exciting. Now that the new staff is assembled and we're working on a new line to deliver, everyone's happy to come to work again, and that's gratifying."

"I'm glad you're still happy about your decision." Anna smiled. "But remember there are only twenty-four hours in a day. Make sure you schedule a couple of those hours for yourself and your family."

"I think what Anna's hinting at is that being not just CEO but owner as well can become all-consuming—to the detriment of other parts of one's life. I know I wasn't as available as I should have been in the early years of Klassik, when our kids were still young. I probably didn't attend as many school events as I should have, and even when I was home, I spent too many hours holed up in here instead of being with Anna and the kids."

"You got better over time," Anna laughed.

"But the point stands: You can never get those missed opportunities back. We never know how many days we have left, so it's worth finding a way to make each one special—not just for the business and employees but also for our families."

"I hear you. Though my situation is a bit different in that Kate is all grown up, and Mike has his own career that occupies him, so he understands I have to spend more than eight hours a day on Sandia right now."

"If you say so." Gerry sounded skeptical. "Just be sure you don't push yourself so hard that you break down. Then you'll be no use to anyone—kinda like this knee I'm getting replaced next week!"

The next morning, just as Kris was about to get on the elliptical machine, she heard her phone ping. Kate was still asleep in the next room, so who would be texting her at this hour?

Sorry to bother you so early, but I thought you'd want to know asap that there's a problem with delivery of the Italian equipment. I just forwarded you an email with all the details. I'll be in a few minutes early this morning if you want to confer when you get to the office. Gotta drop my kid at summer camp on the way in, though. —Eugene

Her heart rate spiked. She sat down and opened Eugene's email. Though the customized manufacturing equipment was to have shipped from Italy the previous week for arrival mid-July, now the vendor was saying they couldn't have three of the components ready to ship until the end of July, earliest. Eugene and the manufacturer had determined the schedule required three weeks' travel time door to door, so that put equipment on the shop floor three weeks before the Vegas show—at best. Subtract at least two weeks for the onboarding, as Gerry advised, and that left maybe one week. Not enough time.

29

"Paolo, I need your help." Kris was at the door of the office Paolo shared with Eugene.

"What do you need?"

"I need your Italian cultural and linguistic skills."

"Well, they're a bit rusty, and I was never totally fluent, you know."

"They'll be just fine for today. Eugene, I need you too. Thanks for sending that text early this morning."

"I didn't want to respond to them until we talked, and I thought you'd want to know right away."

"Know what?" Paolo had just arrived and was still holding several plastic bags of soil samples, each bearing detailed labels. He placed the bags on his desk and turned to Eugene.

"Our frame-making equipment has been delayed. It didn't leave Italy, as promised, last week. They say it won't all be ready to ship till the end of the month."

Paolo's full eyebrows rose a half inch and stayed there. "So …"

"So we need a Plan B. We need to find out how they are

going to make this right. We could push the financial recourse in our contract, but that doesn't solve the immediate problem, which is getting the tools we need to start up the production line." Kris's mind had been racing through potential scenarios and she'd settled on one preferred and one alternate plan. "First, we need to schedule a video conference with your contact before he leaves work today. Could you set that up, Eugene? Paolo and I will be on call at five minutes' notice to join the video call."

"I was headed out to the production office later this morning to do some final materials tests, but I can go this afternoon," Paolo confirmed.

"Then, Paolo, I'd like you to initiate the meeting. We need you to turn on every ounce of Italian charm to convince them that they absolutely must find a way to get us access to their equipment in time to produce at least prototypes of the launch designs. I know they have offered to produce quick-turn prototypes at their facility in Italy, but that's my last-resort option."

"I wondered if you'd want to go that route," Eugene said. "But that would require providing them with our proprietary materials, which I thought you'd be reluctant to share."

"Exactly. That's why I think our best option might be to have them arrange for us to rent time on a line that's already set up in the U.S. You mentioned they have an existing customer in New Orleans that's leasing equipment, so the Italians would need to be involved in working out a deal where a skeleton crew—you two and two production leads—could work extended days over a couple of weekends. We'd have to do hand-finishing back in Albuquerque, but if we at least—"

"I see where you're going, but it's going to take more than two weekends to get what we need. We'll have to have at least a week of continuous access to the whole production line. And we'd have to reconfigure everything, which could be problematic for the current lessee and for us."

"I know it's less than ideal, Eugene, but we have to have at least a full set of samples by mid-September. If they've delayed shipping once, they may delay again, and we can't take that risk."

"How about suggesting something along the lines of what Kris proposes and see what they say? They may have other options to offer. Who knows what's holding things up on their end. It may be a renegotiation ploy." For a design pro—and a young one at that—Paolo showed unexpected business acumen.

"We accepted their standard leasing terms, so if they're looking for more money, it would be a strike against them. I suspect something else is going on. If you can figure that out, we may be able to find a way forward. I've got a quick phone call to make, but let me know when you get the video call set up." Kris left Eugene to email his Italian contact and Paolo to ponder his comments. She hoped she'd struck the appropriate balance between leadership and delegation.

She was still processing exactly what this schedule setback would mean when she turned into her office and saw flowers on her desk. Kate, who was on front desk duty that week, had just dropped them off. "They're from Gerry and Anna," she said, admiring the dozen roses. "Hope you don't mind that I looked. I knew they weren't from Dad—he knows tulips are your favorite—and I wanted to be ready to respond if you asked me to."

"Thanks, Kate. I'll take care of that."

The card stuck in the roses—several luscious shades of pink—read: *Dear Kris, This is your friendly reminder to stop and smell the roses! You're doing a beautiful job, and we're so happy to be involved. Anna & Gerry*

Should she tell them the latest development? Would Gerry feel vindicated in his warning, or just sad and disappointed? It was Monday, July 2. Just a day to get this resolved before everyone in the Albuquerque office cleared out for the Fourth of July. A few were taking vacation time to extend the holiday, though not, thank goodness, Paolo or Eugene. No point in sharing problems that weren't Gerry's to solve. She'd give him an update once she had equipment on site or prototypes in hand.

As she was texting her thanks to Gerry and Anna, Eugene's head appeared around the corner of her door. "Video in five? Can we postpone the leadership meeting?"

"Of course. I'll have Kate let the others know."

Was it by chance or fate that she'd grabbed her one Italian-made white shirt that morning? Paolo was wearing the same woven Italian shirt he'd worn the day she introduced him. That had to be a good omen, didn't it? Eugene wore one of his signature button-down blue denim shirts.

"Buongiorno!" said the Italian halfway around the world as he joined the call. Michael Rinaldi looked to be in his mid-forties and wore gold, antique-style round metal frames below his wavy, brown hair. An American businessman would have considered it on the long side, but the expert cut signaled that the length was a fashion choice. Beneath his white linen jacket he wore a black t-shirt with a drape that suggested its provenance was more elevated than a big box store.

"Buongiorno," Paolo replied, and from then on, Kris only caught the occasional word she recognized. As Paolo

continued in Italian—which, from the speed of his delivery, seemed proficient to her—Michael beamed. He was clearly surprised but delighted to hear his mother tongue spoken by an American. Paolo introduced himself, said something about his father being from Italy and that he himself had lived there a brief while, and then began addressing the business snag. From what she could guess at, and from the two men's faces, she gathered there were expressions of concern about the delay. Then Paolo inquired about the cause of the delay and underscored the importance of the equipment to the entire Sandia enterprise and to the careers and financial prospects of "all its many employees."

"I understand," Michael shifted to English. "Perhaps we should speak English now, so Signora Wright and Signore Pullman can join us."

"Of course," Paolo smiled and shifted chairs so Kris could be seated in the center, fully visible on the screen of Eugene's laptop.

After introducing himself to Kris and commending her on her choice of the very finest frame-making equipment— marrying traditional Italian attention to detail with the latest digitally enabled accuracy and easily configurable customized settings—Michael apologized again, in English, for the delivery delay. Kris was impressed but not distracted by his ability to convey sincerity and lack of culpability while never actually identifying the root cause of the holdup.

Kris signaled to Eugene that he should propose temporary access to an existing production line in the U.S. As he laid out the scenario, Michael appeared to give it serious consideration but then quickly responded, "No. No, I'm afraid that will not work. Not enough time for what you need, and the disruption to our customer's configurations could be significant—if they would even allow you into their facility. No … there may be a better way."

So get to it, already, Kris wanted to cajole the Italian. She did not like being teased with supposedly solid deals only to have terms changed at the eleventh hour, though it appeared she might need to get used to such business renegotiations—may even need to develop her own armory of arrows and shields.

"We have another customer in America—I mean, we *had* another customer. You see, they recently declared bankruptcy, but our equipment is still on site, in California."

Aha! So that's where we're going with this little kabuki theater piece, she realized. If they leased to the bankrupt client, the Italians own the machines, but they're losing income every month the equipment just sits there. And they want to move it someplace where it can generate revenue—preferably without incurring freighter charges, so that means somewhere in North America.

"What are you proposing?" she asked, not wanting Michael to immediately see how much she suspected.

"Well, although we cannot get a completely new line of equipment to you on the schedule you wish, we could possibly transfer the idle equipment from California to New Mexico much sooner."

"How soon?"

"If we can contract for appropriate transport, as soon as two weeks from today."

"How old is the line you've got in California, and how many production hours has it logged?" Eugene asked.

"Very good questions." Now that he had their attention and the promise of a delivery date to nearly match what they'd originally agreed to, all hesitation was gone as Michael's speech sped up. "The machines are less than a year from our factory and are precisely the same as you ordered. The same model numbers. There even is included in the California production line one specialty tool that we can include for no extra cost. And the hours, they are very low, as this customer produced only small numbers of one season's line. I can get you precise numbers after this call."

"Can you tell us the name of your California customer —*former* customer—and why they declared bankruptcy?" As they'd been talking, Kris had been combing her memory of industry news items to figure out who had gone belly up. She thought she had it figured out but wanted confirmation.

"Ah, it was a small company, two young men from Venice Beach—funny the connection to Italy, no? They had used an online financing method—crowd-funding, I think you call it? —in addition to personal capital. It seems they didn't raise enough to carry them far enough. And, as well, they did not have a distribution system that was strong enough. So, they sadly suffered the fate of many young entrepreneurs."

Listening to his story and looking at his face, you could almost imagine Michael's sympathies were for the failed entrepreneurs. But Kris was not distracted. This was potentially great news for Sandia. For a split second, the story of the hopeful indies sounded a lot like the story of Sandia Design … could Sandia crash and burn as the Venice Beach brand had? No! Sandia's staff had decades of experience and the business had a well-established distribution system, even if that system needed redirecting.

"Michael, I'm sorry to hear of their business failure. It's always a sad day when a new, independent brand fails to create a space in the eyewear market, which has been so dominated by the big conglomerates."

"Yes, yes indeed."

"But I want to remind you that, although Sandia Design is a new brand, we are not a completely new company. Our key personnel bring decades of experience in this industry to our new enterprise, and we understand the essential distribution aspect in ways no newcomer could. Sandia Design will not be defaulting on its lease agreement with you." Kris was not particularly religious, but she offered a micro-prayer that her promise was one she'd be able to keep.

"Yes, Kris, we are happy to know that your deep background in the industry—as well as your talented young designer—give you a strong chance of success."

"So let's discuss the details, if we may. I hate to rush you, but everyone here is working on tight deadlines at the moment."

"Yes, of course. I can make inquiries about shipping the equipment before I leave my office today. I will have delivery details to send you by the end of your business day tomorrow."

"That sounds good. Please send that information to Eugene, and he'll share it with me. As for our original contract, there are a few details I believe we will need to revise and update." Michael was quiet for a beat, so Kris continued. "In addition to updating the delivery schedule, we'll want to revise the fee, because we'll be taking delivery of used equipment."

"Yes, but rest assured you will have the same warranty and maintenance support as with new equipment."

"Good to know. Nevertheless, the machinery *is* used, and a production interruption—even if you can promise rapid technician response—is still a production interruption, and that's something that we are especially sensitive to as we begin supplying our customers. And, given the speed of technology change, industrial machines like yours now have a shorter useful life. Even though your machines are built to last a very long time, we both know you will have enhanced models available in just a few years, and those new models you will want to lease at a higher rate, so for now, with this used equipment, we would need a 20% discount on the lease price we agreed to for new machines." Now Kris was the one speaking at a faster clip, determined not to be interrupted.

"Oh! We cannot do 20%. This is nearly new equipment ..." Kris let the silence hang. "I understand your view, but maybe 5% ..."

"15% is as low as I'm prepared to go," Kris interrupted. "That's more than fair, especially given the unexpected delay."

"OK ..."

"And we'll be withholding the first lease payment until after we have confirmed that each piece of equipment is operating perfectly and until your technician-trainer has completed all the previously agreed-upon training of our staff."

"That is not something our CEO will agree to."

"If he is concerned about nonpayment, we can send confirmation that the funds have been set aside in escrow. Rest assured," she said, mirroring his language, "you will be paid, but given the bumpy start to our agreement, we need to know that we will be on a smooth path from now on."

"I understand, Kris. We do hope Sandia Design will be a happy, long-term customer."

"So, with our new schedule, you will have your trainer here for three days, starting July 16, correct?"

"I believe that is correct."

"Good. Please send your trainer's contact information to Eugene, and we will have someone here assist with travel logistics."

"Thank you. And may I say, CEO Kris Wright, that with your business sense, with Mr. Pullman's production expertise, and with Paolo's design talents, I am certain Sandia Design will be very successful! Perhaps one day we will even see your eyewear here in Italia."

"That is my hope, too, Signore Rinaldi."

30

Diana: I have news about Roger!!!

Kris: What???

*Diana: I'll share at the G7 next Fri. Too much info for text &
don't want to get into it at work.*

Diana had kept just a couple of dog-walking clients after she
returned to full-time work at Sandia Design. One was on her
block.

Elsie, a widow in her seventies, had a three-year-old pug,
Penny, whom Diana admired when their dog-walking paths
crossed occasionally. So, naturally, after Elsie tripped on an
uneven piece of sidewalk and broke her ankle in June, she
yelled out at Diana from behind her screen door one evening.
"I'm so glad to see you! I was hoping you and Luna would be
out this evening."

"It's a beautiful evening," Diana responded.

"Would you mind coming to the door? I broke my ankle
and can't get around easily."

"Sure."

"I'd let you in, but I'm worried your lovely lab might nudge me a bit too hard and put me off balance. It doesn't take much these days," she laughed.

"We'll just stay out here. Luna, sit!"

"I called you over because I was wondering if I could hire you to walk Penny once in a while. Home healthcare aides come a couple times a week to do physical therapy, and my kids come by every weekend to clean and restock the fridge and such, but nobody has time to walk the dog. If you wouldn't mind? I'm on schedule to be fully mobile in about three months."

"Of course. Luna and I take a short walk after dinner every evening anyhow. I'll just swing by here first for Penny. Does seven work for you?" Diana was a little embarrassed to feel relief. She didn't mind helping out an older neighbor temporarily, but she didn't want long-term responsibility for an ailing elder. She'd had enough of that with her parents.

"Perfect. You mentioned once when we chatted that you walk dogs for other people. Let me know your rate, and I'll prepay you a week at a time."

And so, for the next three months, Luna and Penny loped and trotted alongside each other every weekday evening, gleefully sniffing and wagging and competing for treats from Diana's pocket.

But the real surprise in Diana's dog-walking life came from an entirely different neighborhood.

As soon as Kris asked her to consider joining Sandia Design, Diana gave all her clients notice that she was exiting the doggy nanny business and provided names of other dog-walkers. Everyone was sorry to hear the news, but a couple flat-out refused to look for a new companion.

One was a single woman in her thirties, Brenda, who worked for the federal government during the week (Diana suspected she might be CIA) and went rock-climbing, sometimes out of state, on weekends. They'd connected through the animal shelter when Brenda was looking for someone to come to her house weekend mornings and evenings to feed and walk her German shepherd, Nemo. (Brenda had a quirky sense of humor and loved the idea that the name Nemo, or "nobody," gave her pup a clever way to deny involvement in any mischief.)

Diana had established a standard fee schedule for all dog-handling duties when it was her main source of income. But when Brenda pleaded with her to stay on as Nemo's weekend human, she demurred and listened to the woman sing her praises until Brenda offered to double her previous rate. That was a deal worth making.

Another long-time client, Heather, also refused to part ways with Diana. Heather and her husband Chuck were in their late forties and had "just kicked our two wonderful kids out into the world to figure it out for themselves," as Heather put it. Chuck owned a well-established roofing company; Heather, who had been his office manager for two decades, had retired from that role when the kids finished college. The two empty nesters were determined to make the most of their weekends, so they refused to schedule any work or social engagements from Friday evening through Sunday night. Some weekends they'd just follow their whims, riding bikes from one end of the city to the other along the Rio Grande, taking side trips for fuel whenever they got hungry or thirsty. (The brewery stops were their favorite.) Other weekends, they looked for last-minute airfare bargains and flew off to Mexico (Beaches!), Montana (Fishing!), Louisiana (New Orleans!) or wherever the fares and their frequent flier miles would take them. That left Merle, their rambunctious blue merle Australian shepherd, all alone.

Though Heather and Chuck doted on Merle and faithfully walked him twice a day during the week, they weren't about to let the youngest member of their family leash them to the house on weekends. So they were ecstatic when, last November, Diana agreed to adopt Merle for the whole weekend. She picked him up after work on Friday and dropped him off on her way to work Monday morning.

When Diana announced her doggy care services retirement on an early Monday drop-off, Heather protested as Merle sat obediently between them in the driveway. "I know you need your weekends now that you're working full time again, but Merle *loves* you. I swear, he sulks all Monday after spending the weekend with you. We don't want to change his routine— or ours. What can we do to make this work?"

Diana listened as Heather pleaded. A small flush of pride at being so needed and appreciated warmed her from head to toe. Her dog clients didn't see her as an overweight woman; they saw her as a loving human who provided a change of scene with new scents and an engaging four-footed pal, Luna. Her human clients never looked at her in a way that suggested they were sizing her up to judge her by her weight; they were overwhelmingly grateful for a reliable dog-sitter. Finally, she spoke. "I love Merle too. He's a doll, and he and Luna get along really well, but you're right. I need fewer responsibilities on the weekends now, so that's why I've had to mostly get out of the doggy care business."

"Mostly?" Heather hadn't missed the critical adjective.

"I've only made two exceptions. One is a temporary client

on my block who is recovering from an injury. The other is another weekend client, but the only reason I'm still taking on her dog is that she offered to pay me double my previous rate, which makes the extra time worth it, and we've dialed my services back to three weekends a month."

"Done! We'll double your old rate too. And we'll figure something out for the weekend off each month. *Please*, Diana …"

"OK," she laughed, as Merle's blue eyes gazed up adoringly at her. "You have a deal—but even though the money helps, I'm only keeping you on as clients because I like both Merle and Merle's humans!" They both laughed. Merle gave an assenting bark.

Coincidentally, Heather and Chuck lived on the same block as Roger, his wife Sally, and Rex. Diana had discovered this fact about a month into her engagement with Heather and Chuck. When she had stopped to pick up Merle one Friday afternoon in February, she noticed a silver Range Rover in the driveway two doors down. "My former boss has an SUV like that. I've seen him get out of it at a park we take our dogs to."

"You mean Roger? And Rex? The rotten rottweiler? That's what we call him around here. He's always aggressive toward other dogs, so we make sure to have Merle safely on-leash if Rex is out with Roger. It's always Roger. His wife, Sally, never walks him."

"Yes, Roger Kohl used to be my boss." Diana noted that it was half-past four. Roger had left the office early, even though she was sure he had an internal spy ensuring that the staff worked all the way to the top of five.

"So he's the one who laid you off," Heather sneered. "What a fool. Well, you're better off not working for that jerk. He's so full of himself. Leaves his fancy new SUV in the driveway to show it off to the neighbors. Not like the Jeep, which he kept in the garage." Heather had driven a mom van for years but replaced it with a red Prius once both kids were finally in college. It was her way of standing out while leaving a smaller environmental footprint. Chuck, on the other hand, drove a standard contractor set of wheels: a Ford F-250 equipped with toolboxes and emblazoned with his company's logo.

At least Diana knew her clients shared her assessment of Roger.

It was the first Friday in July and everyone was back to their usual summer routines after the mid-week Fourth of July holiday. Most yards were showing the effects of drought added to watering restrictions and topped off with mid-summer neglect. Roger's yard, though, seemed more unkempt than average as Diana passed it on the way to Merle's home. The rose bushes hadn't been deadheaded. The patch of grass out front was a mix of too-long clumps, dandelions, and dead spots. A juniper bush was starting to spread over the edge of the driveway.

Diana hadn't seen Roger at the public park since March—for the obvious reason. She hadn't seen him in person since the May Monday she startled him at the front desk of Sandia Design. She hadn't heard anything about what he was up to since he received the shock of his career that day. That was odd. As receptionist and office manager, she was used to being the nexus of office gossip. Then again, Roger's most loyal sidekicks weren't around, so nobody had a direct line to the source. Except for Heather and Chuck.

Heather and Merle met Diana at the door. They chatted a bit, as usual. This weekend, the couple was headed up to southern Colorado for some hiking and hot springs fun. Diana commented that she hadn't seen Roger's Range Rover in the driveway the past few weekends.

"You haven't heard? They got divorced. We know the folks on the far side of their house. They could hear Sally screaming at Roger one night. It was late May. They couldn't hear all the details through the open windows, but the next morning, Angela, our friend, waved to Sally, who was having her morning coffee on the portal and said hello. Sally apologized for the previous night's noise and invited Angela over for coffee."

"You know, no one at Klassik ever met Sally, that I know of. We never had staff-and-spouse social gatherings, and she never came to the office. I wouldn't know her if I ran into her —unless she was walking Rex!"

"She's nice-looking. Long blonde hair. Petite. Actually, a bit scrawny. Spends most of her time 'looking after herself'— going to the gym, going to the salon, regular spa days, eating the latest trendy health food—according to Angela. She's a couple years younger than Roger. They're both from back East, you know; she never really seemed at home here. Maybe thought she was too refined for dusty New Mexico? She served on a couple of nonprofit boards, but other than that, she never worked during the decade they lived here. Anyhow, Angela had always been friendly with her, but they weren't really friends, so she was shocked when Sally spilled everything that morning."

Merle—eager to get into the vehicle where Luna was waiting, her head hanging out the window—gave Diana a head butt. She ignored him. "So what was the fight about? Why did they divorce?"

"Well, it seems there were a few problems that all came to a head after he sold the business. Not only was Roger bad with money at work, he also was reckless with his personal finances. Sally was expecting a windfall from the sale, but it turns out Roger owed money everywhere. He'd borrowed against the house multiple times without telling her, he'd put far too much of their retirement savings in questionable invest-ments—even losing the capital in some cases, and he had no prospects for a new job, let alone an executive salary. Oh, and he'd borrowed money from his father repeatedly but never paid him back. Besides whatever he was paying himself as CEO, he was regularly asking daddy for money. He said it was to build the business, but a lot of it went to pricey vacations Sally planned for them—cruises, five-star resort weekends, ski vacations in Aspen. She didn't know the money was coming from her father-in-law until he hinted at Christmas last year when they were back in New York that he'd cut his son off for good. She was shocked, but at that point she still believed the business was profitable and that they'd be fine.

"Roger had been hanging around the house a lot more after the sale, and he apparently started questioning Sally's expen-ditures—too much money for a subscription supplement service, too many meals out, too much spent on designer clothes ordered online. Sally, who had never had her spending questioned by her parents or her husband, grumbled back and wanted to know why her credit card bills were suddenly such a big deal. That's when Sally forced Roger to come clean on the true state of their personal balance sheet. It took some pres-sure, but he finally fessed up, and she lost it. But that wasn't the final straw."

Diana raised her eyebrows, "Do tell."

"So, she's finally had to admit she's married to a total loser who can't support her desired lifestyle. But then he admits he's been having an affair with someone at work."

"It has to be Sandy from HR," Diana gasped. "They were always eating lunch together. She was totally his yes-woman."

"Yeah, I think that was her name. He told Sally this woman at work understood him and supported him in ways that Sally didn't. They'd started out as friends, but this woman was divorced and apparently on the lookout for a sugar daddy. Thinking Roger had the assets to back his lifestyle, she nudged the relationship along. For the past couple of years, they'd been leaving work separately each Wednesday afternoon and meeting up at a hotel—and not a cheap one. They'd alternate between a couple of nice business hotels downtown and a couple of casino hotels, order room service, and … you get the picture. Roger always paid cash, drawn from his personal slush fund. He'd been telling Sally that Wednesday was his weekly 'catch-up' night to work late at the office and get take-out pizza. She, apparently, was just fine with that. Still, you think she'd have gotten suspicious."

"Wow. Well, I have to give them credit for hiding the extent of their relationship at work. Sandy did suck up to Roger at work, but I had no idea it went, ahem, beyond that!"

"So, Sally filed for divorce and is planning to move back East. She got the house—what little equity they still have in it—and is putting it on the market next week. Roger got to keep his Range Rover and, last Angela heard, he'd driven it out to Las Vegas."

As Diana opened the rear door of her used, 2010 white Toyota

Highlander for Merle to jump in, she felt almost lightheaded. So Roger wasn't just a jerk to his employees. He wasn't just an incompetent businessman. He was a two-timing, self-right-eous, lying husband. And a loser. He'd lost it all: business, wife, family financial support.

She didn't normally take pleasure in others' pain, but this was different. This was Roger. She wondered how Rex was handling the Vegas heat. She couldn't help feeling sympathy for the poor animal, whose temperament was more Roger's fault than Rex's.

She couldn't wait to tell Kris. But she'd have to. They were too busy at work to indulge in a gossip saga. It would make for gleeful conversation at next week's G7, though. She'd prob-ably have to share with Janice tonight. She couldn't keep news like this from her for an entire week. They'd become closer friends—like Luna and Merle—having spent more time together these past several months. Janice would see she was hiding something and would poke around until Diana's willpower broke.

As she drove home, Diana was grateful that divorce was one trauma she'd been spared. No spouse, no divorce. Of course, marriage doesn't always end in divorce—only about half the time. Her parents, though, had enjoyed a happy marriage, as far as she could tell.

Even her friends hadn't had much experience with divorce. Sharon, of course, but her breakup was more a result of having married too young. Janice and Will, well, as Janice told it, they just grew apart. Her erratic work schedule annoyed him, but he wasn't willing to juggle his schedule to help with Amy. When his sales job took him to the Midwest, she didn't want to leave. Amy was just finishing high school and Janice had a good job. No real catastrophe there. Janice said the day Will moved out, she felt the tension in her shoulders relax for the first time in years. The rest of them—Susie, Jo, Marie, Kris— she couldn't imagine them divorcing. Sure, their husbands drove them crazy now and then, but you could tell the love ran deep.

31

Kris found the mid-week Fourth of July holiday annoying. She wished they could automatically move the celebration to a Monday, like they did with MLK Day and Columbus Day. There was so much to do, and people were bound to lose momentum with a mid-week day off. The afternoon before, you had to let staff leave early. The morning after was, well, the morning after for some.

Their own Independence Day celebration had been low-key. Kate had made plans with friends, so Mike and Kris accepted an invitation from neighbors to join their backyard barbeque. Though she had worked from home that morning, she forced herself to kick back with the neighbors in the afternoon and evening. It had been fun, she had to admit. The hosts even made a toast to Kris's first Independence Day as an independent business owner.

But Kris never fully unwound, even though things were largely going well. Her employees (it still felt weird, two months in, to call them her employees) had done her proud. They were showing fresh enthusiasm, creativity, and, most important, collaboration. And she was figuring out—she hoped—how to be the boss without being bossy.

She realized that she tended to impose her perfectionism on others. She'd always been careful to not let that tendency get out of control and burst into micromanagement. But now, especially now as they were completely rebuilding the business and brand, she *had* to micromanage a bit. Still, she had to be careful about when to meddle in daily details. She had to trust her people. That resolve was put to the test the day after the holiday.

"Got a minute?" Terry asked.

"For you, always. What's up?"

"Actually, it's what's down," he said as he entered her office. "Our coding speed is a bit slower than what I originally estimated—and I thought I was creating a conservative schedule, but there are always more surprises than anyone anticipates with a brand new project like our website's virtual shop. While we've hit most of our milestones, there are a couple that have repeatedly been dropped in queue priority. I've been focusing on the revamp of our main site—the architectural backbone, if you will—while Lee has been working mostly as an internal team member with the contractor building out the 3D virtual try-on function."

"Is Lee slowing progress because he's new to all of this?"

"Maybe a bit, but we expected him to take time getting up to speed, and he's actually a quick and eager learner—even has offered some good process suggestions of his own, like using Paolo's CAD drawings of the designs right now as stand-ins for the finished frames. It's more that he's too inexperienced to have sufficient clout to keep the contractor accountable, so I've had to step away from my work more than expected to manage that piece of the rebuild. But there's another consideration that could add time to the new site launch schedule."

"OK, I'm ready for the bandage to be pulled ..."

"It's a good-news/bad-news situation. As you know, we've been consulting regularly with Meredith on the site changes, as the website effectively falls under her purview. Well, earlier this week, she and Kate sat in on our status review and preliminary demos, and Kate made an interesting comment. She said she'd noticed on other eyewear commerce sites that it was often kludgy to navigate back and forth from a prescreened list of frames to a style you're trying on. (She's clearly done more than the required homework!) Then she asked if it would be possible for our site to have a split screen, where the list of styles you'd selected to try on could be minimized but always visible so you don't have to mess with the back button and lose your list or your current selection. I said I'd look into it, and I've talked with the contractor, who says it's possible, but it will add two weeks to the schedule."

"So, let me be sure I understand the potential change in user experience as well as in schedule. What Kate suggested would effectively give the customer a collection of frames to keep reaching back to—like taking a pile of clothes into a dressing room—without having to navigate back to a master list of styles?"

"Yes. She's correct in observing that this approach creates a better UX. But it does add time and contractor cost."

"I'm less worried about the capital cost if this is a feature that will set us apart over the long haul. Details on the schedule?"

"We might still be able to squeak through a full-scale launch by Vision Expo, but if not, I think we can arrange a stripped-down version where we show the functionality but can't provide full access to all the styles and colors right away."

"That sounds like a reasonable alternative—that I hope we don't need. How did Meredith respond to the suggestion and schedule change?"

"She liked the idea and assumed we could push the changes through in time for Vegas."

"Is there anything else?"

"Not today. I know this was your area of responsibility in the past, and the site is a critical component of the public roll-out, so I wanted to let you know, but if you want me to only report through Meredith on this, just say so."

"No, I'm glad you told me. Meredith may be thinking we have more technical resources at our disposal than we actually have. She's used to working with a larger firm. Everyone from Sales to Customer Service to Finance is counting on this site redesign, so I do want to know if you run into any major snafus. When can I see a demo of the new design and functionality?"

"I'd like to clean up a few details first so we don't waste your time. How's next Monday afternoon?"

"I'll try to be patient!" Then, realizing she and Terry hadn't had a personal catch-up in forever, she asked, "How was your Fourth? I hope you made the most of the day off."

"I did!" he said, brightening at the chance to grab a moment of personal time with his friend-boss. "I spent it with a few other NOLA transplants, and we had a Cajun feast. Made me a bit homesick, but I met a couple of new folks who've joined the group ...," he hesitated, wondering how much Kris would think it appropriate for him to share, given her new role.

"And ...," she encouraged. "Anyone special?"

"Maybe," he offered, his eyes dancing. "We'll see!"

The week of the Fourth, Kate was out on Friday night for dinner with friends. She'd been vague about the who, what, and where when she mentioned her schedule at breakfast. "Don't plan on me for dinner tonight. I'm meeting friends and will get picked up from work. Enjoy your romantic dinner for two!" Now that she was of legal drinking age and a college graduate, Kris and Mike fought the parental instinct to ask details or dish out unwelcome cautions every time she exited the door. The only thing they insisted on was that she call them if she ever needed a safe ride home.

Mike must have mentioned something to Kate—or maybe she gave him the idea—but when Kris walked in the door at 6 p.m. (she'd stayed late, knowing Kate didn't need a ride home), he had a bottle of nice cabernet open and aerating in the wine decanter; steaks were ready to throw on the grill.

"What's the occasion?"

"An evening alone with my beautiful wife." Mike greeted her with a lingering kiss.

"How nice. Sorry I'm late." Without commenting on the time, Mike poured her a glass of wine. "The mid-week holiday threw things off-course a bit, and I wanted to tidy some loose ends so I'd have less to do over the weekend. Mmm. Nice wine." She'd taken a quick sip but now held the glass up, swirled it, sniffed, and sipped again.

"It's not seriously pricey, but I figured now that you're drawing a regular salary again, we deserved a step up from the bargain bin."

"Let me change out of these office clothes. I'll be back in five to help with prep."

. . .

They took the last of the wine out on the portal and settled into cushioned patio chairs. Kris kicked off her sandals and tucked her feet up on the seat. "I love long summer days."

"We should get back in the habit of taking a neighborhood walk after dinner during these long summer days," Mike suggested. "Of course, you'd have to get out of your habit of working in the evenings."

"Are you suggesting I need the exercise? I guess maybe I do, though I hit our workout room every morning."

"The exercise is always good, but I thought a walk might help you decompress at the end of the day, and it would give us time together."

"Do we not spend enough time together?"

"Well ..." Mike hesitated. "We're in the house together, but you're usually in front of your laptop. I know you're busy at work, and I fully support what you're doing," he added quickly. "But more than wanting more unscheduled time with you for selfish reasons, I worry you're working yourself too hard. Maybe fight the urge to work every hour of daylight?"

"You're right. I do bring work home. I'm trying to follow Gerry's example and not stay late in the office so others feel they have to stay late just to be seen as dedicated workers. But at the end of the day, the work needs to get done. A lot of people are counting on Sandia to be successful so they can support themselves and their families."

"I get that, and I think the company has a far better chance of long-term profitability in your hands, but you only have two hands. Do you need to hire more staff?"

"Maybe on the production side, once we ramp up there,

but right now there are a lot of decisions that only I can make. It's a function of being in startup mode."

"So, when does startup mode end? After the show?"

"Vegas is certainly the first public milestone. If things go well there, it will help smooth the way forward, but there will be a lot of firsts through the end of the year and, really, through the end of the first operating year."

"Well, you can't keep up this pace for an entire year— nobody could. It's just not healthy or balanced. You used to be so good at taking care of yourself, giving yourself downtime."

"I used to not be a business owner. I'm sorry if that sounds snappy, but it's true. Neither of us comes from a family where we were involved with or saw small business ownership, entrepreneurship. The responsibilities are different than when one is a corporate employee or professional. The rhythm and stresses are different."

"Is there any joy in your day? If it's all stress, you'll crash and burn no matter how smart, wise, and diligent you are."

"Of course! I love seeing how the new team is shaping up. The creative work with Paolo and Meredith is energizing. And once we start generating revenue again"—she raised her right hand, fingers crossed—"that will feel good. And, if I haven't reminded you lately, Paolo and I really appreciate your consulting on the materials issues. He says you've been a big help. I know it's been a stretch to zip down to the other office on your lunch breaks."

"It's been a fun 'special project,' and my boss has taken extended lunch breaks for a decade, so he's not going to say anything if I take an extra fifteen. He knows it's work for your company, and he's always had a crush on you, so he wouldn't make it an issue."

"What? Max, a crush? That's a little weird. I've certainly never said or done anything to encourage that."

"Other than simply being your gorgeous, charming self!"

"Since you mentioned your boss, how's your full-time job these days?" Mike had worked for defense contractors since graduating from MIT. It was one of the standard career paths for the tech grads. Kris's father had also worked for a defense contractor, so she had gotten used to minimal, circumspect talk about work from the men in her life.

"I actually wanted to talk with you about that. The company has been hammering out a new long-term staffing strategy since last fall. Like a lot of government research labs and contractors, our average employee age is skewing higher than it's ever been. Management wants to widen the pipeline, get more recent grads and more diversity in the door. They're looking at various scenarios for early retirement packages. In general, the earlier you retire—fifty-five is the lower cutoff—the more you stand to get in the buyout package."

"Are you seriously considering that? We always said we wouldn't retire until we hit our maximum Social Security age. Seventy is still fifteen years off."

"I know, but I wouldn't be spending the time in front of the TV. I should have a decent chance of doing some consulting. Even if it's part-time, that would be at a higher hourly than I make now. Or I could come work for you!"

Kris shot him a WTF look.

"What? You don't think I could learn to operate your manufacturing plant's equipment? Or maybe I should shift gears entirely and move into sales. You were just saying that the sales team is a bit wobbly. I have no bad habits or expectations; I'm the perfect tabula rasa."

Kris laughed, assuming he was joking with her.

"You think I'm too old to learn a new skill, a new industry?"

"You'd make a fraction, in any role at Sandia, of what you make now."

"With a 'transition career' I don't need to be so concerned about that. I've been in R&D for so long that a change would be welcome."

It was the first time Kris had heard such talk from Mike. "Seriously? I thought you loved your job."

"I do, but I've never stopped to think about what it might be like to do something different. The younger generation thinks nothing of career hopping. We chose a path and stayed on it. It was the fiscally responsible thing to do, but, at least in my case, I also enjoyed the work. Still do. But it might be fun to end my working years doing something completely different. Might keep me young." He grinned.

"Is this a midlife crisis taking shape? If so, at least the change would be something you choose. It's not like you'll be laid off if you don't take the buyout, right?" Her voice carried a twinge of nervousness.

"That's not in the plan right now. The buyout just gets smaller as your age increases, so grabbing it sooner rather than later makes sense if you're going to do it at all."

"So, what happens if you take early buyout in a year or two and Sandia, God forbid, fails to be profitable?"

"We wouldn't be destitute, and we'd still have our retirement savings. Besides, I know you're going to make Sandia a great success—if you don't work yourself to death first."

Kris shot him an enough-with-the-nagging look. "You're changing the timeframe for retirement—or at least income shifting—awfully suddenly," Kris pointed out.

"I've been thinking about it for several months, but when

you were laid off, I didn't want to broach the issue with you. You were under enough stress."

"And I'm not now?"

"I know. But, as you said yourself, your work load isn't going to lighten much in the near future, and I wanted you to know what was happening in my world so we could discuss it. Besides, the shift in my thinking may be all your fault." She could just make out a twinkle in his eye in the low light. "Maybe your leap into business ownership is partly responsible for my itch to do something new too."

They talked awhile longer. Mike assured Kris that his employer's buyout plan hadn't been finalized and that he was just playing with options for now. They talked until the saturated colors of dusk that made the Sandia Mountains glow had dissolved. All that was left were rich, dark shadows.

32

"To Kris and Sandia Design!" Marie shouted as the G7 raised glasses of champagne.

As soon as the cheers ebbed, Marie demanded, "Tell us everything."

"You'd better pull up a bar chair first," Kris laughed.

Late afternoons were still toasty, even on the shaded portal, so the women huddled around Kris's kitchen island, strewn with glasses, Janice's watermelon and mint agua fresca—in homage to Sandia [watermelon] Design—Janice's shrimp ceviche, Jo's chips and salsa, Susie's quinoa salad, and cocktail napkins that read, "If you want a job done right, get a woman!"

The July gathering had the feel of a class reunion. The friends had cancelled their May date because graduations for Kris, Janice, Marie, and Susie's kids took up all but one weekend, and that one immediately preceded Kris's big reveal. News of Sandia Design's launch had filtered through the G7 via text and phone calls, but they needed a flesh-embracing visit to fully celebrate Kris's emergence from the depths of unemployment despair to the apex of the CEO's chair.

After Kris's condensed summary of most developments to date and Diana's recounting of the Roger divorce gossip, Janice proposed another toast: "Good riddance to Roger!"

"It does seem as if he finally got what he deserved, and now you two can fully focus on the future," Susie said, gesturing to Kris and Diana.

"I have one more toast for Kris," Jo announced. "Welcome to the club of business owners!" As they raised glasses yet again, Kris confessed, "It's not all been good news. I've already had to fire someone."

"Besides Roger, Sandy, and Ashley?" Jo asked.

"I'm afraid so. I had hoped that, given a fresh start, the remaining employees would be able to leave old bad habits behind and adapt to the necessary changes in organizational structure, processes, and practices. Unfortunately, one guy just couldn't let go of the bad old days. About a month ago, Kate brought the problem to my attention. Our VP of Sales and Customer Service, who briefly had held responsibility for Sales and Marketing, couldn't play nicely with Meredith and couldn't accept the new approach to marketing and sales. Kate did a great job initially, soft-selling the need for change, but while he didn't contradict her, he also didn't follow through on the action plan he agreed to.

"Long story short, I found out—in part by having Terry give me access to Mark's emails, something I hated having to ask—that Mark had been trying to undermine the sales pivot from the start. The sales rep who supposedly was upset about having no commissions for four months was incited by Mark to take a negative view of the situation. And thanks to Kate's sleuthing in Salesforce, we learned that he'd contacted very

few of our old customers to explain the rebranding. Fortunately, he hadn't reached out to any of our new prospects.
Nevertheless, that put us behind schedule with our critical
distributor communications."

"Well," Jo empathized, "firing someone is never fun, but it
sounds as if you had no choice with this guy. Better to cut your
losses."

"You gave him every opportunity to change," Marie added.
"So, what are you doing about Sales now that Mark's gone?"

"Well, Mike had recently joked about leaving his job to
come and work for me in Sales, and I gave that a half-second's
consideration the day I let Mark go! But it was actually
Meredith who saved the day. Before I fired Mark—after giving
him a month from Kate's intervention to fix his attitude—
Meredith and Kate and I sat down one afternoon to hammer
out script templates for conversations with Klassik customers
and with Sandia prospects. As soon as Mark was gone, we
held a quick conference call with the two remote sales reps and
got their buy-in. They've been chewing through the list of
former customers.

"In the meantime, Meredith recruited another California
transplant to head up Sales, but just as manager, not VP. It's a
young man—well, he's early thirties. It's someone Meredith
worked with in her former job. The guy's long-time girlfriend
was recently transferred to Denver, so his move puts them a bit
closer. They're hoping that eventually she'll be able to telecom-
mute from Albuquerque, where home prices are more affordable. Carlos started this week but is telecommuting through
the end of this month. He happens to have an aunt and uncle
and cousins here, which was an added incentive. He's going to
live with them until he can find a more permanent place."

"I've been getting play-by-play updates from Diana, of

course, but when you string the developments all together like this, *I'm* exhausted," Janice said with a mix of admiration and concern. "That's a lot to tackle in just a few months. Are you happy you made the leap into startup land?"

"Ask me at the end of the first fiscal year! I'll admit there are moments when I wonder if I can pull it off, but I know the plan is worth giving my all."

"That's just as Sharon would have wanted. She told us to experiment, to take a chance. She'd be proud of you," Susie declared as she gestured to a memorial candle with Sharon's picture on the outside of the glass. Jo had offered to bring it every time the G7 gathered.

"Speaking of our dear Sharon, what are the rest of you cooking up with her seed money?" Kris inquired.

"I'm literally cooking, as you know!" Susie said, passing her tray of appetizers.

Janice bit into a baby bibb lettuce leaf filled with quinoa, redolent with spices and a green mango chutney. "Mmm!" she sighed as she chewed. "You've done the impossible, Susie," she gushed after finishing the morsel. "You've made quinoa appetizing!"

Susie squeezed Janice's arm and beamed. "High praise from a culinary artist! As you all know from my texts and invites—and your purchases, thank you!—I've been using Sharon's gift as *feed* money to launch a take-out lunch business from the motel's previously unused kitchen. But instead of the Indian hot buffet everyone is familiar with, I've adapted ingredients and recipes to create cold takeaway lunches. I even talked my sons into creating a website to post menus and process online orders. We have a small but loyal group of locals who pick up their lunch on the way to work, or at noon, at least once a week. I wanted to see how this low-pressure business worked out before adding another element."

"What's that?" Janice inquired.

"Starting this month, once a month we're going to host sit-down Indian Fusion dinners for no more than two dozen diners. My sons, if you can believe it, have agreed to serve as waiters! I'm starting with something I call 'Indian American Diner.' Then next month will be a vegan menu, followed by a paleo spread, then a mashup of Eastern Indian and New Mexican, and Thanksgiving will take Indian liberties with traditional American dishes: turkey korma, spicy sweet potatoes, and sweetened cranberries added to a traditional Indian strained yogurt dessert."

"Sign me up for all of them!" Kris raised her hand.

"Me too," Marie seconded.

"Janice, I'd like to talk with you about a co-marketing partnership. We don't have a liquor license and aren't planning to pursue one for just one dinner a month, so I'd like to have a couple of your nonalcoholic specialty drinks available for each dinner, if you're interested."

"Count me in!"

"How *is* the beverage business?" Marie asked.

"Going well so far." Janice crossed her fingers. "It's been great to be in a garden again, where it all starts. Sharon literally provided seed money—and so much more. I love being involved in the full lifecycle of a product that feeds a need. And I'm finding my customer base isn't just those who are avoiding alcohol; it's also folks who want a lower-calorie but sophisticated cocktail, so we're still finessing our marketing message. Amy is helping me this summer, and we're giving out samples at farmers' markets, which we hope will increase visibility and sales. I've been able to get product into several local bars and restaurants, and that's also spreading awareness."

"Sure is. I saw the short write-up about Freeson in *Local Flavor,*" Kris said. "Congratulations!"

"Freeson is still in start-up mode, but we're receiving enthusiastic press from local food bloggers too. I've rented a small production facility, and the next stage is to bottle ready-to-drink individual servings in jelly jars for sale at specialty liquor and grocery stores. Eventually, I'll need to build buzz beyond the state, but that will require a bigger marketing budget than my single shoestring," she laughed.

"You might consider talking with the Santa Fe Opera about selling your buzz-free beverages during their 2019 season. They attract opera-lovers from across the country—and beyond—so it would be a way to cast a wide net without leaving your home shore." Kris had never completely shifted out of marketing mode, and though she knew she didn't have time to formally consult with Janice, she wanted to offer at least some brainstorming ideas.

"Hm. I may have to look into that."

Kris turned to Jo, who was on her second glass of agua fresca. "What are your plans for Sharon's gift?"

"I was thinking about how close Diana came to having a criminal record—," Jo began, only to be interrupted by a wall of laughter. "And I wondered how many women with records had been denied employment for one error in judgment, maybe at a really bad time in their lives. So I've been talking to some ex-cons, social workers, and my insurance agent about how to set up a special apprenticeship with Jo's Plumbing for women who have a record. Naturally, I have to ensure that the women are qualified, but I'm close to getting the details worked out. The money will mostly underwrite extra legal and insurance costs as well as scholarships for those who want to commit to being an apprentice."

"What a great idea. You really are paying it forward," Marie observed.

"That gives me an idea," Kris mused. "If you work out some best practices for vetting employees with a record, let me know. I may be able to find a spot for one in our production facility in the fall."

"OK, my turn," Diana jumped in. "After paying for the water gun, I had most of Sharon's money left." She grinned. "So I tried to think of something that would bring me joy and allow me to share that with others. As you know, having Luna has made a huge improvement in my mood and my ability to deal with stress, so I got to wondering who else might benefit from the tension relief that starts with a wet nose and ends with a wagging tail. There already are animal visitation programs in several hospitals, but there's another group of injured that came to mind. Several years ago, I narrowly avoided becoming a battered woman—"

"What??"

"When?"

"Oh my God!"

"That's a story for another time, but the point is, after that, when I learned our state has the worst statistics for violence against women, I started wondering what I could do. I'm not a social worker, and, to be honest, I don't want to come face to face every day with others who weren't so lucky. But I talked to the director of a local shelter for battered women and children, and she said they would love to have a resident emotional therapy dog, but it's not in their budget. So I'm working with an organization that trains support dogs and I'm underwriting the care and food for a sweet retriever who will live full time at the shelter."

"Aww!"

"What a great idea!"

"I bet that really makes a difference for the kids."

"We'll see," Diana said. "If it works well at this first shelter, I want to expand to as many locations around the state as I can support."

"Marie? You've been unusually quiet," Kris pointed out.

"I'm practicing my listening skills!" Marie said, only half-jokingly, as the others laughed. "I'm in the midst of another career shift."

"Not another layoff?" Diana voiced the first thought they all had at the news.

"No. This time it's of my own choice. You know how grateful I was to land a job as a patient advocate after two years of unemployment, but especially after learning about Sharon's frustrations with the healthcare system, and seeing as how I'm really a *hospital* advocate, I've decided to make a career shift to becoming a *real* patient advocate—an independent advocate," Marie answered in a run-on sentence that, given her delivery speed, seemed short. "I'm using some of Sharon's money to pay for a training course."

"That sounds like a good move for you and for the patients," Susie nodded, approvingly.

"That's not all. I'm writing a book."

"A book?"

"About what?"

"Who knew!"

"It's slow going, because I can only work in fits and starts in the evenings and on weekends, but I'm writing about how to navigate the healthcare system in a way that minimizes the odds of going broke. I'm teaming up with an investigative journalist, Alexandra, who was recently laid off on the West Coast and moved back to New Mexico, so the hope is that we'll develop this into something useful and maybe even profitable."

"That sounds great, but how is that using Sharon's inheritance?" Jo couldn't put the pieces together.

"Well, for starters, I'm paying a small fee to Alex, which doesn't come close to compensating her for actual hours. And then we have access fees for various research tools. And we may have to travel a bit to conduct a few in-person interviews. And, if we don't succeed in getting a traditional publisher to publish the book—they say you have to be famous *before* you attempt to publish a nonfiction book, which neither of us is, at least in this field—then we'll need capital to publish on our own. Alex has some experience with that process, which is another reason I chose her as a collaborator. But honestly, even if a big New York publisher picks up the book, we'd probably have to spend some of our own money—Sharon's money—on marketing to reach the audience we have in mind."

"It sounds as if you stand to lose money rather than make money on a book," Jo concluded, looking puzzled.

"That's the truth in many cases!" Marie admitted. "But I'm not doing this for the money—for a change. It's my way of giving back. Maybe even my reparations for enabling the pharmaceutical industry for so many years."

"That's an interesting way of thinking about it." Kris hoped Marie wasn't too guilt-ridden. "But at least your company wasn't pushing opiates, so you don't have to feel so bad. The drugs you were marketing were literally life-saving in many cases."

"True, but it just seems as if Sharon's gift has brought my

whole career full circle, and writing a book—or cowriting a book—isn't something I'd otherwise *ever* have considered doing, so it's a big experiment for me."

As the G7 wrapped up, Kris said her goodbyes at the front door.

"I left an extra bottle of bubbly in your fridge for you and your sweetie," Marie whispered in Kris's ear as they hugged.

"Ah, you didn't have to, but how nice!"

Before Diana and Janice headed out, Kris held them back a moment. "Diana, I've been wanting to ask you about something work related, but personal, and so I wasn't sure I wanted to bring it up at work."

"What's on your mind?" Diana was caught off-guard by Kris's hesitation.

"It's not about you—or me." Seeing Diana's puzzlement, Kris was eager to dispel any anxiety. "It's about Kate. And Paolo. I want all Sandia employees to feel free to have workplace friendships, but the two of them have been eating lunch together a lot, and a couple of times I wondered if maybe they were flirting, which could potentially be cause for concern with the other employees. It's not a Roger-and-Sandy thing, because they're colleagues, and short-term ones at that, but I just don't want it to be a cause of personnel gossip. And, I know what you're going to ask. No. I haven't talked to Kate about this, because we've gotten into this nice, easy work/home dual-relationship groove, and I don't want to mess that up, so I thought maybe you, as the office know-it-all"—she grinned—"might have a broader perspective on the situation."

Nervous Kris had been motor-mouthing as if she'd taken

lessons from Marie. When she finally took a breath, Diana laughed. "Relax, mama! So what if they are flirting? You worry too much. You don't need to worry about those two. Nobody else is concerned." Diana, who never spoke so directly to Kris in front of others at work, was more blunt outside the office.

"They're young. They're only young once!" Susie, who was ever-so-slowly making her way to the sidewalk so she could eavesdrop, yelled back at Kris and beamed at the thought of a new romance in the extended G7 circle.

33

"Your mother's coming to visit for a couple of weeks."

"What?"

"She called the landline just before you drove up."

"Seriously? Now? Did you invite her?"

"No. Why would you ask that?"

"I know I haven't spent as much time being domestic lately …"

"So what? Kate and I are filling in around the edges."

"So why is she coming now? It seems like a sudden decision. She doesn't exactly love New Mexico."

"She said it was a good time to escape Boston's summer humidity."

It was nearly the middle of July, so this was a plausible motivation, Kris realized. "But I've got so much going on—we all do—there won't be time to play tour guide."

"She's not expecting that. In fact, she said she knows you're incredibly busy and thought she could help out around the house—*if you'll let her.* Those were her words, not mine."

Kris raised an eyebrow. "What about Dad?"

"He's going to New York to visit your brother."

"When does she arrive?"

"Day after tomorrow. She said she got a great deal on a last-minute ticket."

"Where will she sleep?"

"We talked about turning Kate's room into a proper guest room. Now's as good a time as any. If we add a second twin instead of replacing Kate's with a queen, we'd have greater flexibility—like now, when your mom comes. I can imagine some couples would appreciate separate beds too—especially those with one spouse who hogs the covers."

"I do not—well, not in summer. OK, but how will we get a second bed set up in time?"

"I'll take care of it after work tomorrow. Kate can help. I'll pick her up from work if you take her in with you. Do we have authorization to purchase a frame, mattress, and a new set of matching sheets, boss?"

"Of course. You might try Tuesday Morning for the latter. New sheets are crazy expensive. And get fresh duvets and duvet covers. Let Kate choose those—not that I don't trust you, but it is still her room for a few more weeks."

Kris wasn't completely convinced her mother's visit was a good idea. In fact, she was quite sure it wasn't. She didn't need one more person to worry about. She didn't have surplus energy at the end of the day to be an outgoing, gracious host-ess. Of course, her mother was family, but still.

Around her mother, she'd always second-guessed herself. Was always checking the mirror to make sure her clothes were "presentable," that her hair was neat—even when it was in a ponytail for athletics. Even when she wasn't exactly sure where the bar was set, she knew it was set higher than she might reach. Sometimes higher than she wanted to reach. It wasn't that her mother pushed her in any obvious way. She wasn't one of those parents who overscheduled their kids; that trend seemed to have developed more recently, with her own cohort.

In retrospect, Kris realized she'd been parented by two mothers. One was parenting as she'd been parented. That Margaret insisted on Emily Post etiquette, being aware of other people's feelings, and mastering the domestic arts. The other Margaret was the modern mother, eager to have her daughter reach for every opportunity and give each her all, which, of course, was impossible. Taken together, the two models of womanhood were at worst contradictory and at best over-whelming.

Maybe growing up with Margaret Ward would have been easier if she hadn't inherited her mother's perfectionism.

"Gram! We're going to be roomies!" Kate greeted her grand-mother with a fierce hug. "Just like college! Hope you're ready to party!"

Margaret's smile awakened the full suite of facial folds, and she laughed. "Well, my dear, I'm ready to party—but not on school, ah, work nights!"

Mike had picked up his mother-in-law at the airport, and they arrived home just minutes after Kris and Kate.

"Mom—good to see you." Kris gave her mom a long, tender hug. She was surprised how happy she really was to see the seventy-six-year-old now that they were standing face to face. That face. When she was a child, especially a teenager, her mother's face had seemed old. Not *old* old, but just so adult and disconnected from her own existence. Now when she looked at that face she saw herself, or herself as she was becoming. Their skin gave way in the same places —that hint of a hollow in her cheek that was developing, for example. Beneath the color treatment, Kris's hair was transitioning to the same off-white shade as her mother's still-thick, straight hair. Though she'd just finished a long day of air travel, complicated and lengthened by a rerouting due to storms in the Midwest, Margaret's bob was perfectly coiffed.

"Come and sit at the island while we fix dinner. Kate will take your bags to the bedroom. Mike, get mom a drink—G&T or white wine?"

"A G&T would be lovely. Thanks, Mike. Speaking of lovely, I'd forgotten what a nice house you have. It's so open and sunlit—of course, you have brighter sun than we do, especially with all those old trees shading our windows."

"Funny how we always admire what we don't have. When we were out for graduation, I was gushing over those tall, sprawling trees, especially the oaks. We could use more decid-uous trees here, but they take too much water."

"We're making grilled fish tacos—a little bit of New England and a little bit of the Southwest. That sound OK?" Mike was on grill duty while Kate and Kris collaborated on toppings.

"Sounds wonderful."

"We have a new kitchen schedule around here," Mike explained. "If you thought Kris was the drill sergeant and project manager extraordinaire, you should see your grand-daughter in action! Kate wasn't home twenty-four hours and she had decided Kris and I should trade weeks in the kitchen with Kate serving as full-time sous chef, but in reality, I'd say she's been the top chef! She's not a bad cook, either, especially considering she's been a student the past four years."

"Did I hear someone dissing my cooking skills?"

"Quite the opposite. Your dad was just bragging on you."

Kate came up behind Margaret and gave her another quick hug, then gently began massaging her shoulders.

"Ah, Kate, you have the magic touch. How did you know I needed that?"

"You just flew more than halfway across the country in a sardine can. I hope you'll sleep well tonight. Altitude sometimes throws sleep patterns off, but it's pretty quiet here, and I promise to turn out the lights as soon as you want to sleep."

"That may be very early tonight, given the time change," Margaret admitted.

"It's great to see you, Mom, but it would have been nice to see Dad, too. We didn't have much time together over graduation weekend."

"Well," Margaret began slowly, "as I told Mike, your father went down to New York to spend some time with Kevin."

"But Dad hates New York. Couldn't Kevin come up and spend some time at the shore with Dad?"

"He may later, toward the end of the summer, when all the kids are back in school and beaches are quieter. Your father suggested that. But he felt he should go down now for a few days—not as long as I'm staying here, but, you see, Kevin and Elizabeth have been separated for a few months now, and ..."

"What? Nobody said anything about that in May."

"We didn't want to put a damper on the graduation celebrations, and it wouldn't have changed things anyhow. Elizabeth moved back to Boston a couple of months ago—right after Christopher graduated high school—but Kevin has to stay in New York for his job, of course. Christopher is spending the summer at Elizabeth's parents' summer home on the Cape and is headed to Dartmouth in fall, as you know."

"But why? The separation, I mean."

"Kevin says they just grew apart, and with Christopher off to college, they didn't have a strong enough reason to stay together. Elizabeth never warmed to New York, and she had repeatedly pressured Kevin to move back to Boston, but his career was so well-established in New York that it didn't make sense. Elizabeth's work as an art appraiser was stalling out, I gather—the market is still recovering from the financial crisis, I guess—and Kevin says she thought she might do better based back in Boston."

"Poor Kevin. I never liked Elizabeth—and I know you didn't either, but you were too well-mannered to let on. She always acted as if she was too good for Kevin, too good for our family. But what has she ever achieved?"

"Well, it seems we will see even less of her now. Kevin called last week to say Elizabeth had filed for divorce."

"So that's it."

"Sounds like it. I hope he doesn't get hit too hard on alimony. They had already set aside money for Christopher's college tuition. And Elizabeth has always had her trust fund, so I do hope she doesn't get greedy at settlement time."

"Me too. How's Kevin holding up? He didn't share anything with me, though honestly, we haven't been close since he married. I don't know if it was his fault or mine; some blame probably falls on both sides."

"I think a part of him is relieved they're calling it quits. I probably shouldn't say this, but my sense is that Elizabeth is very needy and jealous, which contributed to Kevin distancing himself from old friends and family. At least he has good support at work, from what I hear."

"Needy, jealous, narcissistic, aloof, pretentious ... I could go on! Just getting through official family gatherings with that princess was a pain. She never missed an opportunity to drop some seemingly innocent comment about how she did this or that differently. It didn't matter if it was hair styling or bread buttering, she always let you know her way was the right way."

"My wish now is that Kevin gets through the divorce phase quickly and easily. Then I hope he finds someone new. Someone who loves him for who he is—who actually helps him find his true self again."

"Me too! I'm going to send him a quick text tonight and invite him out here—maybe for Thanksgiving, after things have settled down for me a bit. I'd like to have my brother back in my life."

"I think he'd like that, too, dear."

The next morning, as Kris, Mike, and Kate scurried to prepare for work, Margaret joined them in the kitchen, a lightweight dressing gown wrapped around matching blue-and-white stripped PJs. "Isn't this a hive of activity at 7 a.m.!"

"Morning, Gram!" Kate gave Margaret a quick peck on the cheek before pouring herself a cup of coffee.

"Morning, Mom. I made extra coffee. It will stay warm until you shut off the machine. There's all sorts of breakfast makings in the fridge. Bread and English muffins—do you still like them?—are on the counter. Toaster is in the cupboard on my side of the island."

"I'm sure I won't starve."

"Do you have the house key I gave you yesterday?" Mike asked.

"It's in my purse."

"Oh, how will you get around if you want to go shopping?" Kris suddenly realized they hadn't arranged for a third vehicle.

"I'll just call an Uber."

"You use Uber?"

"Yes, dear, and I have a few other useful apps on my smartphone as well," she replied with a look that said, *Your mother isn't as set in her ways as you think.* "I found Uber was handy when I had a sprained ankle last fall, when your father was out of town. And he'll be using it in New York, I'm sure."

"Well, OK then!"

"Call or text me if there's anything I can do to start on dinner before you get home. In the meantime, I'll try to be useful by watering plants, tidying up—don't worry, I won't move anything that looks business-related."

"You don't have to do housework, Mom."

"I know, but it will keep me occupied. I can't read all day, and I certainly can't watch TV all day. I think I'll take my lunch outside on your patio—but you call it a 'portal,' right?"

"Correct. I made a huge batch of gazpacho two days ago, and we're having that for lunch again today along with some cheese and—for everyone but Dad—crackers. I left a bowl for you in the fridge, Gram."

"Sounds wonderful. I may do a load of laundry too. I noticed some sheets in the laundry room."

"Really, Mom, you don't have to."

"I know, but I'm fully capable of handling a load of laundry. After all, I taught you how to wash and dry and iron clothes."

"Point taken."

"OK, I think I've got everything," Kris said, rinsing her

breakfast dishes. "Give me a minute to check my teeth and face and I'll be ready to go. You ready, Kate?"

"I'll meet you at the car."

"See you around five-thirty. Love you, Mom. Have a good day." Kris gave her mother a quick hug.

"Love you too. And you too, Michael." Mike gave both his mother-in-law and wife a kiss on the cheek, grabbed his lunch, and waved goodbye.

They took more time for dinner that night, wanting to create a pleasant evening for Margaret. Kris set the dining room table with new placemats and napkins she had picked up the end of the previous summer but never used. Their bright floral pattern reminded Kris of Hawaii. When she saw them in the store, it made her remember their last trip to Kauai, five years ago. *We should go the summer after Kate graduates, just the two of us,* she remembered thinking when she purchased them. Ha! That plan was on indefinite hold.

Mike set out the nice wine glasses and opened a bottle of moderately priced chardonnay. Kate, Kris, and Margaret had quickly assembled a colorful meal of whole wheat penne pasta with Italian sausage, red peppers, and zucchini, plus a green salad on the side. As Kate cleared dishes, Margaret rose as well, but Kate tried to stop her. "I've got this, Gram. Do you want some coffee or tea?"

"Either, as long as it's decaf, would be nice. It would go well with the brownies I made this afternoon."

"*Your* brownies?" Kate salivated.

"Oooh. It's been ages since I made brownies. But we usually skip sweets after dinner during the week. Mike and I are fighting the battle of the midlife bulge."

"You can have a small piece—share one. Remember, chocolate is good for your mood." Margaret winked at Kate.

After dishes were taken care of, Mike wandered off to the family room with a book; Kate convinced Margaret to watch the Food Network with her in the exercise room while she set a relaxed pace on the stationary bicycle; and Kris pulled out her laptop at the kitchen island to do homework. She could hear daughter and grandmother providing running commentary on whatever show was broadcasting. It sounded like a good time. *Focus.* She spent most of her office hours meeting with staff, responding to emails, and tracking progress toward goals. Evenings were her only uninterrupted time to step back, evaluate the day, and strategize for the day ahead, recalibrating tasks as the week progressed. That was harder tonight, with a guest in the house. Family, but still a guest. It wasn't the noise level that distracted her but the knowledge that she was missing out on fun. *Just do what must be done before tomorrow, and then you can join them.* But once she settled in, Kris dove deeply, and her fingers flew.

An hour later, it was if a power cord had been pulled. Smack went her attention and energy level. *Damn (delicious) brownie! Might as well join the party.* But then she realized the TV was silent and her daughter and mother had moved to the bedroom. The door was ajar a few inches, so she knocked and opened it wider.

"Sorry to be heading to the pillow so early, but I think I'm still getting over my travel day and time change."

"Completely normal, Mom. Did you sleep OK last night? You've got the new mattress, so if it's not working out, we can return it."

"I slept really well, and the bed is perfect."

"Don't worry, I won't keep Gram awake." Kate was sitting propped up in her bed, phone in hand. "I'm just catching up with friends. I don't need the light."

"OK. Sleep well, you two. Love you."

As Kris turned out the overhead light, she took one last look at the two in the twin beds. She pictured a third twin in the middle. Though in age, she fell between the occupants of the two actual beds, in looks she knew the average person would classify her as closer to her mother than her daughter.

It wasn't aging itself that bothered her—well, the intermittent knee pain was annoying, but not debilitating by any means. She could even live with the inevitable trajectory of facial lines and sags because she knew that inside she was still a smart, vibrant, creative, capable woman. But that's not what others saw when they looked at her. Sure, family and friends would love her as they always had, and they wouldn't take her measure solely on appearance. Most of her staff, she hoped, were also immune to the most obvious strain of ageism. But the general public was quick to make judgments based on age.

She'd already committed to and believed in a multigenerational image campaign for Sandia Design, but the optics of an innovative new indie eyewear brand might be darkened if a fifty-plus female CEO were too visible in social media posts and trade press mentions. Should she request that her image not be used? Would a male owner make that decision? Of course not. The sexism-ageism duo was a bitch. Besides, she couldn't avoid being herself at the show, where they hoped to gain the biggest buzz.

As she prepared for bed and settled in to flip through a recent trade magazine, she couldn't push out of her mind the image of the three of them lined up in three single beds. Together, connected by umbilical cords, but each her own woman.

Just then she heard a faint sound from Kate's room. A bit of chatter. A giggle. Another giggle. They really were like college roomies. Envy tugged at her heart and she longed for a middle bed in their room. Then quiet. Would the chatter, the confidences shared, be as free-flowing if she *were* tucked in between them? Maybe. Probably not. She shouldn't be envious. After all, she wanted the two of them to be close, and they had spent considerable time together over the past four years, so naturally they'd grown tighter. Proximity counted for so much.

34

Kris and her mother had the house to themselves. It was the last Friday of the month, and Margaret would be flying home on Sunday, so Kris made sure she didn't stay late at work. Mike was at a birthday party for his friend Mitch, a colleague who was turning sixty. Kate was attending an opening reception for a weekend exhibit of contemporary art at a pop-up gallery downtown that featured work by Paolo and a couple of his IAIA classmates. Everyone at Sandia Design had been invited, but Kris begged off so she could spend the evening with her mother.

She wasn't sure why she wanted the time alone with her mother. After all, she'd seen her every evening for two weeks, and they'd spent much of the previous weekend together. Last Saturday, Margaret had set the agenda. The three women had gone shopping to buy Kate a new work outfit—a cute but professional sleeveless dress and matching jacket in cerulean blue, plus a pair of nude pumps. Then they had lunch together on an outdoor patio at a popular New Mexican restaurant. As they were finishing their iced teas, Margaret surprised them by announcing she'd made an appointment for all three to have manicures and pedicures. "You both deserve a little pampering," she'd explained. The salon staff had seated Kris between her mother and daughter. Their three pairs of feet soaked in bubbly warm water while their hands were massaged with fragrant oil. It wasn't quite like having a bed between the two of them, but it was close.

On Sunday they all drove up to Bandelier National Monument to see the ancient pueblo and cliff dwellings. Neither Kris's parents nor Mike's had ever visited long enough to work in that day trip, and Kris, mindful that her mother wasn't getting younger, wanted her to experience one of the state's iconic cultural heritage sites. The plan was to take a scenic drive, saunter among the remains of historic dwellings far older than those along Boston's Freedom Trail, and grab a late lunch. It was a carefree day. No work. Just good-natured arguments pre-departure over the soundtrack for their little road trip. (Kate: "You've got to hear Drake's 'God's Plan.' I know you all think you don't like rap, but you know he gave away a million dollars to a whole bunch of people in need while making the video—not unlike Sharon." Mike: " 'More Than a Feeling' by Boston. OK, so I'm feeling nostalgic for *my* youth—and for a fellow MIT student! And there were real melodies back in *my* day." Kris: "Any classic jazz—preferably instrumental, because I have a feeling there'll be plenty of words flying around in the car!" Margaret: "Something by Aaron Copeland, perhaps. This drive seems to call for classical Americana. Can you arrange for that, Kate?")

At breakfast that last Friday together, Kris had asked what her mother wanted to do for dinner. "Shall we go out somewhere? What would you like to eat?"

"Whatever you like, dear. But why don't you get takeout, so we can eat on your lovely portal one more time before I leave. That way we get the best of eating out and eating in: Neither of us has to cook or clean up, and we can enjoy some wine without worrying about driving afterward."

"Sounds like a plan."

The weather, however, modified their plan. A late afternoon thunderstorm blew in, making dinner outside a wet and windy proposition. Instead, Margaret set places for them at the kitchen island, facing the patio doors so they could watch the storm, while Kris unpacked the food.

"Yum, what did you bring?" her mother asked as she caught the first whiffs of a dozen mingled spices.

"Remember my friend Susie? She's doing monthly Indian Fusion dinners, and though it's dine-in only and reservations get snapped up the day the dinners are announced, I talked her into packing up dinner for two. Actually, I didn't have to do much persuading," Kris laughed. "Susie loves to cook for friends; it's her sons who enforce the no-takeout policy for everyone else so they can manage the volume. What I *do* have to work at is getting her to accept payment for meals like this."

"So what did she cook up for tonight? Something smells familiar, but not entirely."

"She's calling tonight's menu Indian American Diner. We've got turkey meatloaf with masala gravy, spicy oven fries with chili dipping sauce instead of ketchup—she said to reheat those in the oven before serving—and a spinach salad with spiced, roasted chickpeas and a mustard-chutney vinaigrette."

"That sounds marvelous. After a couple of weeks here, between the New Mexican cuisine you've shared and tonight's dinner, I'll be adding chili powder and cumin and goodness knows what Indian spices to my pot roast! What will your father say?" Margaret laughed at the thought of her husband taking a bite of supposedly New England braised beef and getting a mouthful of heat. "He still thinks Italian food is spicy!"

"Let's be sure to pick up a bag of New Mexican chile powder for you tomorrow. It's worlds better than what you buy in your grocery story spice aisle. We'll pack it in double-thickness zipper bags to keep your clothes chile-free! Maybe you need to start sneaking little bits of spices into your food so he doesn't realize it's getting hotter!"

"Like the frog in the pot of water that slowly comes to a boil?"

They both laughed, imagining the expression a chile-loaded stew would bring to Richard's face. He was famous for being able to mask whatever he was feeling—a positive trait in a corporate attorney, Kris supposed—except when he tasted something unfamiliar or unwelcome.

"Susie suggested a rosé with this meal, so I picked up a New Mexican one. Hope you like it." She opened the bottle and poured two half glasses to start. "Mike always prefers beer with Indian and New Mexican food, but I know you're not a beer drinker."

"No, but if I were Kate's age, I think I'd be more interested. The experimentation around different styles—from what she has told me—seems to have made it a whole different sort of beverage than it was when my tastes were forming."

"You're absolutely right. And we have some amazing breweries in the state—arguably better than New Mexico wineries."

While they ate, the storm cleared. The low angle of the

early evening sun caught water droplets on every surface, turning leaves in the backyard into jewels and the uncovered area of the concrete patio into a fleeting reflection pool. As Kris set out their dessert—mango frozen yogurt with saffron and cardamom, garnished with chile-coated New Mexico pistachios—Margaret took in the scene. "I love this time of day here. The light is so intense, especially the way it saturates the colors of everything it strikes. And then that glow on the mountains! I can understand how you've come to love it here."

"Yes, it is beautiful. What we lack in lawns and hardwood trees we gain in blue skies and mountains."

"I'm so glad you let me come out for a visit."

"Of course. You're always welcome—Dad too." Kris was surprised to realize she was sincere. The visit had been more comfortable than she'd anticipated. "I was just surprised you wanted to come out. We didn't think you liked it here very much."

"It's different, that's true. I don't think I could live here, but that's just because we have such deep roots in New England. But I think I understand your lives a bit better after spending some non-holiday time with the three of you."

"Yeah, instead of a few days of Christmas madness, you walked into full-time business startup madness!"

"But it's been exciting to see. And so wonderful that Mike and Kate are involved as well. It's become a family enterprise."

"True. I knew we'd all be affected by my decision to buy Klassik, but I was thinking more of the economic impact on our family, which I knew would be negative until the business starts making money." This was the first time she and her mother had ever talked directly about money as two adults. "And our household budget isn't the only one at stake. The staff who stuck around are counting on having a

job over the long term. So much of this is new for me."
Admitting vulnerability, especially to her mother, was new as
well. "And even though I'm a fast learner, there's a narrow
margin for error. Small businesses are notorious for failure.
Roughly a third fail within the first two years, and even
though I've got startup and operating capital for the short
term, in the long term the market will determine if we're
successful."

"I know you two are doing fine, especially now that Kate is
out of college, but why didn't you come to us for a loan when
you were putting the financing together? We wouldn't have
been able to provide as much as Gerry and Anna did, but it
might have helped, and we would have been happy to."

"Honestly, Mom, it never entered my mind. For one, I was
looking for 'traditional' financing initially, and I needed more
than I could raise just from friends and family. But also, at
some level, I didn't want to ask for help. You raised me to be
independent, and I think if I'd asked you and Dad for help—
especially at this age—I'd have felt like a failure."

"A failure? Never. What you're doing is so much braver
than anything anyone in our family has ever done."

Her mother's comment shocked her into silence.

"Your father and brother took predictable professional
paths. I took the options that were easily available to me at the
time. Our extended family is mostly salaried professionals—
lawyers, professors, engineers—not a business owner among
them. What you're doing takes both intelligence and courage.
Becoming an entrepreneur—at any age—would have taken me
too far out of my comfort zone."

"Believe me, I am well beyond my comfort zone and well
into borderline panic zone."

"Maybe so, but I can tell there's a part of you that is also excited and committed and maybe a little afraid to show how confident you are."

"Don't want to tempt fate!"

"I understand. You never did brag about your talents and achievements. But while you're not playing it safe, you're also not approaching this business reshaping in a foolhardy way, from what I can tell. Everything I've heard from the three of you over the past two weeks tells me the business surely would have continued going downhill under the previous owner, so your employees are better off with you leading the way, right?"

"I hope they feel that way. We won't know if I've chosen the right path until year-end at the earliest." The wind had calmed, and the rain had lowered the mercury to a comfortable temperature. "Let's take the end of the wine out on the portal."

"I was just thinking I'd like one more chance to smell the desert after a rain, dear."

As they settled into their seats, Margaret hesitated and spoke slowly as she picked up the conversation again. "I know it may sound old-fashioned when I call you 'dear,' but you truly are dear to me. You are so precious. I realize I didn't often tell you I loved you when you were growing up. Blame that on how I was raised, I suppose. But I always have, and I always will love you. And whatever happens with Sandia Design, I will always be so proud of what you are doing here."

Kris put her right hand to her chest as her eyes got blurry. "Oh Mom, thank you." That was all she could articulate. "Thank you." She couldn't tell Margaret—who had never gone by Maggie or Meg or Peggy or any other diminutive nickname —how she felt she'd never quite measured up to her mother's expectations. Had she simply misinterpreted Margaret's mothering modality all these years? Had she projected her own desire for perfection onto her mother? It didn't really matter now. They were in a good place. A surprisingly close place.

"And you've raised such a wonderful daughter yourself—you and Mike. It's been a joy getting to know Kate as a young woman over the past four years. She's every bit the tomboy you were and just as clear-headed a career woman."

"We did luck out with her, didn't we?"

"Luck, perhaps, but work and attentiveness too. She didn't raise herself."

"Half the time I just crossed my fingers and hoped we were making the right decisions. We talked about sending her to private school, you know. She excelled at academics right from the start. But she wanted to stay with her friends in public school. And she was happy with her college acceptances, and her career looks like it's off to a good start, so I guess that worked out OK. But it's always been a struggle to be there for her without smothering her—still is! Not just being there for games and performances, but *being* there for her when she was dealing with the things kids deal with: boyfriends, girlfriends, body image. I wanted her to feel I was approachable enough that she could come to me with anything, but I didn't want her to feel I needed her to tell me everything. Some of her friends' mothers were like that. It made me cringe that they were so needy or controlling, or whatever it was."

"We both mothered the best way we could figure out," Margaret sighed. "It's never easy, even with the best and smartest children. You always wonder if you're doing enough —or letting your children do enough on their own. You want them to find their own way, follow their own talents and dreams, but you also strive to provide access to wide-ranging opportunities."

"You were a great mother," Kris interjected.

"Maybe in retrospect it seems that way, but I was so conflicted—especially with you. Norms and opportunities for girls were changing in ways that were exciting and positive, but also unfamiliar. I wasn't sure how much freedom to safely give you."

"And I think things changed even more over the two decades Kate was growing up. Just think: She has never lived without computers and mobile phones. That in itself opens up so many more possibilities."

They were silent for a few moments. Then Margaret said, "You do realize Kate thinks the world of you? You're her role model in every way."

"Really?"

"Of course. Why do you think she jumped at the chance to intern with you and delay her start in Austin?"

Kris felt a blush rising. Why should this validation from her daughter, even if it was by way of her mother, feel even more important than her mother's admiration? It should be the other way around. Her job was to support and validate Kate. Which she did, but still. Kris made a mental note to ask Meredith to write a recommendation letter for Kate on LinkedIn, because, of course, a recommendation from one's mother, even if one's mother is the CEO, just wouldn't look right.

They absorbed the cool evening air in quiet for a few more moments.

"Hi, there! Anybody home?" Mike had come in through the garage to the kitchen, ending their shared reverie.

"Next time you visit, bring Dad," Kris invited as they rose to join Mike in the kitchen. "Kate will be in Austin, and you can have her room all to yourselves."

35

"You're taking next weekend off, and I'm not taking no for an answer." Mike was dishing up takeout and carrying it to the table—blistering hot red chile pork posole, chicken and green chile tamales, guacamole and chips. He'd texted mid-afternoon to let Kris know he was picking up dinner. "We didn't properly celebrate our anniversary last month because things were hectic at work, and then your mother came, but I'm starting to think your work will never be less hectic. We need to go now, because summer is quickly coming to an end and you haven't taken any time off, and I know you won't take Labor Day weekend off because it's too close to the show."

"That's a pretty vehement closing argument, councilor," Kris teased as she grabbed a couple of local brews from the fridge. Mike wasn't usually so bossy. They typically made vacation plans together, but she *had* been preoccupied. "If you insist. But I can't leave before five on Friday. Where are we going, by the way?"

"Taos. We haven't been up there in a long time, and we could get in some hiking. I was thinking Wheeler Peak, so I booked us a room at our favorite low-key lodge in the ski valley."

"Ambitious, are we?" she asked at the mention of the state's highest peak. They'd summited 13,159-foot Wheeler as a family when Kate was fifteen, and though Kris regularly joined Mike on local weekend hikes—at least, until this summer—it had been awhile since she'd taken such a long, strenuous, and high-altitude hike.

"Why not? The days are long, the weather looks good, and it will give us an excuse for beer and brats at The Bavarian afterward."

"You drive to Santa Fe, and I'll drive the rest of the way," Mike proposed as they threw their hiking gear in the back of the Subaru at 5:30 p.m. that Friday.

Kris suspected he wanted her to drive the first leg, right after work, to force her hands away from her phone, but she didn't argue.

"Do you want the water bladder for your backpack or just water bottles? I don't know where our hydration packs are." Mike was rustling around in the overloaded garage shelving.

"Look on the second shelf beside your car. They'll need a rinse when we get there, though." Kris couldn't remember the last time she'd needed more than a couple hours' worth of water on a summer hike. This could be painful.

The post-work Friday traffic was heavier headed down from Santa Fe, but with all the summer tourists and local weekenders, the northbound lanes of Interstate 25 were busy enough that Kris had to pay attention while they made light conversation. Kate was getting ready to move out for good. They discussed throwing a small party for her. Mike wondered if they should shop with Kate for a good used car in Albu-querque before she left for Texas or let her figure that out on her own when she arrived in Austin. Kris suggested Kate would love shopping for a car with her dad, especially since she had spent most of the summer with her mom. They agreed to provide $5,000 for a down payment and have Kate shoulder subsequent monthly payments. After all, they'd put her through college, and she was starting a professional job with a decent salary and no student loan debt—a rarity.

"After Kate leaves for Austin, our parenting will officially be over." Kris sounded melancholy. "I know we'll always be her parents, but we won't have financial responsibility for her. She'll have her own real job. She'll make all her own decisions."

"Well, we've been working toward this stage. You should feel good about it. She's prepared. She's sensible. She's had jobs before now, and since she left for college, she's made most decisions on her own anyhow."

"I know. It's just such a big milestone."

"It's been great having her home all summer—the first time since she left for college. Holiday visits were always too short. I never felt as if we settled in to being a family those times."

"I know what you mean. We'd go from operating as a couple to adding Kate, or Kate and a friend or two, and then back to a couple in the blink of an eye."

"I'm going to miss going on bike rides and hikes with her on weekends. She really pushed me this summer."

"You mean because she's younger and stronger and fitter than your usual hiking partner?"

"No denying that, but she also pushed me intellectually. She's turned into a complex adult. Still quirky-funny, but also well-informed and thoughtful. Having her go out of state for college was good for her."

"She's even talking about getting an MBA. She just mentioned that this week."

"Really? Well, that degree will be on her dime!"

"That's what I told her, but she's planning to work at least a couple of years before she takes that step, if she does." They drove in silence for a minute or two before Kris spoke, as if continuing an internal conversation they'd both been party to. "I am going to miss her when she leaves. Not just having her at home but having her help at work. She's really made an impression on everyone as our roving consultant. She seems to have a natural ability to give feedback and advice in a way that prevents others from reacting defensively. That's a rare talent—certainly one I've had to work at over the years."

After grabbing a quick dinner in Santa Fe, Mike took the driver's seat and launched their conversation in a different direction.

"I'm really looking forward to this weekend with you, K, so before we leave all our home stresses behind, I'd like to clear the air about a couple of things."

"OK …" Kris wasn't sure what that warning presaged. Like most men, Mike rarely volunteered to deal with uncomfortable issues.

"We've been navigating a lot of big changes in the past few months. Some of them obviously have affected you more than me, but we share a life, and so anything that affects you affects me too."

This wasn't sounding good. This had the tone of even more changes. Changes she wouldn't like. Had her focus on Sandia

Design been too much for him? Was he jealous of the time she spent on work now? Was he upset that she didn't cook as much as she used to? Her worry brain was revving up. Oh, God, could he be considering a divorce? She'd heard that the period right after a couple's kids graduated was a bad one for breakups. Look at Kevin and Elizabeth.

Mike took her silence as license to continue. "First, let me state for the record ..." (When Mike had first adopted certain lawyerly phrases, she thought he was trying to impress her, to show her that a geeky engineer could speak like an Ivy League lawyer—like her father. Then she noticed that the catch-phrases—"May it please the court ..."—were delivered in a playful or mocking tone, depending on his mood. Over the years, they'd both call on the legal lingo when they were trying to add a note of levity to a serious subject. Wait, what had he just said?) "... wasn't your fault. A layoff can happen to anyone—especially at our age. If you remember, I encouraged you to take time and explore your options. I wasn't worried about us losing our home or suffering serious financial conse-quences. And when you decided to pursue the purchase of Klassik, we both knew that would mean belt-tightening for another few months. And we got through all that just fine."

He paused, but she wasn't going to comment until she knew where this was headed.

"So I want you to know that my concerns about how much time you've been spending on Sandia since the start of the year have nothing to do with money."

"I don't feel right drawing a larger salary while we're in start-up mode." Kris wanted to get her point on the record as well.

"Understood, and again, money's not the issue. It's time and energy and ... well, for lack of a better word, *living*. I see you falling into bed every night mentally exhausted but unable to relax. You toss and turn more than you ever have. It doesn't bother me so much as worry me. I wish you could find a way to unplug from work more often so you can recharge—I realize that metaphor doesn't quite work, Your Honor!"

"I've told you that will be easier once we're past the Vegas show. We're on the last lap of an Olympic race, and I can't lose focus till we cross the finish line." Where she'd pulled that metaphor from, she had no idea, but it gave her just a wee jolt of satisfaction to know she could still spin words, even though marshaling numbers occupied more of her time these days.

"I really hope that's the case." Mike didn't sound convinced. "To be honest, I've been thinking about Sharon a lot lately."

"Sharon Burch?"

"Yeah. We've been so lucky, healthwise, but we never know what might be lurking, what strange illness might take us out of professional action before we want to exit. I guess maybe spending extra time with our folks this summer made me more aware of my own mortality—our mortality. Your folks are doing great. Mine, not so much."

"You mentioned your mom hadn't recovered well from her broken ankle—what is it with our mothers and their ankles?—but I thought it was just a matter of time."

"I hope so. But recovery takes so much longer as we get older. She's still using a cane to manage stairs, as you saw at graduation, and Dad—I don't know what's going on with him. I tried to draw him out while I was there, but you know how private he is. Never wants to worry my sister and me. But something's not right there. I think I noticed a slight tremor in his left hand now and then. And when we walked the dog, his pace was half of what it was even a year ago. Maybe he'll be more forthcoming if I write him. If I'm not literally in his face, maybe he'll feel less threatened by whatever response he thinks I'll have. He did hint again that they were thinking of selling the house and moving into an apartment. I encouraged them to do that while they could still manage the transition."

"I had no idea. You didn't mention this back in May, when we were out there."

"Well, we were deep in graduation festivities, and I didn't want to spoil the mood. Besides, all I had—and have—are suspicions. But my point is that, our health can change unexpectedly, so I don't want us to regret how we spent our time. I want us both to live our lives to the fullest. I know—really, I do —that right now, living to the fullest for you means dedicating the bulk of your time to Sandia. I just hope that once the business is on sure footing you can enjoy other parts of life."

"Like you? Are you jealous? I never saw you as the clingy, needy type." She made sure her tone was light. His eyes were on the road, and he couldn't necessarily see her expression. She reached over and stroked the slight stubble on his cheek.

"Sometimes. When Kate left, I got used to having you all to myself. Then Sandia came along. And then Kate came home— which, don't get me wrong, has been great, but still, it's changed our domestic rhythms."

"And then my mother dropped by for two weeks. I hear you. But we'll be empty nesters again in just a few weeks. So, where are you going with all of this morbid talk?"

"It's not really morbid. At least I didn't intend it to be. But you know how Sharon insisted that you all take advantage of your inheritance from her to experiment in some way? That got me thinking too. I don't want to be so depleted by the time I hit full retirement age that I have no energy to experiment."

"What do you have in mind?"

"Nothing in particular at this point. But it's like I explained when we talked about the possible early retirement package—I'd like to take that opportunity to try out something new before I do whatever people do when they're retired. I've read that a lot of folks, especially men, find retirement stressful. And one of the stressors is not having meaningful work, not having a daily role in society, so that's why I'm thinking a transition career might make sense."

"Well, as long as you don't retire long ahead of me and then do nothing." Kris couldn't hide her concern. "I've seen people retire early and just lose interest in the world around them. I want to come home and have an interesting conversation with someone who brings fresh information and ideas to that conversation. God, the vision of us being retired, unemployed, sitting at the table, and regurgitating the same stories and comments ad infinitum—I'd do anything to avoid that!"

"Don't worry. That's precisely one of the reasons I'm thinking seriously about the buyout package. Between that and whatever I make doing whatever comes next, we'll be fine. Not rich, but fine."

"OK." Kris was still having a hard time picturing Mike retired—even if it was to a transition position—while she was still at the helm of Sandia Design. That's assuming Sandia survived its first year. "Just promise me that you'll give me at least two weeks' notice before you get totally serious about the buyout. And promise that you won't hold it against me for working while you're semi-retired or whatever it is. And promise"—she had one more stipulation to work in before he could respond—"that you won't just turn into an aimless, wandering—or hiking—husband when you take the buyout. Promise that you'll find something meaningful to do at least half the time."

"I promise. I promise. I promise!" He shot her a smile that engaged his irresistible dimples.

After they were beyond Taos and had crossed a broad plain that put Wheeler Peak in profile before them, they entered the river valley up to the ski village. The two-lane road snaked through the narrow cut in the mountains, edged on both sides by forest. Soon the setting sun was hidden. Shaded by the trees and mountainsides, the road in front of them was darker than the sky above, still holding on to the last shades of blue. It was calm and peaceful.

"Ah!" Kris inhaled sharply. An enormous shadow momentarily blocked out everything in front of them. As fast as she gasped, the doe had cleared the road, missing the hood of their car by inches.

"Whoa! That was close. You OK?" Mike reached for Kris with his right hand, left hand on the wheel.

"Yeah, but I think you'd better keep both hands on the steering wheel—and maybe drive below the speed limit till we're out of the woods." She gave his right hand a squeeze before letting it go.

"Agreed. We're not often out on country roads this time of day. I forgot wildlife are most active at dawn and dusk."

They drove the final ten miles cautiously, pulling over several times so faster drivers could pass.

They arrived at their lodging just as full darkness dropped. Fifteen minutes later they fell asleep to the sound of a burbling creek outside their window.

"Oh, Lord, it's just like a work day," Kris moaned as the alarm went off. "Do we really have to get up so early?" It was still completely black on both sides of the window.

"You haven't been for a long mountain hike recently," Mike laughed. "We've got to be well off the summit before noon if we want to minimize the risk of lightning. You can never tell when a thunderstorm is going to hit."

"I know, I know."

After a quick in-room breakfast Mike had packed for them —boiled eggs, bagels with cream cheese, OJ, and mediocre coffee from the room's coffee maker—they headed out. Mike drove extra cautiously on the narrow gravel road heading to the trailhead. Black was slowly turning to gray. The sun wouldn't be visible until they were on the trail.

By the time they reached the Williams Lake parking lot, the soft morning light was bright enough to show the way up the gently climbing path leading to the mountainside trail. "This isn't the way we came up with Kate." Kris was finally starting to wake up.

"You're right. This is a new route, just finished in 2011. It's a little steeper, but it's shorter—roughly eight miles instead of fourteen and a half, and you gain about 3,000 instead of 4,500 feet. Thought you'd appreciate that."

"You thought correctly. Brrrr!" The air outside the car was still below forty degrees. "Guess I'm going to need those warm-up layers."

Theirs was the third car in the lot, so they probably had someone ahead of them on the trail. Always a good thought, especially if there were any black bears in the area.

They were mostly quiet as they started up the trail, following a fork of the Rio Hondo. It was about as lush a New Mexico scene as you could imagine. Fuchsia fireweed, red Indian paintbrush, and periwinkle-blue harebells popped up among grasses, shrubs, and junior spruce protected by senior trees. Mike set a moderate pace for the relatively easy, if long, warm-up section of the hike. They stopped briefly once beside a boulder field to peel off their fleece jackets. They weren't hot enough yet to want water.

Roughly two miles into the hike, when they reached the fork that would start the ascent of Wheeler proper, Mike asked Kris to retrieve their hiking sticks from his backpack. "Let's grab a bite of trail mix and some water before we start up."

"This must mean we're about to get serious." Kris wasn't sure she was excited about the long climb ahead. It had been a hectic week at work, and though she'd slept well, a hike at altitude always meant less oxygen and faster exhaustion.

As they turned left, the grade began to increase. Trees soon gave way to an unending talus slope. Thistles and, later, ground-hugging miniature alpine flowers replaced fireweed and paintbrush.

The trail had been carved across the rock fall in long switchbacks, as if by Zorro. Higher up, the switchbacks shortened and tightened. Though narrow, the path was generally easy to walk, except when it crossed fields of larger rock, where they had to slow down and feel for unstable boulders. A cute little pika poked out of its hiding place, squeaked its caution to other rock-dwelling rodents, and scurried away. Kris took the critter sighting as an opportunity to unzip her windbreaker and sip some water. The sun was now adding extra warmth while physical exertion was doing a fine job on its own.

Mike, with his slightly longer legs, was in the lead but slowed whenever he was more than a few steps in front of her. He was a good man. Considerate. She knew he could probably tackle the climb faster than her, but he didn't chide her for doodling. Um, *dawdling*. That was the word. The effort of constantly gaining altitude while climbing the mountain stair machine in increasingly thin air was making her head pound. She could hear her pulse in her ears. The top of her head under her hat was a little wobbly. "I can't," she said, just loud enough for Mike to hear.

He quickly descended the few steps to her level. "Let's get to that rock over there so you can sit for a minute."

"I don't think I can make it. I just can't suck enough air."

"You've probably got borderline altitude sickness, but you'll be OK if you rest a bit and eat a trail bar and drink more water." He led the way to a couple of flat-top rocks just off the trail. "Here. Eat this." He opened up a bar loaded with nuts and chocolate.

Kris chewed slowly, sipped more water, removed her baseball cap, and held her damp forehead in her left hand. "I guess I didn't train enough for this," she said, ruefully stating the obvious.

"I'll set a slower pace from here to the top. We're almost to the final switchback that takes us along the ridge to the summit. You can do it. Just rest here another couple of minutes. Remember, it will be windy at the top."

She looked down at the switchbacks they'd already traversed. More hikers were visible now, emerging above the tree line in parties of one, two, four. It was good they'd left in the morning chill, because even though the thermometer might not be much over sixty, the intense, direct sun was penetrating. She hadn't been drinking enough water on the way up. She took a long draw on the hydration pack mouthpiece. She couldn't stop now. Her head felt clearer. Blood sugar must be getting back to normal. "OK, let's bag this peak!"

From that point on, the wind picked up. Kris zipped her

windbreaker and added a headband to secure her hat. One. Foot. In. Front. Of. The. Other.

As they reached the ridge, a gust nearly threw Kris off balance. She steadied herself against her hiking pole and carried on.

"The worst is over," Mike yelled over the wind. "We just follow this ridge to the summit."

It was heady to be hiking along what seemed to be the top of the world—the top of the state, at least. Thin clouds were starting to swirl around them, but she could easily look down on ski runs back in the direction from which they'd come.

They reached the summit marker tired, shivering from the cold wind, but triumphant. "We made it!" Mike yelled as they dropped their backpacks. He hugged Kris's back to keep them both warm. "Happy belated anniversary!" They stood there, locked together, for a full minute, taking it all in.

"This view never gets old. Look, you can see the southern Colorado peaks through the cloud breaks." Mike pointed to brushstrokes of snow still clinging to the highest mountains to their north. They looked so close.

"Why does the last half mile always seem the hardest? It wasn't even the steepest."

"Because you're tired, and you've been going full speed the whole way." Something in the way he phrased his response made Kris think Mike wasn't just talking about their morning's hike.

They watched the multicolored ants crawling up the switchbacks behind them and waved encouragement.

They were surrounded by beauty. Rugged, potentially dangerous beauty. This wilderness held massive mountains— the bottom of the Rocky Mountain chain—and tiny botanical wonders of every color. The weather was always changing up here, especially in late summer when the monsoons rolled in. Above them, innocuous cumulus clouds floated against the lapis sky, but they could join forces, turning gray and deadly with little warning.

"We'd better head down before we cool off too much. We'll have to watch our footing going downhill on the rocks."

"Just one more minute." Kris slowly moved in a full circle, breathing deeply, appreciating the payoff from her efforts, memorizing the textures and contours and the myriad shades of gray, green, and sand. Mike followed her silently, taking a 360-degree video on his phone.

Two hours later, they were almost back to the trailhead. Kris took a slug from her nearly empty water bottle. She had not carried too much water. "Ugh. My water's gotten warm. Should have put a tea bag in this bottle. That beer is going to taste *good.*"

"And it's going to feel so good to put my feet up! Are your knees hurting as much as mine?" Mike had stopped running about five years ago, but long hikes triggered old vulnerabilities.

"Probably more! Hey, there it is!" Kris had spotted The Bavarian below. The wide wooden A-frame restaurant looked as if it had been plucked out of the Alps and dropped near the base of a ski lift. The capacious deck was already half-full of hikers and day-trippers soaking in the sun, hoisting pints of beer, and refueling with German brats, pretzels, and sauerkraut.

A few minutes later, Kris and Mike were seated at a wooden picnic table on the deck. Perusing the menu, Kris declared, "This is *not* a salad day. I think we've earned guilt-free wurst and carbs—both solid and liquid!"

When their frosty beer mugs arrived, they toasted their successful summit and drank appreciatively. Kris held the cold mug to her still-flushed cheeks. "Wow. Nothing like a lung-busting hike to clear your head."

"That was the idea." Mike grinned. "Sorry you had a bad stretch near the top. You rallied just fine, though."

"So, what you're saying is that this was your idea of an intervention."

"Sort of. But I knew you'd enjoy it once you got here. What you're doing at Sandia Design is amazing. I'm so proud of you. But you've got to make time for yourself—and for me. If that means I have to settle for scheduled hours here and there, fine; but they have to be commitments you can't break. Life is short, K."

36

The following Monday morning, Kris tucked a notecard into Mike's lunch bag when he wasn't looking.

Dimples,

Thanks for the weekend away. And for your patience. And for your understanding. And for being the best partner I could imagine. And even for your concern and advice. Message received! I can't promise I'll be able to schedule as much free time as you would like in the near term, but I do promise to make it up to you somehow in the next year. This is an IOU for a romantic weekend away.

I love you to the top of Wheeler and back! XOXOXO K

The lunch-box love note itself was an act of spontaneity. She smiled to herself, imagining Mike's surprise when he found it. Then she kissed him goodbye and left for work.

• • •

As she scanned her inbox, she stopped at a message from Paolo.

Kris,

I hope you enjoyed your weekend getaway. Could I have two minutes of your time, privately, today? Whatever works for you.

Paolo

That was odd. Paolo would be at the weekly meeting in an hour, and she had an open-door policy, so nobody made appointments, unless it was an official personnel matter. Paolo seemed to be getting along with everyone really well, so she didn't think it was about any sort of staff tension.

Paolo,

Stop by right after our senior staff meeting. And yes, we had a good (but exhausting) time in Taos.

Kris

"Thanks for meeting with me," Paolo said as he closed the door.

"Not a problem. What's on your mind?"

"First, I want you to know I'm thoroughly enjoying my work here, and I think we're making excellent progress. I also appreciate the schedule flexibility so I can get my final piece ready for Indian Market next week."

"Of course. That's a great showcase for your personal work."

"You know, I've actually made faster progress on my own art since I've been working with you and Sandia Design. I think I need that yin-yang of the uber-practical and the noncommercial—though I do hope to make a few sales at the market! But I have an even more personal reason for requesting this meeting."

Kris raised her left eyebrow but remained silent.

"I'm asking your permission to take Kate along to Indian Market next weekend. I'll be going up on Friday and staying with family friends Friday and Saturday night. They have plenty of room. We'll have separate bedrooms." He was talking quickly to get all the pertinent details laid out before Kris could respond negatively. "I know that means we'll both be out of the office on Friday, but we're on track with our Sandia responsibilities, and we'll stay late any other day this week if it looks like our schedules are slipping. We'll be back late Sunday, but I promise we'll be at the office on time Monday morning."

"Well, this is a surprise." Kris needed to buy some time to process his news. "It's very thoughtful of you to ask my permission, but as you're both adults, it's not really mine to give. I assume you've talked about this with Kate?"

"Yes. We've been spending a little time together outside of work, and she's got a great eye for design—I suspect she gets that from you. She came to the opening of our pop-up show …"

"She mentioned that."

"… and she honestly seemed to enjoy it. She had perceptive comments about all the pieces—not just mine. I was talking about Indian Market and how it's like one big family reunion, and she expressed interest in seeing it again, now that she's older. She said you'd taken her once when she was a teenager?"

Kris nodded.

"So I thought it would be a unique opportunity to meet some of the other artists—my Acoma relatives as well as old friends from IAIA—to get behind the scenes and see how the event unfolds from the artist's perspective. Most of the time she'll be on her own to take in the market or just hang out in Santa Fe while I'm manning my booth. She's really interested in going. I promise to drive carefully, and I never drink and drive."

Kris wondered how long he'd rehearsed that presentation to ensure he covered all the bases. "Well, Paolo, if you think turning on the Italian charm is going to win me over, you might be right." Kris's shock was abating. "My daughter is a very multitalented young woman." She resisted the urge to emphasis *young*. "How could I deny her an opportunity to get an inside look at the most famous cultural event in the state? I do appreciate your giving me a heads-up, though, and I have one request." Kris paused to look deep into Paolo's dark eyes. They were crowned by thick, straight brows, an architectural detail—crown molding on a flawless, elegantly proportioned face. How could any young woman ignore his attentions? She'd always realized he was handsome, of course. She wasn't blind. But their age difference took romance out of the equation and freed them to focus on their creative synergy. She'd thoroughly enjoyed their artistic collaboration. And there was an intellectual sexiness about the way they frequently completed each other's sentences when they were in a brainstorming groove. "Just don't draw attention to your relationship at work, please."

"Understood."

. . .

Kate returned home from work twenty minutes after Kris. She'd gotten caught in a downpour. "Whoa! That was intense!" she laughed as she grabbed the kitchen towel her mother handed her at the door. "They didn't forecast a monsoon for today. If I'd known I was going to get a surround shower on the way home, I'd have ridden with you. Good thing you put new tires on your bike last fall, or I'd have been slippin' and slidin' totally out of control."

"I think you've forgotten we *do* get rain in the desert!" Kris laughed. "Stay there on the mat while I get you a proper towel."

"Woof, woof! I'll be a good, drenched doggy!"

As Kate dried herself off, she addressed the subject that had been in the back of Kris's mind all day. "Paolo texted me before lunch and said he'd talked to you about Indian Market and that you're OK with me going up with him."

"Well, OK might not be precisely the way I'd put it ..."

"If you're worried about the optics of my dating an older guy, remember, he's only six years older. It's not like he could be my father or anything. And if you're worried about him being more worldly, remember, I spent a semester abroad in France; I know how to look out for myself." Now Kate was talking as fast as Paolo had this morning. And she'd used the D word.

"Besides, some of the other staff have been egging us on, trying to get us to hook up—though we are *not hooking up*," she quickly clarified.

"Good to know. Not sure I'd want to know if you were. God, I am not ready for this phase of our mother-daughter relationship."

"Well, it's not as if I haven't had boyfriends before. You do know this is just a summer fling, right? I'm headed to Austin in less than a month."

"If you say so. But I am concerned about how it will look. It's fraught enough when any two coworkers are involved, but when one is the owner's daughter ..."

"Mom, relax. It's not as if one of us is the boss of the other. We both report to you."

"I know, but he's a critical member of the team, which is why I'd be concerned whether I was your mother or not."

Giving her mom a very damp bear hug, Kate pleaded with her. "Mom, I know you're concerned, and I love that you still feel that mama-bear protectiveness, but you raised me well. I can look after myself. I really don't want you to stress about this. You have enough on your mind. Trust me—trust us. We won't turn this into a messy workplace telenovela. In fact, we've already talked through all that."

"You have?"

"Yes. Paolo is like the most considerate guy I've ever dated. And he really loves his consulting gig with Sandia, so he's not going to do anything to screw that up. I'm going to go change into dry clothes."

Change. Kris used to think she handled change well. New business developments energized her. These days, most of the change was of her own instigation, which only upped the stakes. But this change was of a whole other order. She'd never worried about Kate's love life, but mixing work and romance could be dangerous.

37

"May I come in?"

"Of course."

Meredith closed the door behind her and sat down across from Kris. "I have some potentially unsettling news, so I wanted to share it with you privately. I'm not sure there's even any reason to share it with the others."

Kris took her hands off the laptop and gave Meredith her full attention.

"You and I have both done our share of market research over the years, and we know that sometimes it's worth paying attention to—other times not. And I feel confident in the research you conducted initially, before launching Sandia Design, which is one reason I came on board. And because I'm in a somewhat different market now, I've been on the lookout for general trends that might affect Sandia. I found something today that may indicate a potential challenge. The caveat is that focus groups and surveys are demonstrably slippery when it comes to predicting actual consumer behavior, but I wanted you to know what I found out regardless."

"OK, now you're worrying me. Spit it out."

"We've both worked in the past for midrange and popular luxury brands."

"That's being generous to Klassik!"

"Point is, we've never been in a position to launch a new line under a completely new brand at a premium price point. I ran across a study done by a European research firm that found customers won't buy expensive frames from an unfamiliar brand the first time they see them. And that's pretty much our position right now: an unfamiliar brand with pricey product."

"Well, then we'll have to make sure consumers see our frames more than once before they visit their optical shop," Kris countered. "You're already implementing a blitz of social media, traditional PR, and earned media to get us in front of insiders and influencers. Locally, we've got even more lined up. Maybe ramp up the guerrilla marketing beyond the state? Let's review the marketing plan after Las Vegas. We can recalibrate as necessary after we get a reading there."

"Sounds good. I don't think it's necessarily a high-probability risk, but I know how you feel about risk mitigation, so I wanted you to know as soon as I ran across the study."

"What was the sample size?"

"Two hundred across three countries. The subjects were those who had previously bought a pair of luxury brand frames."

"OK. That's not overwhelmingly concerning, especially as the Europeans tend to be less adventurous than Americans in adopting new brands. They prefer that everyone *know* they're wearing Gucci or Chanel."

"True. I have some good news too."

"Please share."

"I have a solid provisional yes from two high-profile Hollywood actors to wear and promote Sandia eyewear."

Kris raised both eyebrows, in the process creating ripple lines above them on her no-Botox forehead. "Who? How?"

Meredith laughed. "I'm feeling a bit superstitious about it, so I won't share names until it's a done deal. They're both working on or scheduled to work on shoots in New Mexico, so I reached out to their reps. I gave them my elevator pitch about the brand and then emailed PDFs of a few CAD drawings—after insisting on complete nondisclosure to anyone but the actors. They said very complimentary things about the designs, and about working in New Mexico; they just don't want to sign until we've officially launched. I think they want to ensure we can deliver what we've promised."

"Me too! How'd you come up with that idea?"

"In LA, designers are always jockeying to get stars clothed or accessorized with their brands—it's a major part of the game. Over the years, I've made some useful contacts with agents, managers, PAs, those sorts of people. We provide celebrities with a free pair of glasses or sunglasses. They wear them, post on social media, get covered in the trades and consumer media, and it all creates free publicity and de facto endorsement. I'm working on a few more names, including a couple of actors who have homes in the state."

"Nice work!"

38

Showtime! Precisely a year after she had been laid off, Kris was back at Vision Expo West.

Getting everything and everyone successfully assembled for the biggest trade show of the year had been the hardest, most stressful, and most invigorating thing she'd ever done. For the past two months, she had asked every employee to work overtime without pay—as necessary to meet milestones, but no more than ten extra hours per week. In exchange, she rolled out the company's first profit-sharing plan. It was modest, but even without that incentive, the staff would have come in early, stayed late, or worked extra hours from home— whatever it took to relaunch the enterprise.

This year, nearly the entire headquarters staff was at her side, and everyone had been briefed on marketing and sales messages. Liz would help take orders. Terry would keep one eye on the demo of their new website—which was running a loop on a large monitor—while scheduling meetings for sales, trading business cards, and talking about the new designs. Everyone had participated in some degree of cross-training to demolish fiefdoms, infuse new ideas, and make common cause throughout the company. Even Production and Sales finally seemed to be in sync. Eugene, who'd been relieved when Mark was let go, had been making an extra effort to help Carlos get up to speed on the company, the product, and the process.

Because Klassik had been cost-cutting the past few years, Sandia had been locked into a suboptimal booth location. It wasn't the worst spot, but it was off to one of the edges of the exhibit hall. Attendees either had to be on a mission to visit a specific booth or have so much time that they covered every aisle. To ensure the crowd wouldn't overlook them, Kris had gone all-out on the display. A four-sided banner suspended from the ceiling announced: *Sandia Design | Elevated eyewear rooted in the Southwest.* At the corner of their booth (at least they were at an aisle and row intersection), a raised service table held small recyclable cups and an enormous glass beverage dispenser. Conference-goers were always on the prowl for a drink or nibble. If nothing else, the free beverage would prompt some extra show floor strollers to give their booth a second look. On the frosty dispenser hung a sign that read: *Enjoy a sip of the Southwest—Sandia (watermelon) agua fresca!*

And then the doors opened. It took a few minutes for the first of the crowd to reach Sandia's booth, but when they saw it they stopped. Even lingered. And looked—approvingly—at the displays. Kris felt her shoulders relax a fraction of an inch.

For the launch, Design and Production had limited themselves to three acetate-based lines with two shapes in each line. The Sky line consisted of a round design called Sun and a cat-eye shape labeled Moon. The Ancestral line's rectangular frame was Adobe, while the modified square frame was Four Corners; both had temples that could be specified with a "carved" sculptural pattern. In the Desert line, the rectangular frame was Mesa and the butterfly shape was Butterfly.

Each staff member was modeling a different pair of Sandia frames and wore a second lanyard that held a postcard describing the style, inspiration, and color options.

Terry, who had called dibs on the bright orange and yellow Blanket Flower palette months ago, wore a smile as bright as his square Four Corners frames. "Blanket Flowers aren't for wallflowers," he pronounced at every opportunity.

When Liz had tried on the semi-rimless Moon frames, Kris had whispered that they made her look younger. That clinched the deal—along with the Cholla Flower fuchsia inside of the front and temple, which peeked through behind the all-business dark gray Piñon Trunk exterior, its subtle color variations mimicking tree bark.

Eugene had declared he was brave enough to wear the Horny Toad palette in an Adobe frame, and he enthusiastically explained to anyone who commented on the name how the desert horned lizard—commonly known as a horny toad for its armature—used its desert camouflage coloring to avoid detection by predators. The mottled tans, browns, and grays were so much more true to the Southwest than the ubiquitous "tortoise" frames, he added.

Carlos also wore an Adobe pair but in a light gray Tuff, which incorporated a small amount of the actual New Mexico volcanic stone dust (for an additional price premium). The temples' indented pattern evoked sculpted pottery.

Diana, who'd never needed to wear prescription glasses and so wore blanks for lenses, had tried every style they'd prototyped before choosing a Mesa design with a Yellow Sandstone front and Piñon Green temples. The shape added some angularity to her round face while the earthy colors drew attention to her rich brown eyes.

Meredith had selected the cat-eye Moon design in White Sand. Mike, Eugene, Paolo, and Robert the intern had engineered a way to give the acetate a subtle glitter that mimicked the sun-catching gypsum grains of New Mexico's White Sands National Monument. The glasses were the perfect foil to Meredith's red hair.

Paolo stood out—as he would in any crowd—with his round Sun frames in Pinyon Jay, a sophisticated blue-gray.

Kris had decided on Sandia Granite, a mottled dusty pink, for her Butterfly frames.

"Oooh! I'm parched!" cooed a thirty-something woman wearing a peplum-skirted dress as she spotted the agua fresca. "What a great idea—I get it. Sandia, like your name," she gushed with a sweet-tea lilt.

"We're a recently rebranded company, so we wanted to make a splash!" Kris smiled. "Take a look around." She was running an experiment to see if the designs would speak for themselves. She was, of course, prepared to share Sandia's design vision and explain their unique approach to materials, but she didn't want to immediately assault visitors with a hard sell.

Beverage in hand, the woman took in the entire booth and sample frames, picking up a couple and carefully inspecting them. "I like what you're doing here. I just know this is going to be a huge hit in Nashville!" the woman exclaimed. "I can really see the musicians lovin' this. It's stylish but earthy."

"Precisely what we are going for," Kris smiled.

"Wait a minute." The woman paused to look more carefully at Kris. "Have we met before? I'm Nella Johnson," she said, extending a flawlessly manicured hand.

"Quite likely," Kris answered as they shook. "I used to be the marketing manager for Klassik Eyewear, but I recently bought, renamed, and reorganized the business. Were you a Klassik customer—because you should have received a rebranding announcement."

"No, we weren't customers previously," Nella said, "but you can bet we will be now! To be honest, I thought the frames you used to represent were more clunky than classic, but these new designs and colors are really intriguing. And congratulations on taking over the company. I always like to support woman-owned businesses, especially when their product or service is special, like yours."

"Thank you! My associates would be happy to sign you up as a distributor, but I have to warn you, we're running a two-month backlog on orders because we're a start-up."

"I can live with that. Just make sure I've got a link to your site and social profiles so I can build excitement when I get home."

"You've got it! Here's my card."

Just as she handed Nella off to Diana, Kris spotted the editor of the most widely respected industry magazine headed her way. Meredith had been able to schedule interviews for Kris with several media outlets prior to the show, but this title, the most prestigious for reaching their target buyers, had not responded to their press packet announcing the rebranding. Coverage in this publication could jump-start awareness and sales—as long as it was positive. The editor was notoriously unmoved by celebrity names and big ad buys. If she thought a marquis brand's product was slipping, she didn't hold back. Kris could feel butterflies swirling in her stomach as the editor approached.

"Kris Wright? I'm Nancy Dale, editor of *Eyes Up.*"

"Delighted to meet you," Kris said as they shook hands.

"You're probably wondering why I didn't get in touch before the show, but I really wanted to see for myself if this turnaround was real. Do you have a few minutes for a video interview?"

"Of course!" Kris led Nancy to a pair of watermelon-colored leather slipper chairs tucked into a corner of the booth. She pegged Nancy's age as a crow's foot younger than hers. Hands were usually a better tell than the face, and Nancy's displayed just a few liver spots.

The young male videographer gave them a countdown, and after introductions, Kris began with a quick, publicity-appropriate narrative about the business turnover. Then she addressed the elephant in the room.

"I realize it may seem foolhardy for a small eyewear firm to insist on setting up a completely new U.S. manufacturing plant when the industry is dominated by less than a handful of megafirms that are largely outsourcing manufacturing and assembly to Asian countries, where labor is cheap. But I've seen optical shops around the country—our customers and others—who are hungry for American-made eyewear. Some just want to take pride in the 'Made in the USA' label. Others want to ensure that supply chains and industry knowhow don't completely atrophy here in North America.

"Look, I'm a realist. I know there will always be enormous demand from cost-conscious consumers for cheap imports. However, there's also a sizable and growing market—Hello, Baby Boomers!—for statement eyewear that offers designs and materials beyond the generic.

"In terms of our design vision, we're drawing on color palettes, design sensibilities, and even materials that have stood the test of time. We're using the most sustainable materials and processes around. And while our unique frames refuse to simply follow current fashions, they're anything but stale and boring." As Kris wrapped up her brand overview, she hoped she hadn't rambled or sounded defensive.

"In addition to your Albuquerque manufacturing operation, you're doing something else that's unusual in this industry: You're not using professional models in your promo materials." Nancy gestured to the displays throughout the booth.

"That's right. Though we *are* using a professional photographer—Paolo, who also happens to be our designer—we decided to use our local fan base for the initial marketing campaigns, because we're targeting more than just the under-thirty demographic. Of course, that's part of our market, but we're also featuring men and women over forty because we know they're the ones with the most discretionary income. And, after all, one of the most iconic eyewear models of all time is designer Iris Apfel ..."

"Famous for her oversize round frames."

"Yes," Kris continued. "And though she's now ninety-seven, she adopted her look long before she actually needed to wear corrective lenses. So Iris is just one example of someone beyond middle age who rocks statement eyewear."

"Tell me about the big family shot you're featuring—it looks like grandparents, children, and grandchildren."

"We're so excited that tableau is resonating. It features the original company's founder and his family. (Disclosure: Gerry and Anna Pearson are investors in Sandia Design.) We wanted to show how our frames appeal across generations. After all, if a customer is seventy, we want to let her know that our boutique eyewear isn't just for ingenues. And, while we do have some shots of fan-models wearing the standard pensive expression (sometimes ironically), we also show real people enjoying life! It was just chance that Gerry's grandson reached up to grab his daughter's frames as we were in the middle of the shoot, but it's a perfect way to demonstrate that our eyewear is tough enough for real life as well as fashion."

"Thank you for talking to *Eyes Up* today, Kris. Enjoy the rest of the show."

After the camera stopped rolling, Nancy asked, "May we take some stills of your booth?"

"Go right ahead. And here's a media kit and my card."

"Thanks. I've saved a slot for Sandia in the next print issue, and we'll have something on the web and social media shortly," Nancy said, with a smile.

"That's terrific!"

"It's about time someone disrupted this industry, and who better than an over-thirty woman!"

That evening, just as the show floor was closing to attendees and the team was tidying up the booth, they heard a resonant voice shout, "Congratulations!" As Gerry strode to the booth, the grin on his face added a couple of extra skin folds around his mouth—a set of exclamation marks. "Forgive me, Kris, but I couldn't help myself," he said as he cocooned her right hand in both of his. "I just couldn't stay away. I had to see for myself how you folks would do here under the new banner."

"Well, I'm happy to say we had a banner day!" Kris laughed. "There's been tremendous interest, and we've landed a record number of pre-orders."

"I know!" Gerry beamed. "I've been spying on you from distant corners of the floor. Terry nearly saw me an hour ago when he was taking a break, but I hustled into someone else's booth and pretended to be interested. I'm so proud of you all and how you've been able to execute Kris's vision of what this outfit could become. Do you all have dinner plans?"

"Eugene and Carlos have dinner meetings, and I was supposed to make an appearance with Carlos," Kris explained.

"Text them that you've got a more important meeting," Gerry ordered. "The rest of you are all having dinner with me."

Kris laughed. Gerry had never been this bossy when he was CEO, but he was still her boss financially, so she walked out on his arm.

The last morning of the show, Kris checked her phone while making a cup of in-room coffee. Before she could scan her email, she got three texts from Meredith in quick succession.

Did you see the Eyes Up Instagram post? Look now!! The editor LOVED us!

And your video interview is on their Facebook feed!

Buzz, buzz! This is great publicity going into our final day! See you on the floor.

Not only had Nancy Dale posted their interview on Facebook and the magazine's website, she'd also posted a link to a feature story on their homepage—an editorial about the event that made Sandia Design the lede.

Vision Expo West's 30th anniversary is set to break records, according to organizers, but numbers don't tell the whole story.

What I look for at major industry events is product, marketing, and branding differentiators. Though the largest names can be relied upon for eye-catching presentations (and sometimes excess), they rarely offer an experience that breaks through to make a lasting impression. In 2018, the name that made the strongest impression was a newcomer: Sandia Design.

Even if you disregard the phenomenally swift turnaround of what used to be a stale, low-end brand (Klassik Eyewear), Sandia Design presented something truly fresh in the eyewear industry. There's heart, soul, and soil (sometimes literally) in the company's frames.

The brand is staking its identity on the terroir of New Mexico. Terroir is a word more commonly associated with food and wine, but Sandia earns the designation for grounding its vision in its New Mexico origins. Rather than leaning on the stereotypical tropes of the Land of Enchantment—coyotes, heavy turquoise jewelry, and chile ristras—the rebranded company is digging deeper. Its entire staff is located in Albuquerque and, for the first time ever, it will be manufacturing all of its eyewear at a new facility in the city.

The brand's unique but face-friendly designs are the result of an unusual collaboration between the new head designer, Paolo Vitale, and CEO Kris Wright. Wright developed the concept for designs and color palettes inspired by New Mexico's landscape (see photos and captions accompanying this article) and persuaded Vitale to come on board as designer, working closely with the firm's production staff.

Vitale brings two strains of traditional artistic sensibility to his role. His mother grew up in New Mexico's Acoma pueblo and is a noted potter; his father trained as an art restorer in his native Italy. Paolo Vitale has studied under both parents as well as other noted mentors in the U.S. and Italy, holds a degree in Studio Arts from Santa Fe's Institute of American Indian Arts, has worked in Silicon Valley as an industrial and consumer products designer, has completed dozens of private commissions, and already has one conceptual sculpture on display at the Smithsonian Institution's National Museum of the American Indian.

Wright brings a rich and varied career in the eyewear industry to her new role as owner and CEO. Perhaps her greatest contribution to the reimagined and renamed brand will be her fearless championing of more-authentic models in the company's marketing.

Wright's inclusive vision goes beyond racial diversity to age diversity. From multigenerational family shots to ones of women well past sixty (Paolo's mother is one of the models), these images convey how remarkably the brand's eyewear complements real people. These are not the flawless, unapproachable faces we've come to expect from prestige product marketing. Instead, they're complex, beautiful faces framed by works of art. The optics are a perfect antidote for this era of fake messaging and manufactured authenticity in so many aspects of our lives.

Kris clutched the phone to her chest as relief spilled from her eyes. She whispered a grateful thank-you to Sharon, to the universe—to any listening higher power, and then sent her morning text to Kate. *We did it! The show has been a great success, and we just won acclaim from the most important editor in the biz (link). Sandia Design could not have achieved this first milestone without your involvement. And, more important, *I* could not have gotten through the last few months without you by my side! In addition to being an amazing daughter, you were the perfect assistant/consultant for this wild ride. I love and appreciate and admire you more than you will ever know! Hugs and kisses all the way from Vegas to Austin!*

After checking the time, she calculated she could squeeze in one more pre-show task. She quickly checked information in another app and then called home.

"Good morning! I didn't expect to hear from you this morning. Something happen since we talked last night?"

"Yes, but it's all good," Kris reassured Mike, catching the apprehension in his tone. "I'll tell you all about it in Denver tonight."

"Denver?"

"I'm making good on that IOU—provided you can leave work a half-hour early."

"Sure!"

"OK then, I think you have just enough time to throw some things in a carry-on before you head to work. I'm hitting 'Purchase' on your eticket right now. Look for confirmation in your email."

"Wow! This is a surprise."

"Spontaneous enough for you?" Kris grinned, acknowledging that her regimented, overloaded schedule the past several months had edged out most of their free-form fun.

"Yeah—this will be great!"

"Our flights arrive fifteen minutes apart. I'll book a hotel and make dinner reservations before I leave my room. We can text to find each other on the B concourse when we arrive."

"Roger! Sorry—I mean, got it!"

Kris laughed. A laugh that released a year's worth of tension.

CLOSING NOTE

Thank you for reading *Optics*. If you enjoyed the book, please consider posting a review on your favorite bookseller's website (such as Amazon) or your favorite site for book lovers. Share your comments with friends on social media. Recommend *Optics* to your local bookstore, your book club, and anyone who has lost a job!

Sign up for my newsletter, Gail's Reading Glasses, at gailreitenbach.com for the back story on this novel and related content as well as sneak peaks at what's next. Bio and more information can be found at gailreitenbach.com. Follow me on Twitter and Instagram @GailReit or on Facebook at GailReitenbachAuthor.

Gail

Made in the USA
Columbia, SC
14 September 2020